RECRUITS

RECRUITS

Sara Jo Cluff

Recruits

Paperback ISBN 9781087453910
Hardcover ISBN 978-1-7321832-4-7

Printed in the United States of America
First Printing, August 2019

Awkward Pepper, LLC
awkwardpepperllc@gmail.com

For Chad

The Batman to my Robin

CHAPTER 1

Funny how a few pieces of paper seemed harmless and insignificant, but the second I added my signature to it, they became binding and permanent.

Life-altering.

Staring at the paper, I tapped the table with my pen, the *clink-clink* in rhythm with my foot. I'd read the contract over twenty times, yet I still couldn't force myself to sign it. I was basically signing my life away, and just the thought of making a permanent choice for my future twisted my insides into knots.

I glanced around the room, taking in the warm hues and overly chatty potential Recruits. More than two dozen different teens had come and gone since I'd first arrived. Most of them signed their contracts with a flourish that would make my easily excitable best friend jealous.

Everyone came dressed in their best. Modeled after the nineteen fifties retro look—which had been the rage for as long as I could remember—they had the proper balance of style, class, cleanliness, and authority. A style I never quite fit into, despite my fifties style dress and pale green cardigan.

Infinity Corp went out of their way to make Recruitment seem voluntary. Like it was our choice.

It wasn't.

Really, for the average seventeen-year-old, the choice should have been simple. Easy. Infinity Corp offered the best of everything in River Springs—the jobs, the pay, the benefits, and the social status.

According to the *Recruitment Guidelines Manual*, Recruits who excelled were guaranteed high-ranking positions from the get-go. Statistics had also proven employees at Infinity Corp lived a happier, healthier, and longer life than the average citizen.

At least, that was what they promised me in big bold print on the front cover. I couldn't finish the book. Most of my friends had read it ten times and had the entire honor code memorized. We were supposed to read the manual to help us prepare for the upcoming weeks. But after reading chapter after chapter of position protocols, Recruitment procedures, and proper etiquette, I found myself wandering over to my brother, Derek, and sitting through his theory on particle-wave acceleration just so I wouldn't have to read.

Out of sheer amusement, I skimmed the honor code. Whoever wrote it must have been insane. Half of the rules made no sense. The other half were just plain silly.

Infinity Corp held Recruitment every single year for all the seventeen-year-olds in the city. Before anyone even sees the contract, applicants had to take a series of written tests, a physical fitness exam, and a psych evaluation. If you passed, you were accepted into Recruitment.

My letter of acceptance had come in the mail the previous week. *You are hereby instructed to report to the Recruitment Office pursuant to filing the appropriate paperwork to embark on your journey. As you know, being invited to Recruitment is a high honor and should be treated* . . . blah, blah, blah.

I didn't finish the letter, either.

My best friend, Dee Jennings, stood near the front desk, chatting with the receptionist, who happened to be Dee's neighbor. Dee's curly brown hair bounced as she laughed. She pulled off the retro, polka dot dress and red lipstick flawlessly.

Dee had signed the contract and turned in her forms within twenty minutes of stepping through the door. It had been over an hour since she handed the receptionist her papers, yet I still stood there, procrastinating. I'd already told Dee multiple times to leave, but she'd insisted on staying until I turned everything in. Knowing her, if I didn't sign the papers, she'd do it for me.

With my mom working as the administrative assistant to the president and CEO of the corporation, and my dad being the head of the IT department, the expectations placed on me were high. It added way too much pressure to something I didn't want to do in the first place.

Not only did my brother work for them, but he'd also been ranked number one when he finished Recruitment a few years ago. Number *one.* He'd held it over my head every single day since graduation. He "excelled" in Recruitment, giving him the highest first-year position in the security and technology division of the corporation.

I rubbed my temple. My thoughts kept running away from me. It only prolonged the inevitable. I'd eventually end up signing the contract. It was what my family wanted. It was what I *had* to do.

My eyes focused on the contract. All I needed to do was put the pen on the line and scribble my name. My brain shouted at me to do it. My heart told me to walk away. My foot and hand were anxious. My eyes were bored.

Many lines on the contract kept standing out to me. They were so intense. So binding. So grave. *Failure to abide by the rules may result in termination.* That line leaped off the page at me, practically punching me in the gut.

"No matter how intensely you stare at your paper, it won't sign itself."

My tapping stopped instantly as I jerked my head around to see a guy standing unbelievably close to me. So close that I could smell fresh mint wafting from his mouth.

He was gorgeous. While most of the guys in the room had on suits and ties, he had on a pair of casual tan trousers, a light blue button-down shirt with the top button undone, and a navy-blue cardigan sweater over it.

The guy smiled, exposing his perfect, white teeth. Actually, besides his slightly crooked nose, everything about him was perfect. "Are you nervous? Unsure?" His blond hair was a little lighter than mine. A slight hint of amusement traced his blue eyes.

I cleared my throat. "A little of both."

He glanced around, taking in all the other teens signing

their contracts. “It's just a signature.”

My eyes went to the dotted line at the bottom of the paper. Just a signature. “It feels like more than that to me.”

He leaned in, his chest barely brushing my arm. “What does it feel like?”

Trying to ignore the fact that I could feel his breath on my neck and that he was undoubtedly the hottest guy I'd ever seen, I forced myself to look at him. My voice stayed low so no one could overhear. “It feels like I'm signing away my rights. My choice. My freedom.” I closed my eyes and sighed. “That sounds weird, doesn't it?”

When I opened my eyes, he was shaking his head. “I felt the same way.” He shrugged. “You have two choices. One, you work for Infinity Corp. Two, you waste your life away in a crummy part of town with a terrible job and hardly a dime to your name.” He tapped my paper. “Sign it. Those pretty green eyes shouldn't be destined to a life of destitution.”

With his face only inches from mine, I suddenly forgot how to breathe. His eyes were so blue, so alive. “When you sign, what name’s going there?”

My cheeks grew warm. “Emmie Woodard.”

He stepped away, pulling out his contract and pointing to his signature. “Eric Greene.” He had a warm and sudden smile, reaching his eyes. “I'll save you a seat Monday morning.” With one last smile, he walked away, his warmth lingering.

Even though I could feel Dee staring at me, I avoided eye contact. It would only make me blush more when I saw her all too knowing smile.

Sign the contract. That was all I had to do.

One signature separated me from having a privileged life.

By signing below, Recruit acknowledges that participation in Recruitment is purely voluntary.

Voluntary.

Nothing in River Springs was voluntary.

Hoping I wouldn't regret it later, I put the pen on the line and scribbled my name.

CHAPTER 2

Some of the water I'd just swallowed came back up, spraying from my lips, barely missing the manual laying in front of me on the kitchen table.

"Emmie!" Mom shook her head and handed me a napkin. She brushed some of her blonde hair out of her face. She always wore it up in a bun at work but took it down the second she came home. It looked better that way. It drew you more to her beautiful, flawless face, accentuating her green eyes. "Wipe yourself up." She pointed to my manual. "You shouldn't even have that at the dinner table."

We were sitting in the kitchen, the furniture modern, but made to look retro. Anyone who didn't know better would think all the appliances were straight out of a nineteen-fifties catalog, with their sleek, curved appearance. My parents had opted for the cherry red color scheme, making our kitchen pop.

"Give her a break, Janice." Dad smiled at me, the gesture showing in his hazel eyes. He was a very soft-spoken man with a gentle tone, making him the easiest person to get along with and love. "It's her last night with us before she begins Recruitment."

I wiped my mouth. "Sorry, Mom. It's just this honor code. Is it a joke?"

Derek stuffed a piece of roast into his mouth. "Aren't all honor codes jokes?" He looked pathetic as he flapped his oversized, square jaw. Luckily, I hadn't inherited those traits from our dad as he had. Same with the brown hair with a receding hairline, thank goodness.

"The honor code used in Recruitment is there for a reason, Emmie," Mom said, tucking her hair behind her ear. "They're strict, so make sure you follow each rule on there."

I looked back down at the rules, only making it two lines before I shook my head. Some of the rules were understandable: no fighting, no swearing, be in your dorm by curfew, respect authority. Most of those applied to our normal lives in River Springs, like no fighting.

Some of the rules were pushing the line for teens: no makeup, no jewelry, no hair dyes. Some were completely ludicrous: no switching places in line, no talking in lines, no rude looks are to be exchanged, use kind words, no chewing gum.

They had a picture index on appropriate hairstyles, ranging from plain to extremely plain. They had a scheduled meal plan for every day, individualized for each person depending on height, sex, weight, race, hair color, and eye color.

What killed me, though, was the wardrobe. It consisted of

long sleeve, crew neck shirts, and make-sure-no-sign-of-an-ankle-is-exposed pants. There were only a few selected colors: red, blue, green, white and black. They gave you a schedule for what colors you were supposed to wear each day.

"This is delicious, Philip," Mom said.

Dad had let me pick 'my last meal.' He'd meant it as a joke since I would be gone for a couple of months, but it rang true in a different sort of way for me. It felt like my last meal before they ripped away my freedom. Not that I had much freedom to begin with. Everything seemed controlled here in River Springs.

Derek held up his hand for me to high five. "You usually can't do anything right, but roast and potatoes are a decent way to go."

I eyed the gravy sliding down his hand and shook my head. Ignoring Derek's glare, I turned my attention to Dad. "It really is, Dad. I'm going to miss your cooking."

Mom usually worked late, so Dad did the cooking in the family. Well, that was the excuse she always used. She had no cooking skills whatsoever, even when she tried. That was one of her few downfalls. Mom was amazing in everything else she did. Except maybe mothering. She didn't try hard in that field, though. Sometimes I felt like an afterthought.

"Thank you, sweetie." Dad took a roll and poured some honey on it. "I think they've added more rules since I went through Recruitment."

Derek grabbed the book from me, getting a smudge of gravy on it. "I think they've added some since *I* went. Wow, looks at Emmie's menu." He whistled under his breath.

"Tough couple months for you, little sis. Oatmeal for breakfast, bologna sandwich and an apple for lunch, and rice and peas for dinner. Every single day. No dessert."

They had selected every meal I didn't like, probably on purpose. I snatched the book back, wiping off his mess before I set it on the table. "I need to learn how to not gag when I eat peas."

"They're just peas, Emmie." Mom gave me a disapproving look. "They won't kill you."

Frowning, I continued flipping through the book. "Do you know we can't talk to our Recruitment partner after lights out? Which is at nine, by the way." I paused, my eyes unfocused on my food before me. "How would they know if we're following these rules? They're not putting us under surveillance, are they?"

My family continued eating in silence.

"Right?" When no one answered, panic set in. "They can't watch us dress! That's just . . . wrong."

"They don't watch you dress," Dad said. I couldn't be certain, but he didn't sound so sure of that. "They just trust you to do as they say."

Mom rolled her eyes. "Calm down, Emmie. They don't observe you. They'll ask you about it, though. Every day. Your dorm and Recruitment leaders are highly skilled in person to person communication and will be able to get to the truth of the matter."

Derek threw a roll at my face, smacking me in the nose. "You need to learn to think fast, sis. There will be some tough challenges. Especially the one with the sharks."

The roll only made it halfway to my mouth before I paused. “Sharks?”

Derek's eyes widened. “Oh, crap. We aren't supposed to tell you about the challenges. Forget I said anything.”

“What sharks?” My eyes darted to Dad.

He wore a wide smile. “Derek's joking. There are no sharks in Recruitment.”

“There better not be.” I shivered at the thought.

Derek's words were slow and deliberate. “Yes. There are no sharks.”

Mom smacked his arm, laughter pulling at her lips. “Knock it off, Derek. You're going to give her a heart attack.” She gave me a reassuring smile. “There are no sharks, Emmie.”

Muttering under my breath, I pushed my plate away from me. Derek always knew how to ruin the moment. Dad stood, grabbed our empty plates, and took them both over to the sink.

“Emmie, I'm going to miss that scowl of yours,” Dad said as he rinsed off our dishes.

“Don't worry, Dad,” I said. “I'm bringing it back with me, hopefully improved.”

Dad laughed. “I'm looking forward to it.” He added some soap to a sponge and scrubbed the plates. “I trust you'll improve your already amazing sarcasm skills, too.”

“But of course.” I stood, went into the kitchen and put my arms around Dad. I would miss him the most. “How often do you get to visit?”

“Twice.” Derek appeared next to us, ruining the moment, again. He looked down at me, an annoying glee in his eye. I hated how he always towered over me. He was tall like Dad and always tried to use it to his advantage.

Dad rubbed my back. "I've already notified work of those visits, so I'll be there."

"Why do they make them in the middle of the week and the middle of the day?" Derek asked. "It never made sense to me."

I pulled back from Dad and looked up at Derek. "Nothing in Recruitment seems to make sense. It's all a bunch of nonsense if you ask me."

Mom tsked. "Emmie, watch that tongue of yours. You're going to get yourself in trouble during Recruitment, I just know it." She stood and came over to the sink, shooing us out of the way so she could wash her dish.

Dad winked at me. "Emmie will stay out of trouble, right?"

"Sure. But I'm not going to like it." I went back to the table, sitting down.

"Promise me you'll take it seriously," Dad said. "There are going to be a lot of things that seem pointless, but everything's important in Recruitment. Remember they're testing you. They want to see how you react to these things and if you can do as you're told."

Derek smiled at me. "You're so screwed. You never do what you're told."

"I can if I want." I shrugged. "Sometimes. It depends on who's watching." When Dad raised his eyebrows at me, I sighed. "I'll be on my best behavior, I promise."

"Let's hope that's good enough." Mom brought a chocolate cake to the table and sat it in front of me. "Mrs.

Jennings dropped this off. She told me to tell you good luck."

Eying the chocolate cake, I licked my lips, realizing it would be my last dessert for a couple of months. "Looks yummy."

"Is Dee excited about starting?" Dad brought me a plate and a fork. Taking a knife, he sliced a piece of cake off for me and set it on my plate.

"Yes." I took a bite and it immediately melted in my mouth. Dee's mom certainly knew how to bake. "It's Dee. She gets excited about everything, including Recruitment."

When Mom and Dad were done cleaning up, they sat back down at the table. Mom leaned forward, resting her hand on mine. "You're going to try your best, right? You know everyone will be watching you closely. Our family is well known in the community."

I grunted. She certainly knew how to ruin my chocolate moment. "Mom, I said I will."

She smiled, but it didn't touch her eyes. "I know, but I want you to do well. This is important to me. It should be to you, too. This will decide the rest of your life."

Did she need to keep on reminding me of that? "Mom, I won't do anything to embarrass you, don't worry. I'll swear an oath if that will make you happy."

Mom sighed, removing her hand from mine. "You're making it tempting."

I held up my arm. "I, Emmie Woodard, do solemnly promise to do my best in Recruitment, not to do anything to jeopardize the Woodard name, and not to gag while I eat my peas."

With another sigh, Mom pointed to my manual. "Take that and go to your bedroom. Finish reading it before the morning."

I gave her a salute, Derek a high five and Dad a quick hug before I left the kitchen. Once I settled into my room, I lay down on my bed, put the book on my chest and stared up at the white ceiling. After a couple of hours of daydreaming about anything and everything except the book and Recruitment, I finally rolled over and pressed the button on the wall beside my bed, turning off the overhead light.

It took me forever to fall asleep. Every time I closed my eyes a shark appeared, swimming in circles around me, anxiously waiting for me to blackout so he could devour me whole.

CHAPTER 3

As soon as I opened my eyes Monday morning, I mentally listed all the reasons why I shouldn't enter Recruitment. For starters, I signed up for my parents, not for me. The thought of eating the same meal for a couple of months, including peas, was worse. Also, black clashed with my pale skin.

Oh, and the rules. How could I follow all those rules without driving myself insane?

But it would make my parents happy. I would be able to see Dee every day. We'd been best friends since we were toddlers and there hadn't been a lot of days in between that we hadn't seen each other. I needed my daily dose of Dee.

Plus, I'd have a break from Mom and Derek. I loved them, but most of the time we didn't get along.

My arm suddenly tingled with Eric's warmth from when we touched in the Recruitment office. Even though we had such a brief conversation, something about him captivated me. It probably had to do with the way he had looked at me. It was stupid to be hung up on a guy I just met, but I couldn't help myself.

While I'd done my civic duty of applying to Recruitment, I still had a chance to walk away. Yeah, that would pretty much screw up my entire life as there seemed to be an unwritten rule that you should never turn down acceptance into Recruitment, but then I wouldn't be legally bound to Infinity Corp for the rest of my life.

It didn't matter now. I'd already signed the contract. That stupid permanent, binding contract.

Though my heart wasn't fully in it, the thought of failing Recruitment terrified me. I didn't want to let my family down. Humiliate them. People tended to remember the ones who didn't make it through Recruitment. Or the ones who were terminated from the program. I didn't want to be an outcast.

I forced myself out of bed to take a quick shower. Infinity Corp had sent a package with the clothes I needed to wear the first day of Recruitment. The long sleeve shirt and cotton pants were both plain white. The trick would be not spilling anything on them. I threw on the tennis shoes included in the package and went into the front room.

Dad smiled as soon as I entered. "Good morning, sunshine. How'd you sleep?"

"Lousy." I rubbed my hand against my eye. I almost freaked out about smearing my mascara, but I wasn't wearing any. Definitely a perk to the "no makeup" rule. "My dreams consisted of one shark attack after another."

Derek strolled into the room, smirking when he saw me. "How long do you think it'll take before you screw up and get kicked out of Recruitment? I know a guy from my group who didn't make the cut. He's somewhere on the south side of town. Selling drugs, I believe. I'll give you his number just in case."

I raised my eyebrows. "It's nice to know you keep a drug dealer's number handy." He started to say something, but I cut him off. "I'm not going to screw up, Derek."

At least, I hoped I wouldn't. When the stakes were high, I tended to make rash decisions.

Dad patted my shoulder, the gesture awkward. He always did that before he delivered bad news. "Mom had to leave already, so she told me to tell you good luck." He smiled, but his eyes looked right past me.

Mom normally left before I got up every morning, but this day wasn't just any other day. I forced a smile. "I'm sure Randall has a long list of things for her to do today."

Derek pointed at me. "President Randall. You better get used to saying that. He requires everyone to be addressed by their proper titles during Recruitment. Also at work."

"What's your title?" I asked Derek.

"Technical and Security Officer." Derek shrugged. "They shorten it, though. If you ever see me at Infinity Corp, you'd call me TSO Woodard."

No one had ever mentioned that to me before. "Is this a new thing he's doing?"

Dad shook his head. "He's done it for a few years now. It's only in the workplace, though, so you wouldn't have heard us use those terms at home. It slips out sometimes when you see someone around town, but not often." He folded his arms.

"I'm TH Woodard and your mom is AA Woodard."

I laughed. "AA?"

"Administrative Assistant." Derek scoffed at me. "Mom doesn't have a drinking problem."

Shrugging, I looked up at him. "I wouldn't blame her. If you were my son, I'd probably end up with a drinking problem."

Derek gave an exaggerated laugh. "Well, don't let your drinking problem affect your time in Recruitment. Do the family a favor and try to cover up the fact that you suck."

"Derek." Dad glared at him, a warning look in his eyes. "You shouldn't talk to your sister like that. Besides, she's going to do great. It's in her blood."

I frowned. "Please don't remind me that I share the same blood as Derek."

"Yeah, no kidding." Derek held out his arms. "I can feel the taint of Em in there."

"That's Emmie to you," I said. "Only close friends and family can call me Em."

Sighing, Dad shook his head. "Sometimes I wonder why I ever had children."

I reached over and put my hand on his arm. "Come on, you know you wouldn't trade us for the world."

A small smile crept onto his lips. "No, I wouldn't. But you both make it tempting at times." He glanced at his watch. "You better get going so you don't miss the bus."

I put my arms around Dad, squeezing tight. "Love you."

"Love you, too," Dad said. "Have fun."

"Don't screw up." Derek held out his arms. "Come here,

little sis. Let's hug this out." Reluctantly, I let him hug me. When he pulled back, he kissed his fingers and then wiped them down my cheek.

Grunting, I wiped my face. "Is it too much to ask for you to not be annoying all the time?"

Derek nodded. "Yes."

"Bye, Dad." I smiled at him, then ran out the door and to the bus stop a few blocks away. When I rounded the corner, the bus was pulling away from the curb. Pumping my legs as fast as I could, I ran after the bus, screaming at it to stop. Once I realized it would keep on going, I changed course and ran toward another bus stop in the area.

That bus had left already, too.

The Recruitment office was too far for me to walk. I thought about running back home and asking Dad to give me a ride, but he would probably be gone by the time I got there.

The thought of not being there in time gave me mixed emotions. Panicked and worried were high on the list. I didn't want to let my family down and this had a huge weight on my future. But there was a part of me that was slightly relieved at not having to deal with all the pressure. I'd just get that number from Derek and be a drug dealer. No problem.

A slight breeze passed by, making me shiver. Fall was already in full swing. The leaves on the trees had changed to red, yellow and orange. A leaf detached itself from the tree nearest me, slowly fluttered down to the ground, landing in a puddle of water in the gutter. If that was a sign of my time in Recruitment, then I would be in deep trouble.

The leaf had distracted me so much that I hadn't heard the

motorcycle approach. "You really like to stare at things, don't you? First your contract and now a leaf."

When I looked up, Eric sat on the motorcycle, his helmet on his knee. His blond hair was slightly disheveled, and his blue eyes held the same amusement they had when we first met. He had on the white Recruitment shirt and pants.

I smiled at him. "I thought you were saving me a seat." I found it odd that we'd crossed paths again, but when I looked in his eyes, I so didn't care.

"Slept through my alarm." Eric looked me over. "I think you pull off these ridiculous outfits better than I do."

Blushing, I tried to shrug it off. "They are going to take some getting used to, that's for sure."

Eric glanced around the quiet street. "Shouldn't you be on your way to Recruitment?" His eyebrows went up. "Unless you've decided not to go."

"Missed the bus," I said. "Barely."

He scooted forward on his bike and patted the seat behind him. "Hop on. I'll give you a ride."

My eyes went wide. "I've never ridden on a motorcycle."

He gave me a playful smile. "I'm a safe driver. I'll even let you wear my helmet."

"What about you? Don't you need a helmet?"

"Nah, I'll be fine. It's not too much farther to the Recruitment Center." He held out his helmet. "Besides, if we crash, I'll just use you as my safety device."

Taking the helmet from his hands, I placed it over my head. "Wow, that's very reassuring."

Eric suddenly took me by the waist, pulled me closer to

him, and adjusted the helmet. "You pull off this helmet look better, too. Now get on."

I could barely breathe being so close to the guy, but I forced myself to climb on behind him.

He smiled over his shoulder at me. "Put your arms around my waist. We wouldn't want to ruin that pretty face of yours." Doing as I was told, I held on tight, not wanting to fall off. Dying right before I started Recruitment probably wouldn't have been the best idea.

Plus, he smelled so good.

CHAPTER 4

The ride ended sooner than I wanted. Being on a motorcycle turned out to be more thrilling than I expected. Plus, I liked being so close to Eric. My cheeks warmed at the thought.

When we pulled into an alley on the side of the Recruitment Center, a young guy was standing against the wall with his head down. He looked up when we came to a stop.

"It's about time," the guy said. "I was beginning to think you weren't going to show up." He was just a little bit taller than me with light brown hair and golden-brown eyes. He was skinny but seemed to be fit. Freckles lightly painted his face.

"Rough morning," Eric said.

Taking off the helmet, I handed it back to Eric.

The guy eyed me suspiciously. "Who's the girl?"

"This is Emmie. Emmie, this is my cousin, Richie." Eric straightened out his hair, making me wonder how wild my hair looked.

"Are you the one who built this?" I asked Richie as I tried

to smooth out my hair.

"You mean Sonya? Yup. From scratch." Richie beamed with pride. Though he was shorter and scrawnier than Eric, his smile told me they were related. It reached all the way to his eyes, just like Eric's smile.

"Sonya? You named your bike?" I asked.

Richie took out a handkerchief from his pocket and wiped a spot off his bike. When he was satisfied, he tucked his handkerchief gently back in his pocket. "Every guy names his ride."

"We better get going," Eric said, checking the watch on his wrist. "We only have two minutes until we have to be in the main hall. I hope to see you again, Sonya."

"What, no goodbye for me?" Richie asked, hopping on his bike.

"Sorry, bud, you just don't give me the same thrills as she does." Eric ran his fingers through his hair and walked toward the front of the building.

"Nice to meet you," I said to Richie.

"Yeah. Nice to meet you, too. Good luck."

I ran to catch up with Eric, who was just getting to the front door. He held it open for me.

"Does your cousin always hang out in alleyways?" I asked, walking into the building.

Eric laughed. "Not usually, no. Only when I ask him to."

We arrived in the main hall seconds before they shut the doors. The two men in uniforms standing near the doors didn't seem too pleased with us. They kept looking back and forth between me and Eric like they were debating whether they should do something with us, but I didn't care. We were there. On time. So, my life wasn't over. Yet.

Besides the chairs in the front for the Recruitment council, there were no other chairs in the hall. Even if Eric had gotten there early, there would be no seat to save. So, we stood there, nervous as all get out. The tension in the room suffocated the air. We all had a lot riding on the outcome of Recruitment.

Eric nudged me in the arm with his elbow and leaned in close to my ear. "Well, this shouldn't be awkward." He stood so close that our arms were touching.

Glancing around the room at all the Recruits, I noticed some familiar faces. Dee stood near the front which didn't surprise me. She liked to be early to everything.

Adjusting his tie, Whit Randall, President and CEO of Infinity Corp, stood and approached the stand in the front. His navy-blue pinstriped suit was perfectly pressed.

From what Mom had told me, in years past he hadn't been actively involved in Recruitment, so I was somewhat surprised to see him there.

Randall wasn't a tall man, but he was bulky. The way he held himself let you know that he was in charge. For the first time, I noticed he had some gray hairs. It wasn't too obvious since he had blond hair, but they were there. Tiredness overwhelmed his blue eyes. I wasn't sure if he had stayed up late, or if life in general was getting to him.

The room went completely silent, everyone waiting in anticipation.

Mom sat to the right of Randall, looking perfect, as always. Her blonde hair was pulled back in a bun, not a strand out of place, and her black uniform was perfectly pressed and fit snugly, highlighting her figure.

I'd been told on countless occasions that I looked just like her, but when I looked in the mirror, I could never see it. I'd gotten her curves, blonde hair, and green eyes, but not her flawless skin and confident manner.

By the stern look on Mom's face, she noticed my late arrival. She also noticed the guy standing right next to me. She probably also noticed my messy hair. I was so dead. I tried to give her my best, 'I'm really okay, I didn't ride on a motorcycle this morning, and I have no idea who this guy is next to me', smile. I don't think she bought it.

The Vice President of Infinity Corp, Frank Oliver, sat to Randall's left. He was taller than the president, and leaner, too. I'd always loved his jet-black hair and dark brown eyes. It made him seem mysterious. But he still had a soft face, which made him lovable.

Every time I went to see my mom at work, I always stopped by his office, and not just because he had a bowl of candy sitting on his desk. Oliver had a fun demeanor and a great sense of humor. I could talk to him about anything and he'd listen and give me an honest opinion. I considered him a second father.

Oliver's big smile greeted me. When we locked eyes, he winked. Even if Mom was upset with me, I still had Oliver on my side.

Next to the vice president sat Dean Johnson, the head of Recruitment. A big, bald, beefy, know it all. For whatever reason, Randall turned to him a lot when he needed advice. To me, it seemed like he needed someone to agree with him when Oliver wouldn't.

Dean clenched his fist, clearly unhappy that he wasn't the one standing at the podium. It was normally his job.

"I would like to welcome you all today." Randall paused and looked around the room. "You're about to embark on the biggest journey of your life. For the next two months, you will each go through a series of trials. Trials that will test your knowledge, your endurance, your strength, and your reliability. Some of you may be pushed to your emotional, mental, or physical limits. But know this: You are not alone. We'll be by your side, watching you every step of the way. Everything you'll go through will be for your own good. It will help us measure your strengths and let us know where each one of you will help us out at Infinity Corp."

Randall went silent for a minute as if each second he didn't speak gave him more power. He took a long, deep breath and continued. "Each one of you has unique abilities that will be a tremendous asset to the community. Let's bring those abilities out. Let's work together to figure out where you'll be most needed. I have faith in each one of you."

He paused again, his eyes flicking over to Dean before he continued. "Unfortunately, the past few years haven't yielded the kind of Recruits Infinity Corp needs. The Recruits have been lacking the fire, determination, will, and the overall competency required to work here."

Dean shifted uncomfortably in his seat, not looking out at the Recruits. He had his jaw locked tight in anger like it was a personal attack against him.

Holding onto the lapel of his blazer, Randall stood up tall and lifted his chin slightly. "You will be seeing more of myself and Vice President Oliver during Recruitment. We're taking a more hands-on approach this year to guarantee you each live up to your potential. We have looked at the tests scores and I'm happy with the results. There are definitely some strong candidates out there."

He lowered his hand, resting it on the podium. "This also means that this year will be tougher, the challenges harder, the competition more aggressive. Everything will be more formal. Each of you are to address your superiors with their given titles. From here on out, you will address us as follows: President Randall, VP Oliver, RH Johnson. Your recruitment leaders will be addressed as RL first name. Likewise, your dorm leaders will be DL first name. Anyone caught using the incorrect names will report to fitness training for a night, which consists of a strenuous workout."

"He's really painting this rosy, isn't he?" Eric whispered to me. I held in a smile.

"I have a good feeling about this year," President Randall said. Calling him that would be an adjustment for me. "I'm determined to find our best set of Recruits yet. Work hard, play smart, and never back down. That is your key to success here at Infinity Corp. Together, we'll build the future." I almost rolled my eyes, but he locked eyes with me. "Welcome to Recruitment."

The room erupted in cheers. I kept my eyes trained on President Randall until he finally pried his away from mine.

Eric shifted next to me. "Shouldn't we be cheering or

something?" He leaned in close to my ear since it was so loud in the room. At least, I told myself that was why he was so close.

I looked up at him, our noses centimeters away from each other. Maybe even millimeters. "Probably."

"But you aren't," Eric said, not moving away.

"Neither are you," I said, trying to keep my feet planted where they were. My heart was doing cartwheels having Eric that close to me.

"I would if I agreed with this whole process." Eric looked deep into my eyes as if he were trying to read my thoughts.

"You don't?" I tried to focus on the reasons I questioned River Springs and not the fact that I found Eric hot, just in case he *could* read my thoughts.

"No. And judging from the look on your face, I'm guessing you don't either." Eric finally pulled back and turned toward the front of the room.

Taking deep breaths, I tried to slow my heart down. I looked up front and noticed that my mom, President Randall, and VP Oliver were all staring at me. None of them smiling.

CHAPTER 5

We were sorted into five different groups. The results of our preliminary tests decided where we were put.

Honestly, the fact that I passed surprised me. My answers were vague and contradictory to one another. When they asked what position I wanted at Infinity Corp, I'd circled every option. Mostly because the whole corporation needed to be fixed, but a small part of me did it because I didn't want to work there at all.

After we were sorted, we were taken outside where buses were waiting for each group. Eric and Will, a guy from my school, were the only ones I knew in my group. Will was a couple of inches taller than me, with square-framed glasses that suited his face well. He kept his black hair slicked back and styled.

I tried desperately to find Dee in the crowd of Recruits, but with so many people walking around, it was hopeless. She wanted to work in the daycare program they had at Infinity Corp. Dee loved to be around children, and they loved to be around her. She'd been born with a compassionate and patient heart. I struggled with patience, so I was somewhat relieved that I hadn't been put in her group.

"Emelia." The sudden voice behind me made me jump. With trepidation, I turned around slowly, knowing the voice.

I forced myself to smile, remembering his title. "President Randall."

He stood with his hands clasped in front of him. "It's been a long time since I last saw you, Emelia. You haven't been by the office in a while. Are you prepared for the upcoming weeks?"

It irked me that he had used my full name. Twice. No one ever called me that. "I hope so." When his eyes narrowed, I quickly added, "Sir."

"Well, you'll need to do much more than hope." President Randall smiled. "You have some big shoes to fill, after all."

I tucked my hair behind my ear. "Yes, I know how well my parents did in Recruitment."

President Randall nodded and reached out to put his hand on my shoulder. "They did. But I was referring to your brother."

"Derek?" My shoulder twitched under his hand. I'd forgotten how he liked to touch people to show he was in charge.

"Yes, of course, Derek. He is your only brother, after all." President Randall smiled at a Recruit that passed by and then turned his attention back to me. He squeezed my shoulder before he lowered his hand. "He's been one of our most talented Recruits in a long time. He's already proven to be a fine asset to Infinity Corp."

My brother told me that daily, so I didn't need to be reminded. I forced another smile. "Yes, I know, sir."

Mom made her way toward me through the crowd of Recruits. President Randall looked over at her and then back at me. "Better hurry and get on your bus. Looks like it's about loaded. Good luck, Emelia."

He gave me a chilling smile and turned away. He went directly to my mom, putting out an arm to stop her from coming to me. She offered me an apologetic smile before she reluctantly walked away with President Randall. She glanced over her shoulder at me, the look of regret one I hadn't seen from her in a while.

I let out a deep breath. There was no way I could live up to Derek's nerdiness. I didn't even want to.

Eric was leaning against the bus when I approached, like he had been waiting for me, causing me to straighten out my hair and tug on my shirt.

He looked past me at President Randall. "Friends with the president?"

I scoffed. "Far from it. That's my mom next to him. She's his personal assistant so I get to see more of him than I want."

"You look just like her," Eric said, looking at her and then at me.

"Yeah, I get that a lot."

We ended up sitting in the back of the bus since we were the last to get on. Will smiled at me as I passed him. I'd had a couple of classes with him in school, but other than that I didn't know him all that well.

"Where do you think they're taking us?" I leaned my head against the windowpane and watched the freshly painted white Recruitment Center fade away.

"To test our knowledge, our endurance, our strength, and our reliability," Eric said, in a very spot on President Randall impression.

I laughed to myself as I stared out the window. The seat in front of us shifted. A guy with brown hair cut close to his head turned around and glared at Eric. His eyes were the darkest brown I had ever seen. By the thickness of his eyebrows, he was the type of guy that had to shave twice a day. The sternness in his eyes detracted from his cute face.

"I can't believe you'd make fun of the president like that," the guy hissed. "Although, I shouldn't expect much from you."

Eric rolled his eyes. "Oh, get over yourself, Luke. It was just a joke."

Luke's eyes narrowed. "This is not something to joke about. Leave it to you to take nothing seriously. You're just like your father."

Eric's jaw tightened. He leaned in close to Luke. "You better shut your mouth, or I swear I will …"

"You'll what, Eric?" Luke asked. "You can't hurt me. You know they'll be watching you closely. They wouldn't want to take their eyes off the son of a traitor."

Eric's hand balled into a fist. He lifted his arm as if to strike Luke, so I gently placed my hand on his arm. Startled, Eric turned to me and I quickly pulled my hand away. His expression slowly softened as he unclenched his fist.

"He's not worth it, Eric," I said quietly. "Just ignore him."

Maybe Luke was worth it, but I didn't think a fight on the first day of Recruitment was a brilliant idea.

Luke turned to me. "I don't know you, but if you want to do well in Recruitment, I wouldn't be friends with a guy like that. He's bad news."

Okay, so maybe he was worth it. Now I wanted to hit him, too.

Before I could respond, a red-headed girl across from us spoke up. "Stop it," she said in a low voice. She had long, beautiful hair, pale skin, and delicate features. Her startling green eyes made mine look dull. She was absolutely stunning. "Just stop it. We need to stay focused. We're about to start Recruitment and you two are already fighting like little boys."

Luke's face reddened. "Sorry, Tina." His voice came out in a mumble.

Eric chuckled. He turned to me. "Could he be any more whipped?"

I raised my eyebrows at Eric. "Are they together, or something?"

"Ha! He wishes," Eric said, folding his arms.

Luke's face turned a shade of red I didn't know existed. He turned around and sat back down in his seat.

Forty minutes later, we came to a stop next near the top of the river. About a mile up was Crow's Bridge. I had been there a few times with my family when I was younger. I used to love to stand on it and look out over the river, watching it flow downstream.

A guy in his early twenties stood at the front of the bus. He was taller and skinnier than my brother, making his arms lanky. He had a long nose, his eyes spread far apart. He rubbed his hand over his buzz-cut hair. "I'm Steven and I'll be your leader for the rest of Recruitment. You'll refer to me as RL Steven. If you have any concerns or problems, you'll bring them to me." He eyed Luke and Eric when he said that. How he had heard anything we said from up there was amazing. But I guess they were probably trained to watch us all closely. "Once we get off the bus, we're going to the bridge. Try to stay orderly and quiet as we walk up there. Follow me." RL Steven turned and walked off the bus.

We headed up a dirt path that followed the river. The sun had come out a little, warming the air up a bit. It was a perfect day for being outdoors.

"Have you been here before?" Eric asked, walking next to me and talking loud enough to be heard over the river.

The water was a lot higher than in recent years, rushing down at an alarming rate.

"A couple of times. That's Crow's Bridge ahead."

"It looks really high," Tina said, falling into step on the other side of me.

"It's not too bad when you're up there. You can see for miles," I said to her. "I'm Emmie."

"Tina. It's nice to meet you." She smiled at me, the sincerity showing in her eyes.

"It's nice to meet you, too. So, what's with that Luke kid?" I pointed at him a few yards ahead of us.

"He's an uptight piece of work, is what he is," Eric said.

Tina gave Eric a sharp look. "He just takes this very seriously, that's all."

"Well," I said, "he seems like he has some anger issues he

needs to work out. He's not going to do very well if he continues to be so uptight."

There was a small smile on Eric's face. I wasn't sure about the history between those two, but I was curious to find out. There was obviously something up with Eric's dad. But I had a feeling that Eric wouldn't want to talk about it.

"How do you all know each other?" I asked. It seemed like a lot of the Recruits in our group knew each other.

Tina's eyes glanced over everyone. "Most of us went to the same schools growing up."

"What part of River Springs did you grow up in?" River Springs was a large city, separated into four different precincts. I'd grown up in the River Precinct, which housed the Recruitment buildings. Infinity Corporation's headquarters sat smack in the middle of all four precincts.

"The Lake Precinct." Eric smiled at me. "Best precinct to grow up in. You?"

I returned the smile. "Here in River. While I do love the lake you have, being near the mountainside is something I wouldn't want to trade."

As we hiked up the path, we got closer to the mountains. The changing colors painted the trees like something straight from a picture.

"It's beautiful here." Tina's voice held a little awe.

"Yes, it is." If Recruitment didn't work out, maybe I'd run away and live up in the mountains. At least then I could make my own choices and have some freedom.

And I'd never have to eat peas. That alone made living a rugged life very tempting.

CHAPTER 6

A short while later, we stopped at the grassy shore below the metal steps leading to the bridge. I glanced up, taking in the red paint chipping away. It has been years since my family had come. I missed those trips.

RL Steven stopped near a bunch of canoes that were lined up on the shore, turned to face us, and waited until we had all stopped and clustered around him so we could hear him over the roar of the rushing river.

"Listen up," RL Steven said, rubbing his head. "You were each put in this group because your test results showed that you would work best in one of the following fields: Security, Management, Research & Development, or Technology. Your challenges in Recruitment will be centered on those."

Tina and Eric shared ecstatic grins. I had no idea how to feel about it. I still wasn't sure what I wanted.

RL Steven continued. "Today is more of a partner building challenge. Before we start, we are going to create two lines. The girls will line up to the left of me and the boys on the right. Line up shortest to tallest with the shortest starting up here near me."

When we all stood there staring at him, RL Steven rolled his eyes. "Now, please."

Surprisingly, it took us a long time to line up. We had a group full of go-getters who liked to take charge, so everyone felt the need to tell others what to do.

I ended up somewhere in the middle. I had a nice height of 5'6"; not too tall and not too short. I expected Tina to be right behind me since she seemed maybe a half an inch taller than me, but at the last second, some super skinny girl slid her way between the two of us. She pushed her glasses up on her face and then forced a smile. I did my best to smile back.

The girl in front of me turned around, looking me up and down. Her glower made me pull back a little. She had a very thick and muscular body. I had a sick feeling I would be partnered up with her, and by the look on her face, I probably wouldn't survive.

RL Steven held up his hand to silence us. Apparently, Thunder Thighs in front of me didn't have enough room because she used her body to shove me backward, making me bump into Skinny behind me.

Rubbing his head, RL Steven looked down the boys' line and then back up the girls' line, taking us all in. "Make sure you keep a straight line, stay in your place, and no talking." RL Steven offered a small smile. "We'll see how well you can obey orders. You wouldn't want to screw up on your first day."

RL Steven kept his voice loud enough to hear. "We'll start upfront with the first two girls being paired together and the first two boys being paired together." He motioned to the canoes. "When I say go, the first set of partners will go to the first set of canoes, strap on the life vests and helmets waiting for you inside, and then push off into the river, using your oars to guide you down. The pairs will continue to enter the water until you're all in. You have one hour to make it to the bottom."

Chatter broke out among the Recruits. I turned around and looked for Eric toward the back of his line. He wore a wide smile as he rubbed his hands together. Luke stood right in front of him, a mask of horror on his face. I hadn't realized that they were practically the same height.

"Enough!" RL Steven yelled, getting everyone's attention. "I said stay quiet and don't move. Don't make me repeat myself. This is Recruitment. You're going to be asked to do things you normally don't do and that'll take you out of your comfort zone. So, deal with it."

If they expected all of us to just stand still and show no facial expressions after we'd been told we had to race down a roaring river, they were crazy.

RL Steven waited for everyone to calm down before he continued. "Besides bonding with your partner, this will also see if you can do as you're told, even if it's frightening. Like every challenge in Recruitment, we can't force you to do it. You have the option of sitting out. Just remember, though, if you choose not to do it, we will consider that at the end of Recruitment."

The thought of rafting down the river sounded exhilarating to me.

"Before each challenge," RL Steven said, "you'll be given a list of rules you must obey. Today's rules are simple. Stay with your assigned partner, no talking until you're in the river, work together to get to the bottom, no stopping to help other Recruits, and most importantly, have fun. This could be a once in a lifetime opportunity for you, so enjoy it. Let's get started with the first pairs of Recruits." When no one moved, he yelled. "Girl one and two, boy one and two, MOVE!" The two girls and boys hurried over to the first set of canoes.

"They can't make us do this," Skinny said behind me, her voice quiet yet shrill. She tried to flatten her brown, frizzy hair, but it wasn't working. At least I knew my hair didn't look that bad. "It's wrong and very dangerous. We'll all be killed."

A girl behind Tina held her finger up to her lips to tell us to be quiet. Skinny had already broken a rule and it had been less than thirty seconds into the challenge.

"I highly doubt they would make us do anything where we'd be killed," I said to Skinny, keeping my voice low and ignoring the stares from quiet girl. "I'm sure they know what they're doing."

Recruits continued to partner up. A pair of girls opted out, not wanting to go in the water. RL Steven made them go back on the bus.

As we drew closer to the front of the line, I counted the girls left, noticing I would be paired with Thunder Thighs. She had already cracked her knuckles, neck, and back five times since we found out we were rafting.

Before I had a chance to process it, RL Steven was ushering me and Thunder Thighs to the next canoe.

Thunder Thighs snatched a life vest from the canoe and shoved it into my chest as she grunted, making me stumble back.

I glanced over my shoulder at Tina, who was trying to calm a silently shrieking Skinny with just the use of her hands.

Skinny yanked at her frizzy hair, prancing around where she stood, and Tina remained calm through it all.

What I wouldn't give to have Tina as a partner instead of Thunder Thighs.

As if she heard my thought, Thunder Thighs punched my arm, motioning for me to put on my life vest. Resisting the urge to rub my arm—man, the girl could throw a punch—I quickly put on my life vest and helmet, securing them in place.

I only had one foot inside the canoe before Thunder Thighs yanked us into the river and jumped in the canoe herself, fierce determination on her face.

I pushed the rest of my body inside—my shoe scraping across the top of the water in the process—causing the canoe to teeter onto its side, rapid water splashing against my face. Thunder Thighs leaned her body to the other side and the canoe thumped back into place, my wet hands snatching up my oar before it could fall into the water.

If I made it to the bottom of the river alive, I'd be lucky.

The two of us were squished in the canoe, her muscular body taking up most of the room.

"Don't slow me down!" Thunder Thighs yelled over her shoulder at me.

"If you waited for me instead of dashing off on your own, I could actually help."

She grunted, which I realized was one of her way of communicating. What it meant, I had no idea.

A shrill scream made us both whip around, losing our balance. The canoe shifted, going sideways down the river. Tina and Skinny's canoe barreled toward us, the cry coming from Skinny, who appeared to have already lost her oar.

"Rotate!" Thunder Thighs yelled, jamming her oar into the river.

"I'm trying!" I pushed my oar against the tide, trying to slow us down, but it did nothing.

Only a blur of the other canoe came into my vision before it smashed into us, sending both of our canoes capsizing, and the four of us plunging into the raging river.

CHAPTER 7

Cold water filled my lungs as I fought my way back to the surface. As soon as my head cleared, I coughed up the water, trying to gasp for air. My fist clenched onto my oar, not wanting to lose it.

The current dragged me downriver at a fast pace. I noticed a huge boulder sticking up from the water at the last second and used my oar to push away from it, barely getting by.

White water surrounded me as I tried to take in my bearings. To my left, Thunder Thighs was working her way to our canoe. To my right, Tina was close to the other one, but struggling to move. Skinny floated down the middle of the river, crying.

If I stayed in the water the entire way down, I risked slamming into rocks, either crippling me or killing me. Neither option was appealing.

I needed to get to one of the canoes. Logically, I should've headed to the canoe Thunder Thighs was currently working her way into with an abundant lack of grace. She was my partner, and one of the rules stated we were supposed to stay together.

But that meant being with her all through Recruitment, which would basically be me fighting against the current every day.

I glanced over at Tina, who was trying to get to the other canoe. I wanted her as my partner. I could survive Recruitment with her. Excel, even.

I normally wasn't one for breaking the rules. I broke many rules in my head where no one would ever find out, but when I was out in public and when it really mattered, I was on my best behavior. The Woodard family was well known in the community. People kept an eye on my family and everything we did. I had a family name to uphold.

But I also wanted to make it through Recruitment with a decent score and some of my sanity intact at the end. Thunder Thighs or Skinny wouldn't provide me with either of those.

I needed to act fast.

Shoving logic aside, I pushed toward Tina's canoe, but by my life vest made it difficult to move. I quickly unbuckled it, letting the river take it away.

With the current helping me, I swam to the canoe, my fingers sliding across the surface a couple of times before I could latch on.

Trying to get it back upright would be tricky with the water carrying us downstream, but I had to try.

Someone bumped into me from behind, sending my legs swinging forward, my toes lightly banging into the bottom of the canoe. Tina appeared next to me, clinging to the canoe and panting for air. She'd taken off her life vest as well.

"Together," Tina shouted.

With a nod, we pushed at the side of the canoe, tipping it back into place. I quickly threw myself inside, set my oar down, and grabbed Tina by the shirt, hauling her in with me.

Neither of us wasted a second getting into place, me in front and her in back.

I spared a glance behind us to see an angry Thunder Thighs in the other canoe, trying to wrangle a freaked-out Skinny in with her, all the while shooting me daggers.

"Is it bad that I'm glad it worked out this way?" Tina asked, watching them as well.

I grinned. "Not at all. I was praying for this from the beginning."

She glanced down at her wet clothes. "Why did they make us wear white today?"

I followed her gaze, only to see that she had opted for a blue bra. Thank goodness I'd worn a white one.

"Stop checking yourself out, Tina," I said. "We got work to do."

She shoved me playfully on the arm, and I knew at that moment I made the right choice.

Together, we worked our way down the river, communicating well and with ease. The two of us were a natural fit.

As the river flattened out, a sense of calm washed over me as we floated downstream. With the beautiful fall colors, tranquil water, and birds chirping, it completely washed out the craziness that had just happened.

We steered the canoe toward the shore where Recruits were starting to gather.

Luke and Eric were arguing with one another, but stopped when they saw me and Tina, both drenched, but grinning.

Eric disappeared as Luke rushed over, helping pull the canoe onto the shore.

"Are you ladies okay?" Luke's gaze slid down to Tina's chest, his eyes widening.

She quickly got out of the canoe and folded her arms across her chest. "We're fine."

I got out as well, wringing the water out from my shirt.

Eric jogged out from around the bus, carrying a couple of blankets with him. He tossed one to me and Tina when he approached.

"I could have sworn you two had different partners when you got in your canoe," Eric said with a sly grin.

I grinned back. "Fate intervened."

"Oh, fate," Tina said, wrapping the blanket around her, "how I love it." She scrunched her nose. "Wait, didn't you two leave after us? How did you beat us?"

Luke's face reddened as he stared at the grassy shore.

Eric narrowed his eyes at him. "I tried to get Luke to stop when we saw you in the water, but he wouldn't."

I'd been so engrossed in trying to get back in my canoe, I didn't notice any others pass us by.

Luke's gaze snapped to his. "I was following the rules!" He turned to Tina, his voice petering out. "I was following the rules."

Tina rubbed Luke's arm. "We're fine. Emmie and I can handle ourselves."

RL Steven approached us, staring at a clipboard. "I must have written this down wrong. I didn't have the two of you as partners."

Tina and I exchanged a look. Should we tell the truth and risk getting put back with our previous partners? Or take the opportunity to change our outcome in Recruitment?

I knew my answer. "Must have. Tina and I are partners."

Tina nodded in agreement.

Thankfully, both Eric and Luke kept their mouths shut. I was putting a lot of faith in people I'd just met.

Suddenly, someone jerked my collar, turning me around. Thunder Thighs. Both she and Skinny stood there, dripping like wet dogs.

"You want to tell me what happened?" Thunder Thighs folded her arms and glared at me.

"What do you mean?" I asked, handing a shivering Skinny my blanket. She needed it more than I did.

Skinny used the blanket to wipe the water off her glasses, then wrapped the blanket around herself, covering her head so only her face was exposed.

"Is there a problem?" RL Steven asked.

"Nope," I quickly said. "Both our canoes tipped over in the water, but we're all fine. We got back to our partners and finished the trip."

RL Steven glanced at everyone, waiting for someone to say otherwise, and for those few moments, I held my breath. I had no idea what would happen to me if someone told him the truth.

Skinny's chin chattered away, her wide eyes telling me she

was too scared to say something. Thunder Thighs, on the other hand, was shivering in anger. I could practically see the wheels turning in her head, weighing her options. She probably didn't want me as a partner anymore.

RL Steven mumbled something under his breath and erased the names on the paper as he walked away.

"You got back in the wrong canoe," Thunder Thighs hissed, just inches away from my face.

"I was trying to survive," I said, backing away from her. Her breath smelled like pickles. "Her canoe was closer."

"You still broke a rule," Thunder Thighs said. "Do you realize what position you put us all in?" She unfolded her arms and shoved her finger into my chest. "If you want to break rules and get yourself in trouble, that's fine. Just don't bring us down with you."

"Listen, it's over and done," I said. "Our partnerships have been changed."

Thunder Thighs let out a few huffs and then backed away.

Day one and I'd already broken a rule. I just hoped it didn't come back to bite me in the butt.

CHAPTER 8

The bus dropped us off outside of the Recruitment dorms, which were right next door to the Center. Side by side, they didn't look that different. They had the same white, up kept stucco, and the same amount of spotless windows. The Center just had one less floor. River Springs, for the most part, looked exactly the same. The leaders liked uniformity.

Once we were all off the bus, RL Steven addressed us. "I hope you all like your Recruitment partners because that's who your dorm mate will be. When we go inside, the girls will go to the left where you'll be met by your dorm leader Jen. She'll show you to your rooms. Guys, I'll be your dorm leader, so follow me to the end of the hall and up the stairs. When you get to your dorms, you'll find everything you'll need for the rest of Recruitment, including clothes and a bathroom kit. Lunch is in twenty, so make sure you're out of your dorms five minutes before so you can walk with your leader. The dining hall is on the first floor. Any questions?"

When no one answered, he ushered us inside.

DL Jen was waiting for us at the bottom of the stairs that led to the girl's dorms. She was a petite girl in her early twenties, with blonde hair cut to just below her ears. Her hazel eyes were warm and inviting, yet her tight mouth let you know she could be tough when she needed to be.

"Hello, ladies," DL Jen said, her tight mouth turning into a smile. "We'll be on the second floor, so you don't have to walk up far. The dining hall is halfway down that hall on the left-hand side." She pointed to the door for us to see. "The stairs at the end of that hall go to the boy's dorms, which is off-limits to you, so don't try going there. Follow me upstairs."

When we got to the second floor, DL Jen assigned rooms for each set of partners. They were tiny, basic rooms with two beds, a nightstand in the middle with a lamp, and a tall dresser near the door for our clothes.

I went to the dresser and checked the drawers. They were neatly piled with shirts, pants, underwear, and socks. The first three drawers were labeled, Recruit 1, while the bottom three were labeled, Recruit 2. A paper was taped to the top of the dresser letting us know what color scheme to wear during the week.

"I'm starving," Tina said, looking over my shoulder at the list. "Should we change into fresh clothes and then go downstairs?"

I patted my stomach. "Yes. I'm starving, too."

The dining hall was packed with Recruits when we got down there. The excitement buzzed in the air as everyone chatted about their day. After what seemed like forever in line, Tina and I found an empty table in the back and sat across from each other. We had barely started eating when Eric came and sat next to me, his arm brushing up against mine. Luke sat across from us, right next to Tina.

"So, have the two of you kissed and made up yet?" I asked the guys, taking a bite of my bologna sandwich. It tasted as gross as I expected it to be.

"Not likely," Luke said. He just stared at the food on his plate.

"Are you going to eat?" Tina asked Luke.

"I'm not hungry," Luke said, pushing his food around on his plate.

Eric, on the other hand, shoveled food into his mouth like an animal.

"Well, Eric is." I tried not to let my mouth hang open as I watched him pack away his food.

"What, does this bother you?" Eric asked me with a full mouth, a few pieces falling out.

I pushed his arm with my hand. "That's so gross!" A small smile formed on Luke's face, surprising me.

"Emmie!" The shout came from behind us. I turned around to see Dee walking toward our table, her big brown eyes shining.

"Dee!" I jumped up and went to her, pulling her tiny body into a hug. Everything about her was small, from her nose to her feet, but her big personality more than made up for it.

I didn't realize how much I'd missed her, and it hadn't even been a full day yet. Seeing her in a plain white outfit with no makeup on took away some of her spunk. I guess that's why they had us all dress the same way. No one stood out. It made us all equals.

"What happened this morning?" Dee asked, pulling away from our embrace. She tucked one of her brown curls behind her ear. I had always been jealous of her perfect curls. But she had always been jealous of my straight blonde hair. "You didn't show up at the bus stop."

"I barely missed it," I said. "I even ran to the other bus stop near us and that one was gone, too."

Dee frowned. "How did you get here?"

I nodded toward Eric. "He gave me a ride."

Dee looked past me with a scandalous smile on her lips. She'd teased me about him the whole ride home from the Recruitment office when we turned in our papers. "Are you going to introduce me?"

"Be on your best behavior," I said quietly to her as we went to the table. The wink she gave me wasn't very comforting. "Everyone, this is my best friend, Dee. Dee, this is Eric, Luke, and my partner in crime for the rest of Recruitment, Tina."

Dee smiled. "It's nice to meet all of you."

"You, too," Tina said.

Luke just grunted in response.

"So, you do have friends." Eric's plate was already empty, not a crumb in sight. He ate faster than my brother. Although, like everyone else in Recruitment, he didn't have much food to begin with.

"Very funny," I said to him. "Oh, Dee, you didn't tell me

who your partner is."

Dee's face went a little pale. "Amber."

My eyes widened. Dean Johnson's daughter. She had everyone wrapped around her tiny little finger. Amber put on quite the show out in public, but I'd had a few run-ins with her growing up.

Once, when we were seven, she had gone ballistic on me when I didn't tell her I liked the painting she'd drawn. All the other kids in our class were raving about it, but I just shrugged and kept my mouth shut. She cornered me in the hallway after school once everyone had left and told me off. She even scratched me and pulled at my hair. I swore she had a multiple personality disorder, but unfortunately, no one else had seen that side of her except me.

"Oh, Dee. I'm so sorry. I guess you two are about the same height. Is that how they paired you up?"

"Yes." Dee had never seen Amber's other side, but she believed me when I told her of our encounters. Everyone else thought I had made it up for attention.

Tina set down her fork. "Who's Amber?" She took a drink of water and then picked her fork back up.

"The Devil incarnate." As soon as the words left my mouth, I regretted them. I didn't need other people to think I had some weird complex about Amber. That list was already pretty long. Even Dad didn't believe me.

"Amber and Emmie are, well, they don't get along very well," Dee said as politely as she could.

I, on the other hand, was not so polite. "Dee, we loathe each other. She's awful. She just exemplifies everything evil." I had a terrible habit of letting my words run away from me. I needed to bite my tongue.

"Wow," Eric said, eyeing me. "She sounds nice."

"Sorry. I've just had some bad experiences with her," I said to him. Wanting to change the subject, I turned to Dee. "How did your first task go?"

"Oh, Emmie, it was awful," Dee said, taking a seat at our table. I sat down between her and Eric. He didn't scoot over to give me more room. I was practically sitting on his lap. "She has to be the worst partner, ever. They took us to the preschool and locked each set of partners in with ten kids." Dee rubbed her temples. "At first she was so nice with the kids. Played with them, laughed at their jokes. Then a switch flipped when one of the boys threw a ball at her head. Luckily, she didn't take it out on the kid, but she was so ornery the rest of the time. She whined and complained and would never work with me. She got so frustrated one time, she shoved me out of her way, and I fell, landing on a huge box of toys." She held up her left arm and pulled up her sleeve to show us some scrapes and bruises.

I took hold of her arm, looking closely at the cuts. "That looks terrible. I can't believe you're going to be stuck with her the whole time."

Dee pulled her sleeve back down. "And share a room. She made us late for lunch because she wanted to take a shower when we got back. Apparently, she takes two showers a day. Sometimes three."

"Someone needs to tell her that no matter how many showers she takes, the evil will never come off," I said, putting my arm around Dee. When I realized what I'd said, I cringed, but Tina and Eric had laughed.

Dee rested her head on my shoulder and sighed. “I wish there were some way to switch groups. I’d much rather be with you.”

“Even if we did switch groups, I’d have to shrink five inches.” I patted her on the head.

Dee sat up as tall she could. “Or I could grow.”

“Dee!” I knew that high pitched, snappy voice. Amber. “Dee! What are you doing?”

Dee closed her eyes and sighed again. When she didn’t respond, Amber approached the table.

“Dee, we should get back to our dorm as soon as possible.” Amber's voice had switched to kind, almost motherly. She smiled at everyone, her lips parting enough to see a gap in the middle of her front two teeth and then looked back at Dee. “We can't be late for the orientation meeting.”

“Oh, shut up Amber,” I said, turning to her. “You aren’t the boss of her. She can do what she wants.” How did she always bring out the anger in me? I needed to learn to control myself.

Amber looked at me as if noticing me for the first time. She let out a deep breath and then smiled, keeping her tone light and sweet. “I’m her partner, Emelia. We need to stay by each other’s sides.”

She had cut her black hair surprisingly short, making her sharp facial features stand out. She looked like her father. “I see you cut your hair. You could just shave it all off and go for a daddy/daughter look.”

Amber rolled her gray eyes then glanced at her perfectly

trimmed nails. "I would get mad at you, Emelia, but you aren't worth my time." She eyed our table. "I'm so sorry you have to put up with Emelia. She has horrible manners." Amber turned on the charm and reached forward, holding out her hand to Eric. "I'm Amber. And you are?"

Eric stared at Amber's hand. His eyes flickered to mine before he shook her hand. "Eric."

Their clasped hands were right in front of me. Amber caressed his hand with her thumb. Eric finally ended up pulling his hand away. Anger flashed briefly in Amber's eyes, but it was gone in a matter of seconds. Underneath the table, Eric wiped his hand off on his pants, making me smile on the inside.

"So nice to meet you." Amber ignored Tina and Luke, keeping her eyes on Eric. A strange glint crossed over her eyes, causing me to squirm. It was almost a look of ownership. Or maybe lust. "You should come eat dinner at my table tonight. Only the best of the best sit there."

"I think I'll stay here," Eric said, smiling at me. "I like the view."

Amber's face turned red. "Are you talking about Emelia? You can't be serious. She's so … so … so … I mean, she's … well, she's …"

"At a loss for words?" Luke asked. When Amber looked over at him, she looked startled. Luke grinned. "Yes, there are other people at the table besides you and Eric. People who can actually form sentences."

"How dare you! You can't talk to me like that, you …" Clearing her throat, Amber brushed off her clothes like she was brushing off the comment. "No bother. Dee, shall we go?" I could tell Amber was trying not to explode.

"What's going on over here?" RL Steven walked up to our group and looked at Amber. "Is there a problem?"

Amber smiled sweetly at RL Steven. "No, Dee and I were just leaving. Come on, Dee."

Dee turned to me. "It was good to see you." She put her arms around me, and I squeezed her tight.

"It's going to be okay," I whispered in her ear.

"I hope so," Dee said in my ear. She got up and walked right past Amber and headed toward the exit.

Amber look mortified, placing her hand on her chest in an exaggerated fashion. "A few minutes with you, Emelia, and her nasty habits are back. Don't worry, I'll fix her. She'll be normal in no time."

"If being like you is normal, Amber, then I can't wait to be completely insane for the rest of my life." I stared into her eyes. Those stupid, ugly, gray eyes. The dullest color ever.

Amber opened her mouth to say something, but RL Steven cut her off. "That's enough. You should be on your way, Amber."

For a second, I was surprised he knew her name. Then I remembered anyone who worked for Recruitment knew the Johnson family name.

She smiled innocently at RL Steven, provocatively at Eric, and tiredly at me.

"That was odd," Tina said, watching Amber walk away.

Eric nodded. "One minute she was mad. The next she was happy."

Tina shrugged. "Maybe it's that time of the month for her."

"Maybe." I still thought she had split personalities. I glanced at Luke. "Your comment was hilarious, by the way."

Blushing, Luke stared at his uneaten food. "I have no idea where that came from. Something about her rubbed me the wrong way. I can't explain it."

Eric wiped both his hands on his pants. "I'll tell you what rubbed me the wrong way. Her handshake."

"She was practically groping you." Tina smiled at him. "I almost told you two to get a room."

"No, thank you." Eric shook his head, his hands still on his pants. "She's not my type." His hand brushed up against mine. For a second, it looked like he was going to grab my hand, but the gesture was so small that I couldn't be certain. My heart fluttered at the thought.

I suddenly realized RL Steven was still standing near us. He cleared his throat. "When you're done eating, head outside. We'll be going next door for an orientation meeting." RL Steven started to walk away but then turned back. "I'm sure you've all read the honor code for Recruitment, but no dating, kissing, hooking up, getting a room or anything like that is allowed."

When RL Steven was out of hearing range, I patted Eric's arm. "Sorry, Eric, but I guess you and Amber will have to hold off on the romance."

He gagged. "That's not even funny."

Tina laughed. "It kinda is."

Amber had never shown that much of her "other" side out in public. It made me wonder if she was getting worse. It did make me happy, though, that others had finally seen that she wasn't always perfect like she pretended to be. So, I wasn't completely delusional.

Only somewhat.

CHAPTER 9

VP Frank Oliver

Clasping my hands in front of me, I leaned against the table and faced the class. "Years ago, the United States broke apart. There were mass earthquakes, floods, and tornadoes. Entire cities and states were completely destroyed. Panic set in amongst the citizens. Neighbors and friends turned on each other. War broke out, causing lots of innocent bloodshed."

Most of the Recruits had seemed bored when I first entered the room. Suddenly, I had their interest. They were all sitting forward, excited to hear more.

"We needed a change. After a lot of negotiations, a treaty was signed, dividing what was left of the United States into four different regions. The land itself had restructured, causing mountains to move, new rivers and lakes to be created, plains to rise and fall. The four regions were made up of what had been the west most part of the United States. The land had settled into livable areas, with good soil and solid ground."

A hand shot up in the front of the classroom. I glanced at his name tag. Luke Nelson. I pointed to him. "Yes, Luke?"

Luke smiled. "We have the best area, right? River Springs? I mean, out of the four regions."

Talking about the other cities was inevitable. Honestly, I wouldn't have minded talking about them. But Whit opposed it. He didn't like the idea of anyone leaving River Springs or the idea of relinquishing control. I hated lying, especially to the Recruits. I had to tell myself it wouldn't be for too much longer. "Of course. River Springs is more advanced. It's safer and cleaner than the others."

Another hand went up. Looking at her name tag, I pointed to her. "Yes, Angela?"

Angela pushed her glasses up on her skinny nose. "Have you been to the other cities? I heard they're horrible. Disease, murder, and strict punishments. My mom says River Springs is the only place to live." A few others in the class nodded in agreement.

I sighed inwardly. I had been to the other cities. They were all different, all held their own advantages and disadvantages to River Springs. But they weren't bad like they were painted. I needed to keep the topic from going too far off course. "River Springs is the best city out of all of them. We were lucky that we had Infinity Corp to help. It was a key element in the rebuilding of our city. It provided all the materials, supplies, organizational structure and support, and the manpower we needed. The fact of the matter was that the government was decimated and didn't have the required resources to provide food, shelter, and safety for the citizens. Infinity Corp did."

Before the divide, Infinity Corp had been a tech company. It strived in the economy, making it one of the most profitable companies in the U.S. Infinity had survived the divide and started to buy out all the companies that had failed or were destroyed. Pretty soon, they owned everything in the city.

"The company has a core set of values it strives on," I said. "Can anyone tell me what they are?"

Luke's hand shot up again. When I nodded at him, he sat up tall. "Honesty, commitment, charity, and the wellbeing of each member of the community."

"Very good, Luke," I said.

Those values had worked flawlessly for so many years. Unfortunately, I'd seen Whit Randall falter on each one of them. His choices of late were based on greed, power, and the need to be in charge. The fact that he'd chosen to involve himself more in Recruitment had proved it.

In the back of the classroom, Emmie stared at the ceiling. I guess I didn't have everyone's attention. "Can anyone tell me how long we've had full functioning water lines throughout the city?"

Luke's hand went up, but I looked around for someone else. I like his eagerness, but someone else needed a chance to respond. A red-haired girl next to him raised her hand. I pointed at her after glancing at her nametag. "Tina?"

"Twenty years ago," Tina said.

I nodded. "Correct. How about electricity?"

Tina's and Luke's hands went up, but I pointed at another boy in the middle of the classroom. "Will?"

"Seventeen years ago," Will said. "The year we were born."

"Correct again," I said.

"Best year ever." A boy next to Emmie had spoken. The same boy she'd shown up with on the first day of Recruitment. His nametag said Eric. "I'm so glad I live now. There's no way I could live without water and electricity."

Tina shook her head. "Me either."

Most of the Recruits paid close attention the rest of the class. Except for Emmie. She was either yawning or staring at Eric. Sometimes I wished she would take things more seriously, but other times I understood where she was coming from. She didn't like River Springs. She didn't believe in our city.

After the class, I headed back to my office where I was expecting some visitors. I'd been keeping in touch with Wallace Brown, who was the Vice President in the city of Kingsland, north of River Springs. They were able to settle with a government that worked for them. From where I stood, I didn't see much difference between how they ran their city and how we ran ours.

If Whit knew I talked frequently with Wallace, he would be upset. He didn't like the other cities interfering with one another, which was how he saw it. I thought by working together, we could have something amazing and each community could prosper and grow more so than they had been. To me, River Springs had been stuck in a rut the past ten years and needed a fresh start.

Wallace and his son, Dante, were on their way to Infinity Corp. I'd told Whit that they wanted to look into our infrastructure and see how we ran Recruitment because they were considering starting something similar. Whit finally agreed when I told them how much they admired him and his work and wanted to be successful like him.

They were really coming to stake out our Recruits to see if one of them fit the description of a revolutionary described in a prophecy.

Years before, a member of the community, Lee Augustine, had prophesied that greed and hate would form in the hearts of the leaders of River Springs and they would resort to violence, even murder, to get what they want. He said the city would self-destruct much faster than the world had. Augustine said that unless something was done, man as we knew it would cease to exist.

The last part of the prophecy drove Whit crazy. It stated that there would be one among the city who would lead a revolution. One who would want to stop the leadership of River Springs and take it down piece by piece.

For many years, the leaders shrugged it off. They declared Augustine insane and told the citizens not to trust in his ranting. What they didn't tell the citizens was that Augustine happened to be a descendent of the same man who had a prophecy foretelling the dividing of the United States.

In my heart, I knew the prophecy would come true and it would be soon. I'd been watching the Recruits every year trying to see if I could find that person. The prophecy stated that each of the four cities would have their own revolutionary. I'd finally found someone in ours that I believed to be the one.

Dante had been confirmed the revolutionary in

Kingsland. Each revolutionary would have a vision of the future, and Dante's had been exactly like Augustine had described. Dante had the right mindset and determination to do well. He still had some growing up to do, though. Dante had barely turned seventeen and proved himself to be a teenage boy over and over again.

A small knock at the door took me from my thoughts. I'd been sitting in my office, contemplating my strategy for the Brown's visit to River Springs.

I turned my chair toward the door. "Come in."

The door opened and Wallace came in, followed by Dante. Wallace smiled at me. "Frank! So good to see you." Tall and strong, Wallace had the demeanor of a leader. Some gray had started to sneak into his otherwise black hair. He had a natural confidence about him that had rubbed off on his son.

I stood and went over near the door, taking Wallace in an embrace. "It's been too long." I pulled back and shook Dante's hand. He wasn't nearly as tall as his dad, but I had a feeling one day he would. His dark skin was a tad bit lighter than his dad's, but not by much. "Dante. You're looking well." I slapped his biceps, which had grown considerably since I'd last seen him.

Dante flexed his arm, flashing a smile that would probably drive the girl's crazy. "Been working on it. I figured if I can't grow in height, I could grow in girth."

I laughed. "Always a good option." Two chairs were sitting near my desk, so I gestured to them. "Please, sit." I took my seat on the other side of the table. "How was the trip?"

"Long." Dante slumped in his chair. He wore a faded blue T-shirt, tucked in only in the front of his pants. His jeans had a rip near the knee, but that seemed to be the fashion in Kingsland. They dressed very casually and basic. Jeans and T-shirts mostly.

Wallace grimaced at his son. "It wasn't too bad. I think we're both a little exhausted." He wore a dark green polo shirt tucked all the way into his jeans, which were free of any tears or holes. That's as fancy as they got in Kingsland.

"Can I get you anything to eat or drink?" I asked, adjusting my tie. I felt overdressed in my suit.

Wallace shook his head. "Not yet." He leaned forward, his eyes eager. "Do you really think you've found the revolutionary?"

The Recruit's exam results from their Recruitment application sat at the edge of my desk. I slid it closer to Wallace. "Her tests say so."

Wallace took the papers and thumbed through them.

"Technically, she shouldn't have been accepted into Recruitment," I said. "She's Whit's worse nightmare. Completely uncontrollable. But he signed off on it. Probably to keep a close eye on her." Wallace nodded and continued flipping through the papers, so I continued speaking. "She's fiery, that's for sure. She resists authority, questions the corporation and absolutely hates Whit." Leaning back in my chair, I clasped my hands behind my head. "Her psych evaluation was extraordinary. She's a hands-on kind of person. She never believed what she was told; she had to figure it out herself. When the psychiatrist showed her flashcards, she completely ignored him and snatched up a model car sitting on his desk. She took the whole thing apart, put it back together, then set it back on his desk."

Dante let out a laugh. "She sounds like me."

"That she does," Wallace said wryly.

Dante ignored his father and leaned forward, suddenly interested in the conversation. "How does she get along with others?"

"Depends on who it is," I said with a shrug. "Overall, she's nice, approachable and caring. She's the type who'd do anything for a friend, even sacrifice herself. But if she doesn't like you, she'll let you know. She can't fake liking a person even if it will benefit her. She'd rather figure out another way to handle a situation just to avoid you."

Dante's laugh was louder. "Again, sounds just like me." He looked at his father. "We're either going to get along just great or get on each other's nerves."

Wallace sighed. "I hope it's not the latter. If she's the revolutionary, you two are going to have to figure out a way to get along if you want to succeed."

"What's her name?" Dante asked.

"Emelia." I smiled at them. "Don't call her that, though. She'll hate you from the start. She goes by Emmie."

Wallace had been reading the papers, but his eyes flashed up to mine when he heard her name. "You've talked about her before, haven't you?"

Dante took the papers from his dad's grasp while he was distracted and sorted through them, smiling and shaking his head every now and then.

"I've known her since she was a baby." I smiled thinking back to all my memories of her. We'd gotten along so well since the moment she could walk. I'd always considered her like a daughter. "She's smart, capable, trustworthy, loyal. She's everything we want and need in a revolutionary. She'll fight for what she wants and won't back down until she gets it." I sighed. "Right now, though, she doesn't seem herself. She doesn't want to be in Recruitment, yet she's here."

A laugh from Dante caught my attention. He held the paper out. "When the psychiatrist asked her to build a tower from some building blocks, she asked why. When he said, 'because I'd like a tower on my desk,' she said, 'stop being so damn lazy and do it yourself.'" Dante snorted. "Man, I really like her. When can we meet?"

The prophecy had never come up around Emmie. Countless times over the past few years, I'd almost mentioned it to her. Back then, I didn't think it was her, but I had this feeling that I should talk to her about it. Every time, I'd shrugged it off. It just hadn't seemed plausible for her to be the one. Recent events had come to light, making me change my mind. "She doesn't know."

Wallace's eyebrows shot up. "About the prophecy?"

"She knows about that." Unclasping my hands, I put them on the table and leaned forward. "Vaguely. Whit made sure there aren't any books or anything on the prophecy in the city. Most of what the citizens hear is what has been passed on from older generations. What she doesn't know is that I think it's her."

"I see," Wallace said with a nod. He pulled his leg up, resting his ankle on his other knee. "Are you going to tell her?"

"Not yet," I said. "I want to be certain that it's her. Once we tell her, it will alter her life. It will change everything."

Dante looked up from the papers. "I know about me and I'm doing fine." He shook the papers. "If she's as amazing as these papers say, then she'll definitely be able to handle it."

Shaking my head, I looked at the picture of my family on my desk. My wife, daughter and son were my pride and joy. Emmie held a special place in my heart next to theirs'. "If it is her, there's more that will unfold than I can tell you about. It will change her life in more ways than one. She's not ready for it." I reached out and adjusted the frame, so it was in its right place on my desk. "Not yet."

"Can we still meet her?" Dante asked. "I'd really like to get to know her better. Maybe I would be able to tell if she's the one."

Wallace looked from his son to me. "I agree. Dante might have more insight into the matter."

"Whit thinks you're here to scout out Recruitment," I said. "Maybe we can have you be in a challenge with her group. We'll tell Whit it's to see if you can handle it, but you can really keep an eye on Emmie."

Dante stood from his chair. "Great. When do we start?"

He really was eager. Standing, I smiled at him. "Tomorrow morning, bright and early."

Dante grunted. "You had me until bright and early."

"Well, you'll fit in quite nicely then," I said with a laugh.

A part of me didn't want it to be Emmie because it would create a hard life for her. But if anyone could handle it, Emmie could.

CHAPTER 10
Emmie

Orientation had been boring and pointless. It dragged on and on. Eating rice and peas for dinner had been worse. I surprised myself by not gagging. But I'd also snuck some of the peas into a folded-up napkin when I thought no one was looking.

"If I have trouble sleeping tonight," Eric said as we walked out of the dining hall, "I'll just replay orientation in my head and I'm sure I'll be out in no time."

Tina laughed. "No kidding."

Luke had sat with us at dinner even though it seemed like he hated Eric. He must have had a crush on Tina because that was the only plausible explanation to it all. He stiffened as we walked. "Everything we were told was important, vital information."

I rolled my eyes. "It was the same crap we've heard our whole life about the divide. I don't know why they feel the need to keep repeating it over and over again."

"That's how you learn things," Luke said. "Unless you have an eidetic memory, there's no way you could remember something after hearing it only once or twice."

Tina opened her mouth to say something, but her eyes widened. Turning around, I saw what had surprised her.

President Randall and RH Johnson approached us, neither of them looking happy. I'd started using their titles in my head so I could get used to saying them out loud.

"Tina and Emmie," President Randall said. "We'd like a word in private with the two of you."

RH Johnson stood there, the veins popping out of his neck. It made me wonder if the anger stemmed from me and Tina, or the fact that President Randall had taken over his position.

President Randall gestured for us to follow him, so we did. I didn't bother looking back at Eric and Luke to see what expressions they had on their faces.

I could hear RH Johnson walking behind us. We'd just rounded the corner in the hallway when I saw Amber and Dee.

Dee mouthed, "What's going on?"

Shrugging, I shook my head. I had no idea.

"Daddy!" Amber ran up and threw her arms around RH Johnson's neck. He patted her back awkwardly and finally removed her from his body.

"Amber, go on to your dorm." RH Johnson's voice was tight.

Amber pouted, looking at us. "Did they do something bad?"

RH Johnson glared at her, but when she returned the glare

tenfold, he cleared his throat and forced a smile. "This isn't your concern. Please go to your dorm, sweetie."

"Is there a problem, Dean?" President Randall asked.

He shook his head. "No, sir." Gently pushing his daughter aside, he started walking again.

There was a small twitch in Amber's eye, her look bordering on hate. Before she followed him, she pulled herself together, smiled innocently at President Randall and continued down the hall. Dee raised her eyebrows at me and then followed Amber.

President Randall took us to a gym at the Recruitment Center next door to the dorms. RL Steven, Thunder Thighs and Skinny stood in the middle of the room with a man I'd seen a few times before but had never met. Tall, strong, and intimidating were the words that came to my head when I looked at him.

The man had short, neatly trimmed red hair and light blue eyes. He had a few days' growth on his upper lip and firm, square jaw. RL Steven stood next to him, his arms folded, trying to look tough. It wasn't working.

President Randall stopped near the center of the gym and adjusted his tie. He waited until all eyes were on him. "An unnerving situation was brought to me earlier this evening. It seems the four of you," he motioned to me, Tina, Thunder Thighs and Skinny, "broke a rule today. As your contract states, you will be punished for any rule breaking. You could also be terminated from Recruitment."

Thunder Thighs' eyes flickered to mine, pure anger etched all around.

"You were told to stay with your partners," President Randall said. "But you switched when you fell in the river."

Skinny's eyes were on the ground, tears rolling down her cheeks.

I stepped forward. "They didn't break a rule. I did. They had nothing to do with it."

Thunder Thighs nodded and pointed to me. "It was all her."

President Randall undid the buttons on his blazer and put his hands in his pocket. "Yet, none of you corrected her when she lied right to RL Steven's face."

"You can't punish us because of *her*!" Thunder Thighs had practically spat the words out at me.

I kept waiting for Skinny to whine and complain, but she kept her head down, staying quiet. She wouldn't make eye contact with any of us.

She'd probably been the one to rat us out.

"Enough!" President Randall yelled. "You signed the contract. You knew what was at stake when you entered Recruitment. You will be held accountable for every decision you make, including not stopping someone else for breaking a rule or turning them in. You each had a chance to report the infraction to your leaders, but you chose not to. You will all be punished." He gestured to the man. "This is Security Officer Mack Clark. You'll address him as SO Clark. You will do as he commands. If one complaint comes out of any of your mouths, then he's been ordered to add ten minutes to the workout."

Thunder Thighs swore under her breath, but not quietly enough.

"Ten minutes right there," President Randall said. When she swore again, he added another ten. I had a feeling that Thunder Thighs and Skinny were going to be the death of me.

President Randall turned to RH Johnson. "Anything you'd like to add to this, Dean?"

RH Johnson shook his head. "I think you covered it all."

"RL Steven will be watching you as well," President Randall said. "If he catches anyone whining, complaining, groaning, swearing, or anything of the likes, he's been ordered to tell SO Clark, who will add to your punishment. Do I make myself clear?"

We all muttered, "Yes, sir."

President Randall and RH Johnson left without another word, but not without a few dirty looks.

SO Clark stood tall in the middle of the room and folded his arms. "Here's how tonight is going to go. We'll start with fifty pushups, fifty crunches, fifty jumping jacks and then twenty laps around the gym. Once the warmup is done, we'll go from there."

Skinny's jaw dropped. "That's the warmup?"

"Are you complaining?" SO Clark asked, his eyes digging into hers.

She shook her head vigorously. "No, sir. I was just trying to clarify." She smiled sheepishly at him. When he looked away, she shot me a death look. Thunder Thighs shot me one, too.

I turned to Tina with an apologetic face. Shrugging, she squeezed my arm. "I could use a good work out. I might have overeaten at dinner with my unseasoned chicken wing and half a cup of corn."

"If I would have known ..." I started.

Tina smiled and leaned in close. "I still would have wanted you to switch." She nodded over at Thunder Thighs and Skinny who were having a glare off. "They deserve each other."

SO Clark suddenly stood next to us, a sliver of a smile on his face. "That they do. Now, let's begin."

Partway during our workout, I'd accidentally kicked a soccer ball into the corner of the gym. When I bent over to pick it up, I heard two voices right outside the door.

"Is this all necessary?" It was VP Oliver.

"Of course it is, Frank," President Randall said. "You know it is. You've read everything I have."

"Whit, she's just a child." VP sounded tired.

President Randall's voice was clipped. "That's enough. I'm through hearing excuses from you. This is for the sake of our city. For Infinity Corp. We have a responsibility to uphold."

VP Oliver sighed. "But at what cost?"

"Whatever it takes," President Randall said. A chill went through my body. I backed away from the door and ran back to where the others were.

The clock had just struck midnight when we walked into our dorm rooms and flopped down on our beds. Thunder Thighs and Skinny had each added more minutes to our workout, but after a little while, they learned to keep their complaints to themselves.

SO Clark had definitely given us a tough workout, but there was something endearing about him. Maybe it was the look of amusement he'd flash me and Tina when Skinny or Thunder Thighs messed up or stumbled.

One of the rules had said not to talk after lights out and there was no way I wanted to break another rule. I'd learned my lesson for the time being. I looked over at Tina and frowned. She held her hand out for me and I took it in mine. She gave it a good squeeze, mouthed, "Goodnight," and fell right asleep.

When her hand finally dropped from mine, I turned over onto my back and stared at the ceiling. Even though I was exhausted, I couldn't fall asleep. The second Mom found out what had happened, she would tear me a new one. But even with the achy muscles, ornery Thunder Thighs and Skinny, and getting my partner in trouble, if I could go back, I'd make the same choice.

My head wouldn't stop buzzing about what I'd overheard. At first, I thought they were talking about our punishment, but President Randall had said that VP Oliver had read everything he had. Read what? What were they talking about? They hadn't mentioned me specifically, but something in my gut said they were talking about me.

I'd just have to find a way to talk to VP Oliver about it. Until then, I needed to find a way to turn off my brain so I could sleep.

When I closed my eyes, the same stupid shark that I'd envisioned last night came to me. Only this time, it had Thunder Thighs' angry face and Skinny's frizzy hair.

It wasn't a very becoming look for the shark.

CHAPTER 11

The next morning, I could barely move. My eyes were so heavy it took a lot of will and determination to pry them open. All they wanted to do was stay closed and take me back into the land of sleep. With my head actively trying to answer questions I didn't have answers to, I didn't fall asleep until four in the morning. Tina jostled me awake at six-thirty.

"Wake up, sleepyhead," Tina said, sitting on the edge of my bed. "We have to be downstairs for breakfast at seven and out to the bus by eight. I wasn't sure how long you take to get ready."

I moaned and threw my blankets over my head.

"Sore from last night?" Tina asked.

"You have no idea," I said through the covers.

Tina tugged on my covers, but I held on tight. She let out a small laugh. "Well, you might want to hurry if you want to take a shower. Who knows if there are any stalls available."

I threw off the covers and slowly sat up, my muscles screaming at me from the movement. "You're probably right."

I slapped my face, hoping that would help wake me up.

"Need help with that?" Tina asked.

"Very funny," I said, giving her a shove.

I ended up having to wait fifteen minutes until a stall opened. I took a quick shower, got dressed in my green clothes and ran a brush through my hair. I looked in the mirror and sighed. I looked terrible. I felt terrible, too. It was going to be a long day.

On the way out of the bathroom, I ran into Amber. Literally. I had just opened the door to walk out when she came waltzing in. I couldn't stop myself in time, so I smacked right into her.

Amber grabbed me by my shirt and threw me against the wall inside the bathroom, the door swinging shut behind her. She may have been short, but she was extremely strong. If I didn't hate her so much, I probably would've been impressed. "You need to watch where you're going, Emelia."

I took her hand and yanked it off my shirt, throwing her backward. She stumbled a little but quickly regained her balance. "Leave me alone, Amber." I wasn't in the mood for her that morning. Not that I was ever in the mood for her.

Amber shoved me into the wall with all her might. "Stay out of my way and I will." She stuck up her nose and turned around, walking toward a stall.

It might have been the strenuous workout, or the conversation I overheard the previous night or the fact that I didn't sleep, but I just snapped. I threw myself at the back of Amber, knocking her down on the ground.

Putting my hand on the back of her head, I pressed her

face into the ground and moved my mouth near her ear. "I really don't want to deal with you right now. Just get over yourself and move on with your life. I don't know why you're obsessed with me, but you need to drop it. I don't want to see your ugly face again."

I gave her head another shove and stood up. My brain was foggy with exhaustion. Somehow, Amber brought out the worst in me. Maybe *I* was the crazy one.

As I walked to the door, Amber came up behind me, grabbed my hair and threw me on the ground. She jumped on top of me and punched me hard on the jaw. She went to punch me again, but I moved my head at the last second, her fist hitting the tiled floor, hard.

Amber screamed out in pain, a sound I could definitely get used to. I took the opportunity to wriggle away from her and stood up, rubbing my jaw.

"You stupid, little, conniving …" Amber started, standing up. Her knuckles were covered in blood. Before she finished her sentence, she flung herself at me again, pushing me up against the wall. She punched me in the stomach with her good hand. When she went to punch me again, I grabbed her wrist and twisted it away from me.

"Knock it off!" The yell came from the door. I looked to see my dorm leader, Jen, standing there with her hands on her hips. When Amber wouldn't get off me, DL Jen came over and pulled her off.

"What's wrong with you two?" DL Jen asked, holding onto Amber.

"She started it," Amber said, trying to shake DL Jen off her.

"Stop it!" DL Jen yelled at Amber. "Just stop!"

When Amber finally quit moving, DL Jen waited a few seconds and then let go. She took out a small device from her pocket and held it up to her mouth. "We have a situation in the girl's bathroom."

"What kind of situation?" A voice came from the device.

DL Jen sighed. "A fight. Just come up here."

"Do you want me to get one of the leaders?" The voice asked.

"No," DL Jen said, eying me. "Just you. Get up here." She put the device back in her pocket.

"I'm not staying here," Amber said, walking toward the door. DL Jen took hold of Amber's arm, stopping her from escaping.

"You're not going anywhere," DL Jen said.

The bathroom door opened, and Tina walked in, stopping in her tracks. "What's going on?"

"Nothing," DL Jen said. She looked at Tina. "There's a medical kit under one of the sinks. Will you get it for me?"

Tina looked at me and then back at DL Jen. "Okay." As Tina went to look for the kit, I sat down on the floor and leaned my head against the wall. I wanted to curl up in a ball and go to sleep.

A minute later, RL Steven came into the bathroom. He looked at Amber, who held her bloody hand close to her, and then at me sitting on the floor. "What happened in here?"

"That stupid brat attacked me!" Amber yelled out, choking on a cry. She held up her hand for RL Steven to see. Tina came back with the kit and handed it to DL Jen.

"Yes, that's right, I made you punch the floor," I said, rolling my eyes. "Seriously, Amber, you have to be the biggest idiot."

"Enough!" DL Jen yelled. She forced Amber to sit down on one of the benches in front of the shower stalls and cleaned her knuckles. She looked at RL Steven. "Should we tell anyone about this?"

RL Steven looked at me. "Are you okay?"

I rubbed my jaw. "I'll live."

"What about you?" RL Steven asked Amber.

She whimpered. "Hello! Look at my hand."

"It's just a few scrapes," DL Jen said, blowing away some hair that had fallen over her eyes. "Nothing major."

"My dad will be furious," Amber said, looking at me.

"Why? Because you didn't do a better job beating me up?"

Amber clenched her jaw. If DL Jen hadn't been holding her hand, I'm sure she would've attacked me again.

RL Steven rubbed his head. "I don't know the history between the two of you, but whatever this is, it needs to stop. We'll leave this between us for now, but if this happens again, I will personally take it to the president." He wasn't going to tell him now?

Amber snorted. "Yes, because the president would have time to talk to you. You'd have to talk to my dad first, which is fine with me. I'll be telling him about this, you can count on that."

RL Steven looked frustrated. "Let's just leave him out of it for now. We don't need to make this bigger than it is."

"She attacked me!" Amber screeched. "She can't get away

with it. She's a danger to everyone in Recruitment."

"A danger? Really? Don't you think you're overreacting?" I asked, rubbing my tired eyes. "I mean, you're the one who punched me in the jaw and stomach."

"You shoved my face into the bathroom floor. Do you know how gross that is?" Amber pouted, bashing her eyelashes innocently. "I had to protect myself. It was self-defense."

"Shut up!" RL Steven yelled. With his jaw held tight, the veins popped out from his forehead. "I don't want to hear another word from either of you. Amber, you also fought. If I report this, you'll both be punished. And it will be a mark against me and Jen and our ability to be leaders in Recruitment." So that's why he didn't want to tell anyone. He looked at Amber. "And don't you breathe a word about this to your father." When Amber didn't respond, RL Steven squatted down in front of her, looking her straight in the eye. "Do you understand me?"

Amber looked away. RL Steven grabbed her chin and pulled her face back toward him. "Do you understand me?" His voice was quiet but firm.

A weird look crossed Amber's face that I couldn't make out. She sighed. "Fine."

That caught me by surprise. Amber told her dad everything. I looked back and forth between RL Steven and Amber, wondering why she had caved so easily. Maybe she didn't want to get in trouble that early on in Recruitment.

RL Steven let go of her face and stood. "Emmie, Tina, let's go. Jen, you can take Amber down in a few minutes." RL Steven stood there waiting for me and Tina. I gave one last hateful look to Amber and then left the bathroom.

We walked down in silence to the dining hall. When we were in line for our food, Tina finally spoke. She glanced around to make sure there weren't leaders close enough to hear us talking. "What happened in there?"

"I accidentally bumped into her on the way out and she grabbed me by the shirt and threw me up against the wall. It went a little crazy after that." I moved my jaw back and forth hoping to alleviate some of the pain.

"Sounds like it. Did she really punch you?" Tina had her long, red hair pulled back in a ponytail, making her eyes stand out. Or maybe it was the green Recruitment clothes that brought out the green in her eyes.

"Yes." I held up two fingers. "Twice."

Tina lifted her eyebrows. "Did it hurt?"

"Surprisingly, yes. She's pretty strong." When we got to the front of the line, the lady scanned my finger to see what my breakfast items were, poured some oatmeal in a bowl and handed it to me.

"I can't believe they just let you go and didn't say anything. You should consider yourself lucky," Tina said as we walked away with our food. All she had on her plate were two slices of dry bread and a pickle.

"I don't feel lucky," I mumbled.

We found Eric and Luke sitting near the back of the dining hall.

"Are you okay, Emmie?" Luke asked as we sat down. "You look horrible."

"You really know the right things to say to a girl, don't

you?" Tina asked as she rolled her eyes. "Boys."

"Long night, that's all." I took a few bites of my oatmeal, but couldn't stomach any more, so I pushed the plate away. I lay my head down on my arms and closed my eyes. Eric rubbed my back and leaned in close.

"Are you sure you're okay?" Eric asked. "Do you feel sick?"

"My stomach's a little uneasy," I said into my arms. "I couldn't sleep."

Eric let out a little laugh. "Are you kidding? On those soft, fluffy mattresses they gave us? I was in heaven."

"You mean the thin piece of cardboard?" Luke asked.

"Oh, I know," Tina said. "I'm going to miss my bed terribly.".

Eric was still rubbing my back, so I sat up. I looked around to find RL Steven. He sat a few tables away, looking at us. Great. The last thing I needed was for him to think something romantic was going on between me and Eric. It would be another rule broken.

"What happened last night?" Eric asked. He dropped his hand, resting it in his lap.

Frowning, I rubbed my arms. Everything on my body screamed in pain. "Our partner switch was reported. We were up until midnight doing a workout."

"Ouch." Eric shook his head. "Sounds rough."

Right as I was about to open my mouth, RL Steven signaled for us to head out to the bus.

Grateful for the interruption, I got up and went to Tina, linking my arm through hers. I let Tina get on the bus first and sat down next to her in the back. I liked Eric and all, but he was a little touchy-feely. I wouldn't want RL Steven to get the wrong impression and report it back to anyone.

"If I fall asleep at any point today, just slap me upside the head," I said to Tina, as I rested my head on her shoulder.

"No problem. I'd be happy to." Tina put her arm around me and gave me a little squeeze.

"You're such a doll," I said.

She shrugged. "I know."

Moments later, the bus stopped. I opened my eyes and looked out the window. "How long have I been asleep?" I asked Tina.

"Right after you told me how wonderful I was you zonked out," Tina said. "I hope your little forty-five-minute nap helped some." Had it really been that long?

"I do feel a little revived. We'll see how long it lasts, though." As I sat up, I noticed something in the back corner of the bus. A camera. The technology for them had been recreated just a few years before. They were in limited supply. At least, that's what I'd been told. It made me wonder if they were in all the Recruitment busses, or just ours.

Everything seemed to be getting more and more complicated, and I had no clue what any of it meant.

CHAPTER 12

When we got off the bus, we were near an orchard of trees. I glanced around and saw that there was a stack of long logs of wood and a stack of smaller logs sitting in an open area near the trees. There was a pile of sacks next to the logs. To the right of the sacks were a bunch of sandboxes on the ground made of wood about four feet by four feet.

"Any of you want to go into the lumber trade?" I asked.

Tina, Eric, and Luke were all standing next to me.

"Yes, that's what I've been dreaming of since I was little," Tina said. "Cutting down trees all day long."

Luke looked at Tina. "I'm sure they do other things besides just cutting down trees."

Eric shook his head and rolled his eyes. "It was a joke."

Luke was about to say something when RL Steven cleared his throat, catching our attention. "Yesterday, your bravery was tested. Today, your strength, endurance, and problem-solving skills will be tested. Each team will start by grabbing two long logs from that stack," he said, pointing to the stack on the left, "and ten short logs from that stack," he said pointing to the stack on the right. "Then you'll take one of the bags from the pile. In each bag, you'll find a bunch of ropes you'll use to tie the smaller logs to the longer logs to create a ladder. Once your ladder is created, you'll take it to one of the trees in the orchard. You'll lean your ladder against the tree and use it to climb."

Tina tapped my arm and pointed to the sky. A blue bird flew around above us, flapping its tiny wings hastily. The bird dove at a few Recruits and then perched itself on RL Steven's shoulder. We all tried to keep from laughing as RL Steven tried to brush it off, but the bird didn't want to go anywhere. RL Steven flailed his arms wildly until the bird got fed up and left.

RL Steven rubbed his head and continued. "On the upper branches of the tree, you'll find a series of bags holding pieces of a puzzle. You and your partner must collect all the bags, six in all, and bring them back down to one of the boxes over there on the right. You'll empty your bags and start putting the pieces together to form an image. Once you think you have the correct image, let me know, and I'll check. If you're right, you'll be done, if not, you'll continue until you finish. Any questions?"

A short girl standing near RL Steven spoke up. "What if we can't lift the logs? My partner and I aren't very big."

"You have two options," RL Steven said. "You do the best you can and work hard until you're done. You can also bow out at any time if you feel you can't do it. This, of course, will be taken into account at the end of Recruitment and may affect the outcome of where you're placed in Infinity Corp."

"How long do we have?" Luke asked.

"As long as you need. Be aware that your time will also be taken into account. So will the way you work together as a team. Your rules for this challenge are to make sure each partner gets three sets of bags from the tree, no talking with the other groups, and one partner will put the puzzle pieces together while the other tells them where to place the pieces. Good luck. You may begin." RL Steven went and sat down on a tree stump near the boxes, looking around the sky for any signs of the bird.

"How do you think we should tackle this?" Tina asked me as we headed toward the logs.

"Let's start with the smaller ones," I said. "Try to find the shortest ones you can. Unless you have some superhuman strength I should know about, we want to minimize the weight. Each step doesn't need to be very wide. We only need to be able to put our hands and feet on them."

"Sounds good to me," Tina said as we sorted through the logs.

Most people had started with the longer logs. We found the ten shortest we could find and set them in an open area where we could work.

"Let's get the big ones," Tina said. We went to the longer logs and found two we thought would be sturdy enough to hold our weight, but not too heavy. "Think we can carry two at a time?"

I eyed the logs. "Well, I'm not Thunder Thighs or anything, but we'll have to eventually when we carry the whole thing. This will be a good test."

"Thunder Thighs?" Tina gave me a questioning look.

I laughed softly. "Oh, yeah, I gave the girl in front of me in line that nickname since I didn't know her real name."

"It fits perfectly," Tina laughed. "Her name is Rachel, by the way." We hoisted the two logs onto our shoulders and made our way back to our small pile of logs.

I twisted my lips in thought. "I think I like Thunder Thighs better."

"What nickname did you give Angela?" Tina asked.

"Angela?" I asked.

"The skinny one."

"Skinny," I said, as we put down the two big logs.

"Not as clever, Emmie," Tina said. "But still appropriate."

"I'll start lining these up. Why don't you go get a bag with the ropes?" I offered.

"Sounds good," Tina said.

As she left me alone, I scooted the two longer logs arms width apart and placed the smaller ones on top one by one. Tina came back with the ropes and dumped them on the ground. "Looks like there are twenty individual pieces of rope."

"Do the smaller logs look spaced well to you?" I asked her, eying my work.

Tina looked down at the logs. "Yeah, they look good. Let's start on the left and work our way to the right."

"Do you know how to tie ropes?" I asked, picking one up in my hand.

"Not really," Tina said. "I say we just wrap them a few times around the two pieces of wood and then tie as many knots as we can with what's left of the rope."

"And hope it doesn't fall apart when we start climbing," I said as I started on my first rope.

"I'll let you go first," Tina said, wrapping her piece of rope around the two logs.

"Thanks. You're such a sweet and giving partner."

Tina smiled. "I try. How are you feeling, by the way? Still tired?"

"I'm surprisingly okay now. I think all this moving around is helping me."

"Then don't stop."

"Not planning on it." I noticed the two shortest girls were sitting near the bus watching everyone work. "Well, that didn't take long. How could they raft down a river, but give up after a few minutes of lifting some logs?"

"Yeah, that doesn't make sense," Tina said, reaching out for another piece of rope. "But everyone has their own strengths and weaknesses. Besides, they were the first to go yesterday. I'm sure they had no idea how scary it would be until after they started rafting. It was the fourth set of girls that chickened out."

"True." I glanced around at the other Recruits. "Speaking of those girls, where are they?" Now that I thought about it, I hadn't seen them since we got off the bus after we rafted.

Tina looked around, her forehead creased in confusion. "Good question."

"Do you think they left Recruitment or were they kicked out?" The thought intrigued me. We'd signed a contract saying it was all purely voluntary, but I wouldn't put it past President Randall or RH Johnson to kick them out.

"I don't know," Tina said with a shrug.

I looked over at Eric and Luke who were silently working on their ladder. "Yesterday morning on the bus, Luke mentioned something about Eric's father being a traitor. What was that all about?"

Tina paused for a minute. "I don't know all the details. I've just heard a lot of rumors."

When she didn't continue, I spoke up. "What did you hear?"

"Listen, Emmie," she said, pulling tight on a piece of rope, "I know we're partners and everything, and I hope you won't take offense to this, but I don't think it's my place to tell. I don't want you to get the wrong idea about Eric. He's a nice guy. I feel bad for him." Tina glanced over at Eric and then looked back at me. "Everyone has given him a hard time since it all went down. I can tell you his father is gone. I'm not sure where and or why, but he has been out of the picture for almost two years now."

"Oh." I couldn't imagine not having my dad around. I was used to my mom never being home, but my dad and I had a close bond even though he sometimes worked a lot.

"You should ask Eric. It's his story to tell, not mine. You aren't mad, are you?" Tina bit her lip, concern in her eyes.

"Of course not." I picked up another piece of rope. "I completely understand. Besides, that makes me like you that much more."

She raised her eyebrows. "Really?"

"Not many people are that loyal to their friends or even family members," I said. "My brother would rat me out in a second if I ever did anything bad. I respect the fact that you won't talk about something you don't know the complete facts about. But I don't think Eric would tell me."

"I think he will," Tina said. We were working on our sixth log and were getting better with the ropes. "I've known Eric since we were toddlers. I've never seen him attach to someone so quickly. I think he really likes you."

My cheeks grew hot. "I'm not sure about that."

Tina laughed. "I'm not trying to embarrass you, Emmie. I'm just stating a fact. All the talking, the touches, the rubbing of the back this morning …"

My cheeks grew hotter. "You noticed that?"

She smirked. "Who didn't?"

"He was just trying to be nice," I said, shrugging.

"Uh huh. It's not a big deal, Emmie. So what if he likes you? He's nice and cute. And he's already concerned about you. Not many guys are like that." She smiled. "I could tell he was disappointed when you didn't sit by him on the bus."

I kept my focus on my rope. "I thought I should sit by my partner."

"I don't mind if you sit by Eric. That just means I can sit by Luke." Now Tina's face was getting a little red.

"You return the feeling?" I asked, a smile on my face.

She looked up at me with wide eyes. "Return the feeling?"

"Eric told me yesterday on the bus that Luke liked you." I wrapped my next rope around the logs.

"Really? He said that?" Hope filled in her eyes.

"Well, not in those exact words, but that's what he was hinting at," I said, finishing off the knot I was working on. I wondered what she saw in him. A part of me didn't like him, but if Tina did, there must be more to him than I could see.

A car pulled up near the bus and VP Oliver got out. Two other guys got out with him. The older one was the epitome of tall, dark and handsome. The younger guy wasn't as tall, but he was still dark and handsome. You could tell by their eyes that they were related. From the way they were dressed, I knew they weren't from River Springs.

The younger guy looked at me, causing me to pause. The intense look in his eyes told me he was there to see me. But why?

When he finally looked away, a sense of longing washed over me. I felt a connection to him that I couldn't explain. I wanted to know more about him.

I had a feeling I was about to get my chance.

CHAPTER 13

VP Oliver spoke briefly with RL Steven and then came over to me and Tina. We both stood and brushed off our hands.

"Emmie." VP Oliver smiled at me. "Are you too old for hugs now?"

I shook my head. "Never." He hugged me tightly.

He pointed to the two guys next to him. "Emmie, Tina, this is Wallace Brown and his son, Dante. They are visiting from Kingsland."

I reached out and shook their hands. "So nice to meet you."

"You, too." Wallace shook Tina's hand next. "And you, too."

"They're here to learn a little more about Recruitment," VP Oliver said. "I hope you don't mind, but I thought Dante could trail you for the next couple of days so he could get a feel for how it works."

I eyed Dante's muscles. "Can he help out?"

Dante laughed. "Nope. Sorry. Frank said I could just watch."

Wallace looked at his son. "And be quiet, too." He turned to me and Tina. "He's not to interfere with your challenges. Just observe. If he becomes too much of a hassle, please let me know."

"You won't notice I'm here, promise." Dante winked at us. "You can continue talking about your hair, boys and whatever girls talk about."

"You forgot about nails," Tina said with an eye roll.

I let out a little laugh.

VP Oliver smiled at me. "Well, good luck. We'll get out of your way now." He and Wallace headed back to the car.

After a moment's hesitation, I ran over to them and stopped VP Oliver. "Is there a time we can talk?"

He kept his voice low. "Come see me tonight in my office. I'd like a full report of what happens today."

"Thanks." I gave him another hug and then ran back to Tina and Dante.

Tina pointed to the ladder. "Ready to carry this thing and see if we can actually use it without seriously injuring ourselves?"

"As ready as ever," I said. "You grab the front and I'll grab the back. Let's try to find the closest tree we can."

We both took hold of our ends and lifted. It was heavy, but nothing we couldn't manage. The first few steps weren't very gracious.

"Let's get our steps in synch," I suggested.

"Smart. Let's start with the left foot. Ready?" Tina asked

from up front.

"Yes. Left," I said.

"Right," Tina said.

We continued like that until we reached a tree. I was happy when I looked up to see that there were still bags in the tree we picked. We set the ladder down in front of it.

"Come back here and help me push this side up and rest it on the tree," I said to Tina. I grabbed the left side of the ladder, she took the right, and we lifted it into place. I shook it a little to test it. It seemed sturdy enough. I looked at Dante. "Want to try it out for us?"

With a smile, he shook his head and made a gesture like he was zipping his lips.

Sighing, I placed my hand on my hip. "Well, I guess I'll climb up first and head to the branch on the left. Once I'm up there, you can head up and go to the right. It looks like there are three bags on each side."

"Don't fall." Tina gave me a small smirk.

"I'll try not to. Cross your fingers for me." I looked over at Dante, eyeing his muscles. "Will you at least catch me if I fall?"

When he nodded, I put my left foot on the first step and lifted myself off the ground, bouncing a little to test it out. So far, so good. I slowly made my way up, surprised at how well it held together. As I neared the top, some loud thuds to my right caught my attention. I looked over to see that two guys' ladder had fallen apart and most of the logs were rolling away. "That sucks," I said to no one in particular. I reached over to my left and hoisted myself onto a branch.

"Your turn!" I yelled down to Tina.

"Oh joy," Tina said as she started up the ladder.

I watched her until I was certain she was stable, and then reached out for my first bag. I untied it and then tied the bag to one of my belt loops.

"Smart," Tina said as she got to the top of the ladder.

"I figured it would be better than trying to hold onto it. I also figured if I dropped it on the ground, those two short girls might make a dash for them."

"I wonder if that would disqualify someone?" Tina asked, untying her first bag.

I already had my second bag in my hand, working at the rope to untie it. "They never specifically said you couldn't."

"True. But that would be very daring of someone."

I put my hand on the branch next to me and pulled myself onto it. "It would prove you would be a good leader. Let someone else do the dirty work for you, and then sweep in at the last second to take credit and finish the job."

"No kidding," Tina said with a laugh.

She reached out for another branch, losing her footing for a second and slipping. She grabbed ahold of another branch at the last second and steadied herself.

"Be careful over there," I said to her. "I don't want to have to carry you back."

"Hey, just be grateful I'm not Thunder Thighs. I'd like to see you carry her around."

I laughed as I untied my last bag. "I have all my bags. I'll meet you on the ground."

I worked my way back to the ladder, resisting the urge to

swing around like a monkey, and climbed down. As I waited for Tina, I took a look around.

Eric and Luke were a few trees over, almost done getting their bags. There were maybe six other groups of guys working on their trees. Quiet girl from the line the day before and her partner were just getting to a tree.

The rest of the Recruits were still working on their ladders, including the ones whose ladder had fallen apart. Thunder Thighs was giving Skinny an earful. It didn't seem like they worked too well together which again made me grateful for my swap.

I turned my attention to Dante. The connection to him was still there. I knew exactly where he had been standing before I looked. "Have you been to River Springs before?"

Dante glanced around, hesitating.

"Oh, come on," I said, giving his arm a little shove. "You can talk to me. Nothing bad will happen. Promise." I felt so comfortable around him. Why? Who was he?

He finally caved. "First time. It's nice. Different than Kingsland, that's for sure."

"How so?" I asked.

Tina came back down the ladder, interrupting us. "Let's go finish this."

Dante closed himself back up and wouldn't talk any more. With an inward sigh, I went over to one of the boxes. Dante sat down nearby, keeping his mouth shut. Eric and Luke came up to a box next to us.

Eric gave me a mischievous smile, telling me he wanted to race. I always loved a challenge. I smiled back and then Tina and I dumped out our pieces and sorted through them.

"Are you a puzzle person?" Tina asked me.

"Yes. I used to do jigsaw puzzles all the time with my Great Grandma Mae when I was little. She always said it relaxed her soul."

"Good. I am, too. Why don't I place them, and you tell me what to do?"

She placed the pieces in the sandbox and I directed her movements, arranging the pieces one by one. Tina had no trouble following my instructions. Within minutes, we had put together the pieces as we thought they should go. In the center stood a huge lion with a golden mane. With his chest puffed out, he looked bold and confident.

"RL Steven! I think we have it!" Tina shouted over to him.

RL Steven jogged over and looked over our puzzle. "Nice work. First ones done."

Tina and I jumped up and hugged. I looked over at Eric and Luke. They were only about halfway through their puzzle. I gave Eric a shrug and he shook his head, half smiling, half glaring.

RL Steven cleared his throat. "Take some of the sand and cover up your puzzle so the other teams won't see it."

"Sure thing," I said.

Tina and I bent down and pushed the sand over the puzzle. I picked up a handful of sand, running it through my fingers. The soft, cold feel of it made me smile.

"You can go sit by the bus with the other girls," RL Steven said, pointing at the two short girls.

I reluctantly walked away from the sand, went over to the

bus, and took a seat on the ground. I looked at Tina as she sat down next to me. "So, Eric and Luke, they seemed to work things out pretty quick. The first day Luke talked as if he hated Eric."

"As I said before," Tina said, tucking her legs to the side, "Luke takes this whole process very seriously. He's the type who would put aside any feelings to get the job done."

"Any way he can talk to Amber about that? That would be nice for Dee." I stretched my legs, trying to work out the stiff muscles from the hard work out last night.

"I feel so bad for her," Tina said, looking up at the clear blue sky. It was a beautiful day. "Luckily, Luke isn't that bad. What he said the other day to Eric, well that was just his dad talking. His dad is very opinionated. I've noticed Luke sometimes gives an opinion that sounds more like his dad's than his own. But deep down inside, I'm not sure if he feels the same way."

"Well, at least they're being civil around each other now." I watched them as they worked on their puzzle. "They seem to be working well together."

"Let's just hope they can stay that way."

Dante sat nearby, watching us with an amused smile. I turned toward him. "Will you talk now, or are you just going to continue to observe?"

"Listen," Dante said. "I know I'm irresistible, but you're going to have to pretend like I'm not here. It will make it easier for everyone."

I rolled my eyes at Tina. "What a charmer."

Dante responded with a smile.

Eric and Luke ended up finishing their puzzle ten minutes later. They joined us over at the bus, giving Tina and me high fives.

Some of the stress of the previous night melted away as we sat and talked. The thought of finishing first made me giddy. It would make Mom proud.

During our chat, I kept looking over at Dante. I figured VP Oliver had chosen me and Tina because he knew me well, but it would have made more sense to put him with some guys. I had a nagging sensation that there was more behind it than what VP Oliver had said.

I guess I would have to wait until tonight before I found out.

CHAPTER 14

After dinner, I wanted to go and talk to VP Oliver. Once I left the dining hall, it suddenly dawned onto me that I couldn't leave the Recruitment dorms without permission. VP Oliver's office was in the Infinity Corp headquarters located two buildings away.

As my brain tried to come up with a possible solution, a light tap on my shoulder took me by surprise. When I turned around, Dante stood there with a smile on his face. "You look lost."

"I feel lost." My eyes went to a badge that hung around his neck. The word *visitor* sat in the middle of it. "Can you get anywhere with that badge?"

Dante shrugged. "I've been walking around a few different areas and no one has stopped me. Why?"

"I need to go see VP Oliver." I put on the best innocent smile I could muster. "Do you think you could let me borrow your badge for twenty minutes or so?"

"No way," Dante said. "President Randall said I'd be in

big trouble if I lost it. He seems like a guy you don't want to cross."

My smile faltered. "I'll bring it back to you. I promise."

He shook his head. "I'm not going to part with it. I'll go with you. Maybe they won't stop the two of us."

I looked down at my green Recruitment clothes and pointed to them. "It's obvious I'm a Recruit."

Dante shrugged out of his hooded jacket and handed it to me. "Put this on."

I hesitated for a moment and then finally slipped it on. Despite being way too big, it at least covered up my shirt. Nothing I could do for the pants, though. "Let's go." As we walked, I tried to keep a casual demeanor, but I wasn't doing a very good job. I hoped people would completely overlook me and only have eyes for Dante since he was a foreigner.

Dante smirked at me. "Can you at least try to not look so suspicious? You look like you just committed a crime."

"It's not easy. I could get in a lot of trouble if I get caught."

Out of the corner of my eye, I saw two Recruitment leaders headed toward us. I quickly grabbed Dante by the shirt and yanked him down another hallway. I pressed myself up against the wall and positioned Dante so he blocked me.

"I'm just supposed to stand here in the middle of this hall?" Dante asked.

I stole a glance past him, but the leaders hadn't crossed the hall yet. "Yes."

"Can we at least pretend we're kissing or something?"

When I looked at Dante, he wiggled his eyebrows. My face flushed. "No."

Dante sighed. "Fine, then we can really kiss." He leaned in, but I pushed him away.

"What are you doing?" I said through clenched teeth. When I looked past him again, the leaders were walking by, so I snapped my head back, using Dante's body as a shield.

"I'm trying to see how red your face can get," Dante said with a small laugh.

"Shhh! They might hear you." I suddenly realized that our bodies were touching. I stepped back and pulled his jacket tighter around me. I cleared my throat. "That's another rule in Recruitment. No kissing."

Dante frowned. "This Recruitment isn't sounding all that great. Lots of physical labor and nothing physical with a girl."

I wished I could stop my face from turning red, but it was a hopeless cause. "I think we're clear now."

Without looking at him, I started walking again. We made it outside without further incident. As we walked down the sidewalk, I pulled the hood over my head, ignoring Dante's snicker. Every time we passed by someone, I stepped in closer to Dante.

We finally arrived at Infinity Corp. I let out a sigh of relief when we walked in and no one was in the lobby. I drummed my fingers along my arm as we waited for the elevator.

"Are you always this anxious?" Dante asked, eyeing me. He had his hands stuffed in his jean pockets. I wondered what they felt like. I'd never worn jeans, just seen them in some old photos.

I shook my head. "Not usually. But after last night's punishment, I'm not ready for another workout."

The elevator door opened, so we stepped in. I pressed the button for the thirtieth floor and watched the door close.

Dante's eyebrow shot up. “Punishment? You got in trouble on the first day of Recruitment?” He shook his head, smiling. “Sounds like something I would do.”

I ignored him the rest of the way. My anxiety melted away when I walked into VP Oliver's office and saw him standing near the window. He smiled when he saw us walk in. “Good, you came.” He looked at Dante. “Mind if I speak with Emmie alone?”

With a wink at me, Dante left the room, closing the door behind him.

VP Oliver laughed. “How did the two of you hit it off?”

My cheeks colored again. “We didn't hit it off!”

“I meant with him tagging along in Recruitment.” VP Oliver sat down in his chair, motioning to a chair across the table from him. “Not a relationship.”

“Oh.” I sat down in the chair, pulling my legs up close to me. “It went fine, I guess. He kept his mouth closed as you told him to. VP Oliver, can I ask why you picked me and Tina for Dante to follow?”

He leaned back in his chair. “In my office, you can call me Frank. As for Dante, because I knew the two of you would get along.”

I laughed. “Hardly. He's a little full of himself and quite rash. He loves to tease people, too.”

“Sounds an awful lot like someone I know.” He smiled dryly.

“I may be rash and tease people,” I said, crossing my arms,

"but I'm not full of myself." When he raised his eyebrow, I rolled my eyes. "Well, maybe a little." I played with the zipper on Dante's jacket. "Frank, why is he really here?"

He held my gaze. "To find out more about Recruitment."

I shook my head. "I'm not buying that. I know there's another reason."

Sighing, he interlocked his fingers. "Emmie, you're observant. I could never get anything passed you. Unfortunately, I can't tell you much right now. What I can tell you is that President Randall is keeping a close eye on you and everyone you're around. Be careful, Emmie. One wrong move and you'll be in serious trouble."

Trouble? I'd only broken one rule. It couldn't have been that serious. "What do you mean? Why is he watching me?"

"Emmie, promise me you'll be on your best behavior." He gave me a similar look my dad did when he worried about me. "You need to be mindful of every move you make."

I opened my mouth to say something, but the phone rang in his office.

"Hello?" He kept his eyes on mine as he listened. "Understood." He hung up the phone. "You need to get back to the dorms. Now."

"Why?" I asked, standing at the same time he did.

"They're doing a sweep of the entire building." He went over to his office door, his hand resting on the knob. "Emmie, how well do you know Eric Greene?"

I pulled back in surprise. "Not too well. We just met in Recruitment."

He mulled that over. Finally, he nodded. "President

Randall seems interested in the fact that you two are around each other so much. Try to keep your distance if possible." He paused. "And don't put too much trust in Eric." He opened the door. Dante was leaning against the wall outside. "Get her back to her dorms without being seen."

"What's a sweep?" I looked at VP Oliver.

His forehead creased in worry. "It's standard practice during Recruitment. They just want to make sure no one is hiding any contraband or doing things they aren't supposed to." He grabbed me by my arms. "Promise me you'll be careful."

His intensity troubled me. I'd never seen him act this way before. "I promise."

VP Oliver gave me a tight hug and then looked at Dante. "Hurry."

I wanted to continue talking, but Dante grabbed my arms and dragged me down the hall. He pressed the button for the elevator repeatedly until it opened.

When we were inside the elevator, I looked at him. "What's going on? Why are you here?" He opened his mouth, so I held up my hand. "And don't give me any crap about wanting to know more about Recruitment."

"It's complicated." Dante stayed silent until the doors opened, and we were running out the front door. He took my hand in his as we ran down the sidewalk. "Do you know anything about a prophecy?"

I'd heard rumors about one, but never anything specific. Mom always said it was complete garbage and to not believe in it. "Not much."

An Infinity Corp security vehicle rounded the corner. Dante stopped me and pushed me up against the wall, still holding onto my hand and putting his other hand on my hip. "A long time ago a man prophesied that a rebellion would break out in all four cities left in the U.S." He looked to make sure the vehicle was out of sight and then we continued running. "Each city would have a citizen who would lead the revolution."

We arrived at the dorms, so Dante opened the door and pulled me inside. He took his jacket off me and put it back on himself. "Does any of this ring a bell?"

"Not really." I glanced past him. Tons of Recruits were heading up the stairs, going back to their dorm rooms. All the leaders were directing them. "So, we're going to have a rebellion?" The thought terrified me for a moment. Then it intrigued me.

Dante looked at the crowd. "You better get in there before you get caught." He looked at me, a smile on his lips. "I won't be there tomorrow, but I'll be at the challenge the following day. It sounds like it's going to be a blast. We can talk then."

With that, he was out the door. I quickly joined in with the female Recruits going up the stairs. When I got to the second floor, I ran down to my room. Tina was standing outside.

She let out a breath when she saw me. "Where have you been?" She pointed to our room. "Two security guards are in there right now. They say it's just routine, but it feels more serious than that." He looked at me. "They asked where you were."

"What did you say?" I asked.

"That you had to use the restroom." Tina leaned up against the wall. "Where have you been?"

As I filled her in on everything, I tried to get my heart to calm down. I went to go talk to VP Oliver so I could get some questions answered.

I ended up with no answers and a ton more questions.

CHAPTER 15

When the security sweep ended, I took Tina with me to find Dee and then went to the bathroom on the top floor. I did a quick check to make sure it was empty before I spoke. Tina and Dee both patiently watched me, exchanging looks between each other when they thought I wasn't looking.

I sat down on a bench. "I went and saw VP Oliver tonight."

"When?" Dee took a seat beside me.

"After dinner," I said, crossing my legs. "I wanted to find out more about Dante."

"Who's Dante?" Dee asked.

Tina rested against one of the sinks with her arms folded. "He's visiting from Kingsland."

Dee's eyes went wide. "We have visitors from Kingsland?" She smiled. "I've always wanted to go there. Or any of the other cities. I want to know what it's like out there."

"Me, too." I'd always wanted to step outside of River Springs, but I never had. They didn't forbid anyone from leaving, but they frowned upon it so much and would always say how much better it was in River Springs. President Randall would say over and over again that we had everything we needed here and that the outside world was dangerous.

He made it sound so terrifying. It had been fear that had kept me inside my whole life. The past few years, intrigue took over. I wanted to know what was outside the walls. I wanted to explore. To be free.

"What did he tell you?" Tina took out a ponytail holder and threw her long, red hair up. The girl could pull off a sloppy ponytail. Really, she could pull off anything.

"Not much." I sighed. "They keep saying Dante's here to check out Recruitment, but I feel like there's more to it."

Tina nodded. "I got the same feeling. He kept staring at you all day long."

Dee smiled and gently squeezed my arm. "Maybe he thinks you're cute." She fanned her face. "Oh, what must it be like to have two guys swooning over you?"

My eyebrows shot up. "First of all, no one is swooning over me. Second, Dante's interest is not romantic. It's curiosity."

"I agree with Emmie," Tina said. "About it being curiosity. But I agree with Dee about Eric. He definitely likes you."

Ignoring the heat rising in my cheeks, I brushed off my clothes. "Can we please keep focus here?"

"Yes." Dee looked at me. "But not before you answer one question for me: Do you like Eric?"

"Dee …" I started.

Dee rolled her eyes. "Come on, Em. Just tell me. Your facial expressions and body language tell me everything I need to know, but I want to hear it out of your mouth." She looked at Tina. "She's never admitted to liking a guy, ever."

I sighed. "Fine. I think he's hot, okay? My heart races when he gets close to me or touches me. And a couple of times I've wondered what it would be like to kiss him. Satisfied?"

"Completely." Dee stretched out her legs. "Continue, please."

Tina shook her head and laughed.

"Anyway, VP Oliver told me that President Randall is watching me closely."

Tina looked taken aback. "Why?"

"I don't know," I said with a shrug. "He wouldn't tell me. All he said was that I needed to be on my best behavior and if I made one wrong move I'd be in trouble."

"Wow." Dee tucked one of her curls behind her ear. "That sounds serious."

Tina took the seat on the other side of me. "He didn't give you a hint as to why?"

"He got a phone call about the security sweep before he could tell me anymore." I glanced over at Tina. "How well do you know Eric? VP Oliver told me not to trust him."

The expression on her face told me she was genuinely surprised by my comment. "Not trust Eric? Emmie, you can trust him. I swear. I'm not sure what VP Oliver is talking about, but Eric's a good guy."

Hope. Trust. My world seemed to be relying on two simple words. I folded my arms. "VP Oliver made me promise to be good."

Dee laughed. "Oh, dear. You may be in big trouble then." She looked around me at Tina. "Good and Emmie don't usually go in the same sentence."

I slapped her arm. "Not true. I'm good." I twisted my lips. "Most of the time." I sighed. "When it counts."

Curiosity usually got the better of me growing up. I tried to listen to my parents and not to get in trouble, but I had a hard time knowing when to back down. Plus, Derek liked to push my buttons, so it had become a habit to push back.

"Uh hmm," Dee said. "Only when it counts. But that's why I love you. Life is more fun with you in it."

I glanced at both of them. "You should know, he's watching everyone close to me, so that includes the two of you."

Tina groaned sarcastically. "Oh, so now I have to be good, too?"

"Sorry," I said. "Unless you want to get a new partner."

"Speaking of partners," Dee said, sitting forward, "did you know Amber has a little sister?"

She'd never once mentioned a sister to me, nor had I seen another girl with their family. "What?"

Dee nodded. "She said something about her today, but I could tell it was a slip. She instantly changed the subject and snapped at me when I tried to bring it up again." She furrowed her eyebrows. "It's been weird being around her so much. She was always so polite growing up and got along with others. Now she seems … different. One second she's happy and content, complimenting me on my hair, and then the next thing I know she'll freak out, yell, and tell me how much she hates me."

"She sounds bipolar if you ask me," Tina said.

"No," Dee said, shaking her head. "It seems more complicated than that. I can't really pin down the problem, but there's something not right. Every now and then I'll see this weird twitch in her eyes. It's like she's not herself for a brief second."

I'd have to have Derek look into it when family day came around. They hadn't mentioned when that would be, but I crossed my fingers it would be soon. I needed my dad's advice on everything.

Dad could probably look more into the Kingsland and President Randall situations. My brother could also check it out. He had access to documents that most people in the city didn't. Getting my answers depended entirely on whether he'd be willing to help me out. He usually liked to cause me more grief than be of assistance.

But just like me, curiosity usually got the better of him. If I dangled enough bait in front of his face, Derek would snatch it up in a heartbeat. Especially if it meant using his programming skills to do something he shouldn't. I'd learned most of my bad habits from him.

Maybe I wasn't as good as I thought. For now, all I needed to do was pretend to be good.

I also had to trust that VP Oliver and my family would help me out. It made me wonder if you could ever really trust someone, especially in dire situations. The only thing I could do was hope.

CHAPTER 16

The next day we ended up at a maze. There were five different colored flags placed throughout the maze that each group had to get. They gave no other rules beside retrieve the flags. They had four entrances to the maze, so they had six groups of two at each entrance.

"You may enter," RL Steven said to us, rubbing his head. "See you on the other side."

All the groups ran in, going in all different directions. After talking with VP Oliver, the security sweep, and hardly getting any sleep, I was all worked up. All my common sense had left. I just wanted to get it over with. I stopped Tina, Eric, and Luke right when we entered the maze, but made sure we were out of RL Steven's sight. "Let's work together. I think four heads are better than two."

"I don't think that's allowed." Luke shifted uncomfortably where he stood.

"They never said anything about not working together," I said. "They just said go grab the flags."

"She's right," Eric said. "I think it's a good plan."

Tina eyed me. I knew she was thinking we needed to be on our best behavior, but I didn't care. And I was sure the look on my face expressed that.

"Okay," Tina said with a shrug. "How should we start?"

"We've already lost time just standing here," Luke said, stuffing his hands in his pockets.

"Well, everyone else is running around like crazy, with no strategy." Eric ran his fingers through his hair. "Let's work this in sections."

"I like that idea," I said. "Let's start with the front left and then work our way over to the front right. If you can, try to keep track of how we're turning."

Luke immediately took off, so we all followed him. He seemed nervous, constantly shifting his head back and forth like he was waiting for someone to catch us.

"Maybe we should look for anything that sticks out, so we'll know if we've been down a row before," Tina said as we were walking. We turned right onto a different row and she pointed at a dent in the hedge. "Like right there. There's a small hole. If we see it again, we'll know that we've been down here before."

"Good thinking," Luke said to Tina.

We made a few more turns and came across a row with yellow flags scattered about. Luke and Tina each grabbed one.

"One down, four to go," Tina said as she shoved our flag into her pocket.

"We need to head right before we go forward too much," Eric said, making his way to the right.

We worked together like that, section by section. We found the red flags and then the greens flag a little while later.

Eric glanced over his shoulder at us. "There was a flag in the front left section, one in the front right section, and one in the back right section. That means there's probably one in the back left section."

"Where do you think the fifth one is?" Tina asked.

"I'm guessing the middle or toward the exit," I said.

Luke scratched his head. "But we should've passed through the middle already, right?"

"Yes," Eric said.

We passed a lot of other groups as we worked our way through the maze. Most of them looked frantic. Some looked annoyed. A couple looked defeated. It was funny that something like that maze should have been a simple task. It wasn't that complicated. But put a bunch of teenagers in a maze who'd had controlled lives and chaos ensued.

We soon found the fourth flag, blue. One left.

"Exit?" I suggested.

Tina nodded. "It's our best bet. We should've been through all of the other sections already."

We wandered to where we thought the exit should be. We were right that the exit was there, but we were wrong about the flag.

"Where could it be?" Luke's voice was laced with frustration.

Tina shook her head. "I don't know. It doesn't make sense."

I looked up at the sky, trying to clear my head and think.

A bird flew overhead, flapping its wings with grace, making me think of the little blue bird the other day. I needed to focus, so I closed my eyes and took a deep breath.

My eyes flew open as a thought came to my head. "How tall do you think these hedges are?"

"Maybe eight or nine feet?" Eric said. "Why?"

"How much can you lift?" I asked him, looking at his arms.

Eric smiled. "Definitely a tiny girl like you." He clasped his hands together and bent down. "Hop on."

"You're a smart guy to say I'm tiny," I said, putting my foot in his hands and my hand on his shoulder.

"I aim to please," Eric said, lifting me into the air.

I grabbed onto the hedge to balance myself as Eric held me up. I looked over the top of the maze and glanced around.

"You see anything?" Tina asked from down below.

"A bunch of wild teenagers running around," I shouted down to her. "Oh! Thunder Thighs is screaming at Skinny! I wish you could see this, Tina!"

"Who?" Luke asked.

"Shhhhhh!" I said, waving my hand at him. Thunder Thighs and Skinny were in hearing range.

"How did you get this far in life without knowing left from right?" Thunder Thighs flailed her arms as she talked.

Skinny shrieked, pulling at her frizzy hair. "I know my left from right! I was just going where you were pointing!"

"You went the opposite way of where I was pointing!" Thunder Thighs yelled.

Skinny let out a scream and stomped her feet on the

ground. "This maze is just so confusing! There are so many twists and turns!"

Thunder Thighs slammed her fist into the hedge. "That's what a maze is, dummy!" She pulled out some of the leaves and threw them in Skinny's face. Skinny let out another scream and then stormed away, brushing out some leaves that landed in her hair.

"Take your time up there," Eric said, not trying to hide the sarcasm in his voice. "I can hold you up all day."

"Good. It's a beautiful view up here." I sighed in frustration. "I don't see any flags we don't have. I can see all the other ones."

As I was turning around to tell Eric to bring me down, something in the very top right corner of the maze caught my eye. Forgetting that I was being held up, I leaned in so I could get a better look, setting us off balance. Eric tried to move with me, but it was too late. He stumbled back and forth a little and soon my feet slipped from his hands. He tried to catch me, but I just ended up falling into him, sending us both to the ground. I landed on top of him, knocking the wind out of me. Rolling off him, I lay on my back and gasped for breath.

"Emmie, are you okay?" Tina asked, running to my side. She bent down next to me and brushed some hair off my face. "Slow, easy breaths."

Eric grunted next to me. I reached over and took his hand. "Sorry, Eric," I said between breaths.

"Next time, tell me when you're going to move, okay?" Eric said, squeezing my hand. "Luke, what were you doing that you couldn't help?"

Luke's face went red. "Oh, uh, sorry, I was just …"

Tina's face was a little red, too. "We were just talking to each other and didn't realize what was happening until you were already falling."

I smiled. "Don't worry. We're both alive. I have no broken bones." I turned to Eric. "You?"

Eric ran his hands down his torso and then his legs. "Everything's intact."

"And on a positive note, I found the last flag," I said. Side note: Eric was still holding my hand.

"Where?" Luke asked, all the excitement back.

"The very top right corner," I said. "They're on the bottom of the hedge, tucked in a little. I could barely see them, but they're there."

"Let's go get it," Luke said.

Eric stood and reached out his hand, helping me up. He gave my hand a quick squeeze and then let go. "Point us in the right direction, Emmie."

We weaved our way to that corner rather quickly. The purple flags were tucked in on the bottom, barely visible.

"They made these flags hard to find, didn't they?" Luke asked. "I hate to admit this, but that was a brilliant idea, Emmie."

"Why thank you, Luke," I said with a smile, placing a hand over my heart. "A compliment coming from you is something I'll treasure for the rest of my life."

He rolled his eyes in response.

We were soon at the exit. Luke, Tina, me and then Eric walked out, all smiling. We stopped outside the maze, reliving our experience. RL Steven sat on the ground a few yards away. Surprise flashed in his eyes when he saw us all standing there talking. Crap. I didn't think about the fact that we should've spaced ourselves, so we didn't come out at the same time. I think we were all so excited that it went well, and we finished.

"Already done?" RL Steven checked his watch. "That only took you an hour. Who came out first?"

"Does it matter?" Eric asked.

RL Steven's jaw twitched in annoyance. "Yes, it does matter, Eric. I need to make note of who was first and who was second. Ties aren't allowed."

"Luke stepped out first," I said to RL Steven. "So that puts him and Eric in first place. Tina and I were second."

RL Steven pulled out a piece of paper to write it down. "Okay, so Luke and Eric came out first, followed by Tina and Emmie."

Before anyone else could respond, I spoke. "Yep. That's what happened."

All three of them looked at me, but I shook my head. It didn't matter the order. Besides, after looking around, we were the only ones out of the maze. I didn't want to be first again. That would cause more attention on me than I wanted. Plus, it would mean a lot to Luke to come in first.

"Okay," RL Steven said. "Come over here and sit down. We'll probably have a long time to wait for everyone to finish. Yesterday it took one group eight hours."

"I hope we don't have to wait that long today," Eric said as we walked over to sit next to RL Steven. I thought of Thunder Thighs and Skinny standing around fighting, making me think we might be there longer than that.

Tina and I tried to keep the conversation light as we sat around and waited since we knew RL Steven would report everything we said back to President Randall.

I stretched out my legs after we sat down. "So, Tina, what position do you hope they place you in? Besides lumber."

Tina had her legs tucked into her chest. She rested her chin on her knee and smiled. "Security, actually."

"Me, too," Luke said.

Security was the job everyone wanted. They worked in Infinity Corp's headquarters and got to use the latest technology and equipment. It was considered the most important job besides the president and vice president. But I never saw it that way.

"What about you, Eric?" I asked.

He shrugged. "I don't know. There have been a couple of things I've wanted throughout the years. Like automotive." He flashed me his perfect smile. "Or dental."

Tina nudged me. "What about you?"

I opened my mouth but shut it when I saw RL Steven staring at me, obviously intrigued to hear my answer. I'd come to realize I wanted to go into management so I could try to fix the city, but it would be pointless since President Randall would overrule any changes. So, I tried to give a safe answer, which was what my mom wanted me to do. "Probably secretarial."

RL Steven frowned in disappointment as the others pulled back in surprise.

Luke scratched his head. "I wouldn't have chosen that for you."

"What would you choose for her?" Eric asked.

Luke mulled it over for a minute. "I don't know, maybe management?"

Tina and Eric nodded in agreement. I tried to keep my face straight as I changed the subject.

There had been something bothering me since we'd arrived at the maze. "Hey, RL Steven, two groups of girls aren't here anymore. The ones who didn't raft and then the ones that sat out yesterday. Where are they?"

RL Steven watched me for a while, looking like he was trying to piece together what he wanted to say. He finally cleared his throat. "They removed themselves from Recruitment."

"Removed themselves?" Luke shook his head. "Why would they do that?"

RL Steven shrugged, still looking at me. "Don't know. It happens now and then. Remember, Recruitment is voluntary. I wouldn't dwell on it if I were you."

Voluntary. There was that stupid word again. I wondered if the girls really did want to remove themselves or if they were coerced into doing it.

After that, we mostly talked about what it was like growing up in our precincts, trying to see if there was anything different. From what we gathered, everything was exactly the same: boring.

CHAPTER 17

Our leaders must have been ordered to keep an eye on us. RL Steven watched us like a hawk throughout dinner and even DL Jen walked with Tina and me back to our dorm room. Having a constant babysitter was getting rather annoying.

The next morning, DL Jen hovered around while we were getting ready and then RL Steven sat near us during breakfast. Multiple times I had to resist the urge to flick my oatmeal at his face.

My annoyance didn't last very long. Once we arrived at our destination for the day, there was a sudden shift in the energy of the Recruits. We were doing a security mission. Tina squeezed my arm in excitement and Luke jumped up and down where he stood, getting his blood flowing. With a determined scowl plastered on his face, he was ready for the challenge.

Dante stood near us but didn't speak to anyone. He kept getting weird looks from all the Recruits. If it bothered him, he didn't show it.

They suited us up in a protective vest, knee and elbow pads, a helmet, goggles, and then rounded the outfit off with a paint gun in the form of a rifle. I'd never once seen real security guys with pads, helmets, or goggles. Or a paint gun for that matter. But they obviously couldn't give us real weapons. Thunder Thighs would be sure to "accidentally" kill Skinny within two seconds of the gun being put in her sturdy hands.

As RL Steven shouted out our instructions, I took in the obstacle course. The area was filled with ropes, half walls, mud, tires, stairs, trees, a few towers, and a small section had been covered in barbed wire.

I looked over at Tina and almost asked her what about the scenario before us enticed her, but by the giddy smile on her face and the fact that she bounced on her heels in anticipation, I already knew the answer. All of it.

Nothing about it appealed to me in the slightest. It looked like a lot of hard work and I saw multiple opportunities for serious injuries. Having Tina for my partner was comforting, though. She was tough and most importantly, excited for the challenge.

Eric nudged me. "Are you even listening?"

"Huh?" I turned to him.

An amused smile tugged on his lips. "I guess not."

The Recruits had been sorted into groups, already talking about their strategy. Eric, Luke, Tina, Thunder Thighs, Skinny, and two guys I didn't know were standing near me. Most of them looking at me.

"Thanks for joining us," Luke said, looking at me with obvious annoyance. He glanced around at the others. "I say

Tina and I take lead on this. Everyone else, follow what we're doing and stay close."

Luke turned toward the entrance to the course, but Thunder Thighs put her hand on his chest to stop him. "Why do you get to choose who's in charge of our group?" He glanced down at her hand still on his chest and she immediately snapped it away.

"Because it's what Luke and I want to do for our career," Tina said.

One of the other guys shifted his gun awkwardly in his hand. The gun went off, sending a paintball flying into the air. "Whoops." He was tall like the other guys in our group, but he was super scrawny. His untamable, frizzy, brown hair reminded me of Skinny's. A long nose sat in the middle of his face, distracting from the large dimple in his chin.

Luke sighed. "Simon, keep your finger off the trigger."

"You're going to shoot one of us before anyone else gets a chance." The other guy had spoken. He playfully shoved Simon in the arm as he smiled at all of us. Even though his physique matched Eric's, he didn't carry himself with the same amount of confidence. He covered it up with an abundance of happiness.

"What if I want to do it as my career, too?" Thunder Thighs asked.

Skinny blew some hair out of her face. "You know you don't get to choose your career, right?"

Thunder Thighs glared at her. "Of course, we know that. But we want to show them we're serious about it and will do it well."

"Well, arguing about it isn't going to help," Tina said.

"RL Steven said we could only have two leaders," Eric said, ignoring Thunder Thighs' death stare. "Let's just have Tina and Luke be in charge."

Happy Guy slapped Thunder Thighs on the shoulder. "It'll work out. You'll still be able to shine."

Skinny looked over at Dante, who lingered behind. He had also put on protective gear, but he didn't have a gun. "What's he doing here?"

RL Steven came up to our group. "He's just observing. Ignore him. Your group is up next. Get ready to enter."

Two angled walls lead to the entrance. Luke, Eric, me, and Simon lined up against the left wall. Tina, Thunder Thighs, Happy Guy, and Skinny lined up against the right.

I put my hand on Eric's arm and reached up on my tiptoes so I could talk into his ear. "What's the happy guy's name?"

Eric smiled down at me. "Theo."

When I realized how close our faces were, I blushed and put my feet back down on the ground. Tina smirked at me, but I acted like I didn't notice.

Luke looked inside the entrance. "There are some tires off to the right that we have to run through. My group will head in first, followed by Tina's. Be on the constant lookout for shooters."

I reached up to Eric again, still ignoring Tina. "Are we fighting other Recruits?"

"No," Eric said, moving his face so he could see me. Our faces were inches away from each other. "There will be random people trying to shoot us, so be careful." The side of his mouth turned up into a smile. "Just stay close to me and you'll be fine."

I nodded and scooted closer to him, telling myself it was for the good of the mission. It had nothing to do with the fact that he had gorgeous blue eyes or a smile that made my heart flip.

Luke turned to us. "Let's move out." He held his gun close to him as he went through the entrance. Eric, me, and Simon were right at his heels. As soon as we entered, I looked around. The tires Luke had mentioned were off to the left. Behind them was a short wall, but one we'd have to climb over. As we ran through the tires, I tried to focus on each step so I wouldn't trip. Luke and Eric fired off their guns a few times.

Movement to my right caught my eye. A bulky man in camouflage was perched on a small platform. Aiming my gun at him, I pulled the trigger, hitting him on his shoulder. I smiled for a moment and then lost my footing and fell forward, smacking my helmet against the tire in front of me.

Simon fell right on top of me, his gun going off like a wildfire. I felt him get pulled off me and then someone pulled on the back of my vest and lifted me up. Eric smiled at me and took my hand, holding it tight as we finished running through the tires.

When we got to the half-wall, Luke ran at it and jumped, throwing his body over the top in one swift movement. He landed with a thud, then immediately fired his gun.

With my eyes wide, I looked over at Eric. "Uh, yeah, I can't do that."

"Neither can I," Simon said, his voice shaking. I turned to

him and saw that he was already covered in paint. Most of it had probably come from his own gun.

Eric let go of my hand. "Don't think about it. Just run and jump. I'll be right behind you."

Taking a deep breath, I ran at the wall, pushed my right foot against it and jumped up, gripping tight onto the top of it. I pulled myself up and over the top. I landed clumsily on the other side, but Luke was right there, helping me steady myself. Eric came over seconds later but then had to hop back up to help Simon over. We didn't wait for Tina and the others before we continued.

A building filled the area before us, so we ran toward it, stopping near the door. Both Eric and Luke peered inside.

"Clear," Luke said, stepping into the room. We followed him in.

It was set up like a classroom, with desks and chairs lined up in rows. No one was in the room, so we shuffled through the desks until we got to a door on the right hand wall.

Luke slowly looked in and then pulled his head back. "There's a door on the north side of that room. I can see men out there waiting for us."

"Is there anything else in the room?" Eric asked.

Luke nodded. "A large desk in the middle of the room, plus some cabinets lined up on the east wall."

Tina, Theo, Thunder Thighs, and Skinny joined us in the room. Skinny was covered in more paint than Simon. Theo had one hit on his left leg.

I looked down at myself, marveled that I couldn't see any paint yet. I would probably feel it when I did get hit.

"What's the plan?" Tina asked.

"Can we knock over the table and use it as a cover?" Eric asked.

"I think so," Luke said. "Tina and Rachel, cover me and Eric while we run in and knock the table on its side. Once that's done, everyone take cover behind the table or one of the cabinets."

Tina and Thunder Thighs positioned themselves on either side of the door and nodded at Luke. He and Eric ran into the room as Tina and Thunder Thighs fired away. I heard a loud thump of the desk hitting the ground. The two girls disappeared into the room, leaving me, Theo, Simon, and Skinny in the classroom. They all turned to me.

I just shrugged. "See you on the other side." I ran in, keeping my body low as I did. Men were shooting at our group, who, besides Eric, were hiding behind the desk.

Eric stood behind one of the cabinets, peeking out just a little to shoot the enemy. The men outside wore similar helmets to ours and their entire uniform was in camouflage. Their guns were slightly bigger than ours, giving them an advantage.

A stinging sensation went through my left arm. I dove down behind the desk near Tina and glanced at my arm. A big, blue paint mark sat there staring at me. I glared back at it.

Turning to my knees, I put my gun over the desk and fired, not bothering to look where I aimed. I figured if I shot toward the door, it was close enough.

Theo, Skinny, and Simon clumsily made their way into the room, all getting hit a couple of times before they fell behind the desk. Once they were with us, it became way too crowded. Thunder Thighs hopped up and ran to a cabinet near Eric, using it for cover.

"Emmie!" Eric motioned for me to join him. Taking a deep breath, I rolled over there, narrowly avoiding getting hit. Eric pulled me up, continuing to fire toward the door. "Nice roll."

I fired a few times, one of my shots hitting an enemy in the face. "Thanks."

After a few more minutes, the firing finally stopped. Luke and Tina slowly made their way toward the door, peering out to see what awaited us.

"No more men," Tina said.

"Just a set of stairs," Luke said. "Everyone run as fast as you can up the stairs. Tina and I will go out first. Rachel and Eric, stay in back."

Tina and Luke exited the room, their footsteps fading away as they ran up the stairs. Simon and Theo ran out next, followed by a shrieking Skinny.

"Let's go," Eric said, taking my hand and guiding me toward the door. I went out first and ran as fast as I could up the stairs. I let go of Eric's hand after a few steps so I could run faster. Thunder Thighs grunted with each step she took.

When we got to the top, we were standing in a tower, overlooking the entire course. What I saw didn't give me any comfort.

"Looks like the fun is just getting started," Eric said with a smile.

Fun wasn't the word bouncing around in my head, but we weren't allowed to swear in Recruitment.

CHAPTER 18

Looking down, I saw a patch of barbed wire low to the ground on our right. To the left stood a small forest, bundled with thick trees and a small river running down the middle. Other Recruits were in there, some screaming out, some giving a warrior cry. Neither seemed to be very effective.

What lay in front of us truly scared me. There was a rope attached to the tower that angled down to the ground. It ended near a mud pit, nearly a hundred yards out.

Luke handed out a bunch of L shaped bars with rubber grips on each end. There was a small rope loop attached to each end to put your wrists through. "Set the angled part on the rope and go down. Try not to land in the mud."

My eyes widened as I went to the edge of the tower and looked down. It was a far way to the ground, and only grass lay below. I swallowed. "And if we fall?"

"Don't," Luke said, his tone firm as if that closed the argument.

"They're trying to kill us." Skinny stood next to me, her

voice quiet, trembling, yet still grating.

Tina slapped her on the arm. "You'll live. Watch me go first." She put her wrist through one loop, set the angled part on the rope, and then put her left wrist through the other loop, gripping tightly onto the handles. With a deep breath, she pushed off and slid down the rope, plunging toward the ground at an alarmingly fast rate. She made it over the mud pit with ease. She slid her wrists out of the loops and waved up at us.

"See, easy," Eric said to Skinny. He smiled at her, but she just pulled at her hair and shrieked.

Thunder Thighs went next, followed by Theo. Eric turned to me. "Why don't you go next?"

I licked my lips as I took the strap connected to my gun and threw it around my neck, so the gun rested along my back. Putting my right wrist through the rope loop, I took a few breaths before I placed the bar over the rope and hooked my left wrist through the loop. I held onto the handles so tight, my knuckles turned white.

Eric came up behind me and placed his hands over mine. He kept his voice quiet so only I could hear. "You'll do fine, Emmie. Keep your feet up in front of you and don't drop down until you pass the mud pit. Tina will help catch you."

I slowly nodded, trying to work up the courage for the jump. He moved his hands to my waist. "On the count of three. One, two …" He picked me up and gave me a gentle push. Tucking in my legs, I soared downward, heading toward the others. My panic soon turned to laughter and I shouted out in excitement. When I neared the mud, I straightened out my legs and pulled them up, making my body parallel to the rope. I barely made it over, my feet landing near the edge of the pit. Tina and Theo both caught me and helped release my hands from the straps and stand up.

It felt nice to be on solid ground again. I threw my arms around Tina's neck. "That was fun."

"I know," she said. "I wish we could do it again."

Eric soon joined us, followed by Simon. He almost landed in the mud, but Eric and Thunder Thighs caught him just in time.

Skinny's fall wasn't so graceful. She screamed at the top of her lungs. A few times she yelled, "I'm going to die!" Panic filled her eyes when she saw the mud. Losing her grip on the bar, one of her wrists came out of the loop and she fell into the mud. Thunder Thighs and Theo reluctantly helped her out. She shook her body, flinging mud at all of us.

Thunder Thighs swore. "Stop it, Angela!"

I looked wide-eyed at Tina, trying not to laugh. Thunder Thighs had a harder time holding in the swear words. But then again, breaking rules had been a common theme since Recruitment had started.

Once Luke landed on the ground, we headed toward the area covered in barbed wire. Apparently, they were expecting us to crawl underneath it. Mud caked the ground below the wire, making our attempts to avoid the mud pit pointless.

Theo laughed. "Well, Angela, we'll all be covered in mud soon." He rubbed his hands together. "Who's going to go first?"

"You," Thunder Thighs said. "Since you seem so excited

about it."

Theo dove toward the ground and army crawled under the wire. Thunder Thighs went after him, followed by Tina, Simon, and then Luke.

Eric motioned for me to go. "I'll be right behind you."

I got down on my knees before I flattened my body out and slowly scooted my body under the wire. There wasn't too much room to wiggle through, so my gun kept getting caught on the top wire. I ended up moving it to the side so I could move faster. Mud splashed up onto my face a few times, but I couldn't wipe it off, so it stayed there.

After about thirty yards, the wire finally stopped. Luke helped pull me out. I looked down at my mud-covered body and sighed.

"Let's start toward the next wall," Luke said to Tina.

I looked past them and saw another wall, a little bit taller than the first one. A rope hung down from the top. I sighed again. The challenge would never end.

The others took off as I waited for Eric and Skinny. It took Skinny almost fifteen minutes to make it through. Eric and I had to keep shouting words of encouragement to her, so she'd stop whining and keep moving.

When she was almost through, Eric and I bent down, took hold of her vest and pulled her out. She stood and stomped her feet repeatedly. "I hate this, I hate this, I hate this!"

Eric looked at me. "Do you want to tell her about the wall or should I?"

"What wall?" Skinny asked. When she looked past us and saw it, she started crying. "I hate this."

I slapped her on the arm a couple of times, sending mud flying. "There, there, champ. We'll get through this."

Rolling her eyes at me, she stomped away toward the wall. I smiled at Eric before we followed her.

Everyone else was already over the wall when we got to it. Eric shouted as loud as he could. "Luke, Angela's going to need some help over the wall."

A moment later, Luke appeared at the top of the wall. He straddled it as he looked down at Skinny. "Grab the rope and pull yourself up as much as you can."

She whined, but still took the rope and tried to climb up. She only got a few feet before she slid back down. Eric clasped his hands together. "Hop on."

Skinny stepped onto Eric's hands and he lifted her up. She reached her hand toward Luke. He caught hold of her and pulled her up until she was on top of the wall. Before she could whine about the way down, Luke just pushed her off. He looked at me. "Let's go."

Taking hold of the rope, I climbed. Eric stood back up and watched me climb. I held on as tightly as I could but having mud on my hands made it difficult. Luke reached his arm down to me when I got closer. I reached up, just barely out of reach. Suddenly two hands were on my butt, pushing me up. Luke grabbed my hand and pulled me up, so I was on top of the wall. I glared down at Eric, but he just winked at me.

Shaking my head, I jumped down onto the other side. Skinny lay on the ground, faking an injury. At least, it seemed like she was faking. She kept complaining that she'd broken her leg, but she moved it around just fine.

Shots rang out, making everyone pull their guns out and look around. Men had come out behind some trees and fired at us. We fired back as we ran toward the tower. Since Skinny ran right beside me, her leg couldn't have been broken.

Once we arrived under the tower, the shooting stopped. Dante stood in the corner, his arms folded, his face holding no expression. When I looked closer, I corrected myself. Amusement definitely danced in his eyes.

RL Steven stood nearby with a bored expression on his face. "Congratulations. You're halfway done."

CHAPTER 19

Skinny immediately fell to the floor, somehow shrieking, crying, yelling, whining, and whimpering all at the same time. It was quite impressive.

RL Steven ignored her. "For the rest of the challenge, one of you will have sustained an injury and won't be able to continue on their own. The rest of you will have to help carry that person around."

All eyes fell on Skinny and she stopped her tantrum. She sat up, her face excited. "Me?"

Thunder Thighs grunted. "If it will get you to shut up, then yes."

"Plus, she's the lightest," Luke said. Tina nodded in agreement.

"How are we supposed to carry her?" Simon asked, scratching his frizzy head. There were chunks of mud sitting in his hair.

Theo picked Skinny up and threw her over his shoulder, despite her protests. He smiled at RL Steven. "Which way do we go?"

"East," RL Steven said. "You'll see a long log sitting out in the open. Once you reach it, turn north into the forest."

Everyone stood there, waiting for more instructions. Given the look on RL Steven's face, apparently, he had no more to give.

"And then?" Thunder Thighs asked.

"You'll go through the forest," RL Steven said.

She rolled her eyes. "What about when we get out of the forest?"

"If you get out," RL Steven said, "head west. You'll go through an open field until you hit a set of stairs. They'll lead you to a room where you can get cleaned up before we leave." He looked at Dante. "Follow them but keep your distance."

Dante answered with a nod.

Luke clapped his hands together. "Keep your eyes and ears open. I'm sure there will be plenty of camouflaged men waiting for us in the forest." He pulled his gun in front of him and held it close. "Let's move out." He moved east, with all of us trailing behind him.

It was eerily quiet as we walked. The group before us must have made it through the forest already. If they made it through. That *if* loomed over me as we crept toward the trees.

We came across the log five minutes later. I looked to the north only to see an endless amount of tall sycamore and pine trees. Besides random chirps from some birds, silence sat in the air. The day had started nice, but thick gray clouds rolled in overhead.

Pausing in front of the log, we all stared out, none of us

taking the first step. Thunder ripped through the silence making me jump in surprise. Eric laughed next to me, easing the unwanted tension.

"What do you think is out there?" Skinny asked, her head pressed up against Theo's back. Her hands were holding on tight to the back of his vest. From the smile on Theo's face, plus the way he stood tall, he didn't mind holding her.

Theo looked eagerly at Luke. "Should we go in?"

Luke and Tina exchanged a look before Luke spoke. "Let's line up in two groups, just like we did when we first entered this challenge. No talking. Keep close together and watch for any signals from me or Tina."

I jumped over the log and went and stood behind Luke and Eric. Simon stood behind me, shaking slightly. I wasn't sure if he was cold, nervous, or both.

A fat raindrop landed on my cheek. I wiped it away, only to smear mud all over my face. I'd forgotten to clean off my face after crawling under the barbed wire. Plus, my hands were muddy, too. I would have wiped them off on my clothes, but they also were covered in mud.

More rain fell as we entered the forest. The trees slowed down the rain, but it made the drops much bigger. I kept close to Eric as I looked around for anything out of place. With the enemy in camouflage, it would make it hard to spot them.

A rustle to the east made me pause. I pointed my gun in that direction, looking for any sign of a person. My eyes passed over a bush but then swept back. Two eyes stared back at me, unblinking. Without hesitating, I pulled down on the trigger, hitting my target in the face a few times.

"Nice shot," Eric whispered.

We continued walking, keeping our pace slow and steady. It would have been much smoother if Simon wasn't clomping along, kicking up leaves, sticks and anything his foot could connect with. I motioned for him to be quiet, but he just gaped at me.

"How am I supposed to be quiet?" His high-pitched voice carried through the forest, making some birds sing out.

"SHHH!" Thunder Thighs' declaration was louder.

Moments later, we were ambushed. Everyone fell to the ground, except for Simon who stood there shaking. I crawled over to him and yanked him down.

Theo set Skinny behind a tree and out of the line of sight of the enemy. He came back around, low to the ground, ready to fight. Even though we were under attack, he was still smiling.

I pulled Simon over to a tree. "Just stay behind here until I come and get you."

He nodded and closed his eyes. I went back over to where Eric and Luke were, getting down on my stomach behind a fallen tree. Perching my gun on the log, I looked out toward the oncoming fire and started shooting. There were easily thirty to forty men out there that I could see. They blended in so well with the scenery, there could have been a lot more I couldn't find.

"You're too high, Emmie," Luke said. He was on the other side of Eric, who lay right next to me. I lowered my gun just a little and continued shooting. "Perfect."

Smiling on the inside, I swept my eyes around, trying to

conserve my ammo and only shooting where there was a person. Eric and Luke seemed to be doing the same thing. Tina, Thunder Thighs, and Theo were to the left of us, hidden behind a couple of trees.

I glanced over at Tina to see how she was doing and saw a bush moving toward her. Shaking my head, I looked closer to make sure it was actually moving. I could see a few pairs of eyes in the bush. "Tina! Behind you!"

She spun around, spotted the approaching bush and fired. When the bush finally stopped moving, she turned toward me. "Thank you."

I nodded at her and turned back. Another group of men were approaching us from the east. I pointed at them. "Luke, over there. More men."

"We won't get to them from this angle," Eric said.

"Let's move east and find cover behind some trees," Luke said, standing up halfway.

We kept our bodies low as we went east. We didn't get very far before they started shooting at us.

Running the rest of the way, Luke took cover behind a sequoia while Eric and I took cover behind a large pine tree. We kept our backs pressed together as he shot around the west side of the tree and I shot around the east.

Tina and the others joined us, helping us shoot down the enemies. Soon, there was no one left firing at us. We all came together near a sad-looking pine tree. Its branches were almost bare, and it drooped to the right.

"Nicely done everyone," Luke said.

"We need to continue north," Tina said. "Let's keep close

together and remember to keep your eyes peeled."

Theo was still smiling. "I need to go back and get Angela."

"And I need to get Simon," I said.

Luke looked at the group as if noticing for the first time that they weren't with us. "That's probably a good idea. Let's head back west before we go north."

I found Simon right where I left him. We'd just started back toward the group when a creak came from my left. Simon had jerked to a stop next to me.

"My shoe's stuck under a root," Simon said, pulling at his leg.

As I turned to see what had caused the noise, a giant tree fell in our direction.

I only had a moment to react. Falling on my knees, I pulled Simon's foot out of his shoe and pushed him with all my might, making sure he was out of harm's way.

When I looked back at the plummeting tree all I could see was a blur of wood and bark headed straight for me. At the last second, my body was propelled away, rolling a few times until I came to a stop on the ground.

Dante lay on top of me, his eyes wide with panic. "Are you okay?"

My gaze shot back to the tree, flat on the ground, the earth smashed underneath it. That would have been me.

CHAPTER 20

It took a minute to work moisture back in my mouth. Dante still hovered on top of me, looking me over for any serious injuries.

"I'm fine," I managed to get out.

Dante stood, held out his hand and helped me up. "That was scary." He went back over to the tree and examined it. "Must have been a pretty old tree …" His voice trailed off. He bent down, looking closely at the stump.

I joined him, squinting to make sure I was seeing it correctly. It had been cut. My eyes found their way to his and he looked back at me. He noticed it, too.

A rustle in the trees caught our attention. I barely caught a blur of someone running away.

Dante grabbed my arm. "Take Simon and get back to the others. I'll go check this out." He took off without another word.

"Where's my shoe?" Simon asked. Well, more whined.

I went over to get it, but the fallen tree covered the area

where his shoe should have been.

"What's going on?" Eric walked up, with the rest of the team behind him.

"Simon's shoe is trapped under this tree." I pointed to it. "Help me roll it away."

Tina came up to me. "Did that fall? Just now? I thought that bang was just thunder."

I nodded. "Yes. I had to pull his foot out so we could get out of the way, but now his shoe is under there."

Eric looked me and Simon over. "Are you injured?" He eyes held concern.

"That's so scary," Tina said under her breath.

"We're wasting time!" Thunder Thighs yelled out.

Luke kicked at the tree. "Even if we all pitched in, there's no way we could roll it in this wet, slippery weather. Sorry, Simon, but you'll have to go shoeless."

Theo nodded in agreement. He had Skinny over his shoulder again.

"Do you want me to take a turn holding her?" Eric asked him.

Theo shook his head, his teeth exposed as he smiled. "Nope. She's light as a feather."

Eric nodded. "Let me know if you change your mind."

Simon stood next to me, his shoulders slumped in defeat. Even though he was covered in mud, I could still see a mass amount of paint.

"Let's get going," Luke said, his eyes on Simon. "We're almost through this."

"Head out," Tina said.

We kept in our two lines, walking a bit faster this time around. Everyone seemed more alert and ready for another attack.

We reached the edge of a hill a little while later. A small stream ran through the forest at the bottom of the hill. The slope downward was free of any trees, which would leave us all exposed. But we had to go down and across the stream to get to the other side of the forest.

"Here's the plan," Tina said. Even with a helmet, goggles, and some mud smeared on her face, she still looked overwhelmingly beautiful. "We're going to go down as fast as we can. Luke and I will keep our eyes trained north. Rachel, you have the west. Eric, you have the east. Theo, Emmie, and Simon keep your eyes on the south."

"What about me?" Skinny rested her elbows against Theo's back while propping her chin on her hands.

"Injured people can't talk," Thunder Thighs said.

Skinny frowned. "Yes, they can."

Thunder Thighs grunted and muttered a swear word under her breath. "Not in this challenge. So, shut up."

Skinny opened her mouth to protest, but Tina held up her hand. "There's no time for arguing right now. You two can argue about this later tonight."

"Alone in your dorm room," I put in. Everyone else nodded in agreement.

"Let's go," Luke said. A slight smile rested on his lips. The whole challenge relaxed him and helped him open.

We filed down the hill as fast as we could. Going down backward was not easy for me or Simon. I held onto his arm the whole way down so he wouldn't fall. A scream to the right of me caught my attention, making me let go of Simon.

"Ah!" Simon yelled out as he fell.

I was too busy looking over at Theo and Skinny to pay him any mind, though. At first, I thought that Theo had slipped at the bottom of the hill, dropping Skinny into the stream. But her screams were from relief. She had jumped off Theo and into the stream herself.

"Finally, I can get this mud off!" Skinny exclaimed, rolling around in the water.

Thunder Thighs approached her, pulling her up by the vest. "This isn't the time for a bath."

All our commotion brought out another set of attackers. We had been so distracted by Skinny that no one had been looking.

"Run for cover!" Tina yelled out.

Theo snatched Skinny out of Thunder Thighs' grasp and we all ran to the nearest trees. I'd been hit a few times in the arms, legs, and torso. If this had been real, I'd be dead. All because Skinny wanted a bath.

As soon as I was behind a tree, I checked my ammunition. Low. I turned to Eric, who stood next to me. "I'm almost out."

"Me, too," he said.

"We're *all* almost out," Luke said.

Simon pulled some mud out of his hair. "I've been out for a while." He smiled sheepishly at Luke.

"I'm out, too," Theo said.

"Great." Thunder Thighs huffed. "What do we do now?"

"Make a run for it." Tina looked down at her legs.

"Thanks to Angela's outburst, we've all been hit. We're dead anyway. Let's run."

Luke nodded. "Sounds good. Run!"

We took off after him, running as fast as we could through the rest of the forest. I stumbled a few times on some exposed roots, but Eric held onto my vest as we ran, easily keeping me upright. By the time we reached the end of the forest, no one was following us anymore.

To the west lay an open field that ended at a set of stairs. The stairs led up to a building in the northwest corner of the field. Rain still fell, smearing the paint and mud all over our bodies.

"I don't like the fact that it's an open field," Thunder Thighs said. "It's a trap."

Our group walked to the edge of the field and stopped. Throughout the field were protruding pieces of grass. As I pointed to them, Eric, Luke, and Tina all nodded. They'd seen them, too. Luke looked around, spotted a rock on the ground, picked it up and hurled it out onto the field near one of the protrusions.

Simon apparently hadn't seen our interaction because he started walking out onto the field before Luke's rock landed. "I just want to get this ov …" His words were cut off by a high-pitched squeal that escaped his mouth. Yellow paint exploded up from the ground, splattering all over him. At the same time, Luke's rock struck the protrusion and red paint flew into the air.

As Simon squealed, Luke looked at all of us. "Land mines. Try to avoid the protruding pieces of grass. Head for the stairs." He smiled at Tina. "I'll see you at the top."

Tina took that as a challenge and the two of them took off, dancing over the mines. Thunder Thighs took off after them, her dance looking more painful and jerky. Theo followed, with Skinny bouncing around at his back, her shrill filling the air. He took hold of Simon's arm and pulled him along after them.

Eric held out his hand and smiled at me. "Ready?"

Taking hold of his hand, I smiled back. "Sure."

We took off running, keeping our eyes down and watching for the mines. We jumped around them and over them, smiling the whole time. The rain came down on us, adding to the fun. Holding Eric's hand comforted me because I slipped a few times on the wet grass. We were almost to the end of the field when I lost my footing and almost stepped onto a mine. Eric noticed and lifted me up, pulling my body toward him. He wrapped his arms around my waist and carried me the rest of the way.

He set me down when we got to the stairs and we ran up until we got inside the building. After shutting the door, I took off my gun, my helmet, and my goggles and threw them in a pile with all the others. The floor was covered in mud and paint, along with previous Recruit's equipment. There were a few benches along one wall and then a bunch of showerheads along another.

Tina hurried over and turned on one of the showerheads.

Skinny gasped at her. "We can't all shower in here!" Her face reddened. "Together …"

Tina just laughed. "Don't take off your clothes and we'll

all be fine." She stood, completely clothed, under one of the showerheads, washing off all the mud and paint. I joined her, turning on the showerhead next to her. Eric, Luke, Theo, and Thunder Thighs did the same. Simon and Skinny just gaped at us.

When we were done, they separated the boys and girls and let us go to private stalls so we could take off our wet clothes and get changed into nice, dry, clean clothes.

On the bus ride back to the dorms, Tina and I cuddled under a blanket and talked about the whole experience. Even though it had been messy and completely draining, it had been the best day yet in Recruitment.

Aside from the falling tree. My mind wandered as we talked. Had it been cut? If it had, why? Someone had been there, so they had to have pushed it when they wanted to. Was it meant for Simon? For Dante? For me?

The thought made me shiver.

CHAPTER 21

I hoped I'd be able to talk with Dee, Tina, and Eric about the tree after we got back, but I didn't have the chance. They surprised us with a social event. Everyone was excited but me. It made me suspicious. We were only a few days into Recruitment, and they were already having a party? President Randall showed up and said he wanted to reward us for how well we were doing. Maybe I was just being overly paranoid. They could've had parties often during Recruitment.

We were all taken over to the Recruitment Center, where we met the first day. They had a table with a bunch of treats, like pastries, cookies, chips, and the hard candies VP Oliver used to sneak to me when I was a little girl. Seeing them brought a smile to my face. Music drifted out of the overhead speakers and they let us slow dance, but of course, we still had to have a proper distance between us, according to Recruitment rules.

All our group and dorm leaders were standing around, keeping an eye on everyone. RL Steven stayed close to our group the whole night, not letting us out of listening range, which made for an uncomfortable evening.

Eric and Luke had no idea that I was being watched, so they kept eyeing RL Steven, looking at him as if he'd gone insane.

"So, Ms. Woodard, how are you doing this evening?" Eric asked me.

We were dancing together in the center of the room, his hands on my waist and my hands on his shoulders, spaced out as far as we could go.

I smiled. "Very well, Mr. Greene. And you?"

Eric looked around the room and then at RL Steven, who walked right by us. RL Steven was making a constant loop around all our group. "I don't think there's a word that could convey what I'm feeling right now."

Tina and Luke were dancing next to us, chatting away. It surprised me how relaxed Luke could become when he was around Tina. She brought out the best in him.

Dee and a friend of ours growing up, Tim, were dancing near us too. Tim was a short guy with light brown hair. I think he always felt comfortable with Dee because she was one of the few girls in our school that was shorter than him. Although with her friendly personality, you couldn't help but love her. And I had a feeling Tim did.

"Well whatever you're feeling, is it good or bad?" I asked Eric.

He looked at RL Steven who had just walked by. He waited until he was a little farther away. "For my general feeling about being here tonight, with the way everyone's acting, the feeling isn't great." RL Steven passed by again. He stopped right next to us, bent down and pretended to tie his shoe. Eric and I danced in silence, waiting for RL Steven to finish. Finally, after the longest shoe tying session ever, RL Steven got up, sighed, and started walking again.

Eric looked me in the eye. "But with my present company, the feeling's amazing." A small smile formed on his mouth, making me blush a little.

"If you could change anything about tonight, what would it be?" I asked him.

"For one, we wouldn't all be wearing the same clothes."

"I didn't know guys cared about clothes," I said, laughing.

"We do. Trust me." Eric paused for RL Steven and then continued. "We all want to see the girls in different clothes."

I raised my eyebrows. "Different?"

Eric looked me up and down, taking in my long sleeve shirt and pants. "You wouldn't be so … covered up."

RL Steven still hadn't made his way back around so I took the opportunity to slap Eric upside the head.

"Hey!" Eric said. "You're the one who asked. Don't ask if you can't handle the answer."

I rolled my eyes. "Fine. What else?"

Eric's fingers drummed my waist as he thought. "The music would be different. Maybe a little louder?"

"A lot louder," I said.

"Okay, a lot louder." He looked at RL Steven who passed by. "There wouldn't be sharks swimming all around us, that's for sure. And you," he said, his thumb stroking my side, "wouldn't be so far away."

I blushed.

"Have I ever told you that red is a good color on you?" Eric asked, smiling.

I told myself it was because the color of the day was red, but deep inside I knew it was because my cheeks matched my outfit.

A throat cleared next to me. "The song's over." It was RL Steven.

He, Tina, Luke, Dee, and Tim were all staring at us, Tina and Dee clearly trying not to laugh. It made me wonder how much they'd heard.

"Bathroom break?" Dee said to me and Tina.

"Yes," Tina said, taking me by the arm.

Dee came to my other side and took my hand. I looked back as we were walking away and saw RL Steven looking conflicted. He honestly couldn't have been thinking about coming with us. To answer my question, he pulled something out from his pocket and held it to his mouth. So, DL Jen would be coming with us.

Sure enough, when we got to the bathroom, DL Jen waited inside.

"Hello ladies," DL Jen said as we walked in. She was leaning up against a sink, her arms folded, not trying to hide the fact that she was just there to supervise.

"Hi," I said.

"Having fun?" DL Jen asked us.

"Tons!" Tina said, giving DL Jen a thumbs up. I could tell from her tone and gesture that she was joking and from DL Jen's face, she could tell too.

Disappointment washed over me. I wanted to talk. Dee had suggested going to the bathroom in the first place so we could. So, the three of us just washed our hands and then pretended to fix our hair and make sure we looked good before we headed back out to the social. Right before we walked out, a loud popping sound came from outside, followed by some screaming. A voice came from DL Jen's pocket and she pulled out her device.

"Jen, we need you out here, now," RL Steven said.

DL Jen eyed the three of us. "On my way." She gave us one last look and left us in the bathroom.

Once the door closed, Dee spoke. "Should we go see what happened?"

I shook my head. "All I want to know right now is if RL Steven's going to follow us like that all the time now. Could he have been more annoying?"

"I want to know what's going on with you and Eric," Tina said, raising her eyebrows at me.

My cheeks flared. "Nothing, obviously."

Dee tilted her head, making her curls bounce a little. "Obviously?"

I tucked my hair behind my ear. "Because we can't date during Recruitment. You two know that." Before I could touch my hair again, I put my hands in my pocket so I wouldn't fidget.

"The only thing that's obvious is how much he flirts with you," Tina said with a smile.

"Who's flirting with you?" I turned to see Amber standing in the doorway with her two sidekicks, Stacy and Tiffy.

I sighed, stuffing my hands farther into my pocket.

Amber's two friends were opposites in looks. Stacy was short and stocky, while Tiffy was tall and slender. They weren't opposites in attitudes, though. Or in the way they did anything and everything Amber did. They had even cut their hair short like Amber.

"You need to stop following me to the bathroom, Amber," I said, forcing myself to keep my hands in my pockets. Only this time it was to keep from punching her. "It's really creepy."

Amber huffed. "Please, Emelia. I wouldn't follow you anywhere. I came to check the bathrooms. We're being evacuated."

"Evacuated?" Tina asked. "Why?"

"Some technical malfunction," Amber said, waving her hand in the air. "One of the speakers blew out and its spark started a small fire. They're overreacting, but whatever. The dance was boring anyway." Amber folded her arms and shifted her weight to her hip.

I pouted. "So, I take it no one would dance with you?"

Amber's cheeks flared, but she tried to sound casual as she talked. "I wouldn't dance with any of these pathetic boys anyway. I prefer older, mature men."

"My Grandpa's available," I said. "I could introduce the two of you if you'd like."

"That's not what I . . ." Amber took a deep breath, calming herself. "Never mind. We need to leave the premises."

"Whatever." I moved toward the door, but the three idiots stood there blocking the exit. I looked at Amber. "Uh, apparently you don't know how this works, but you have to move your butt if you want us to leave."

Amber grabbed me by my shirt just like she had a few days earlier, only this time she didn't throw me against the wall. She pulled me down to her face, only inches away. "You better watch it, Emelia. We don't want a recap of the other morning."

I laughed. "What? Where you punched the ground? I don't need to be here for that. How's your hand doing, by the way?"

Amber grunted while she let go of my shirt and threw her arm back ready to punch me. I didn't want to have another fight. I tried to move out of the way, but she nailed my chin. The sudden need to defend myself overwhelmed me.

Before she could connect with my face again, I threw my whole weight into her body, knocking her to the ground. I got off two punches, one to her eye and one to her nose, before Stacy and Tiffy grabbed me by my arms and pulled me off her.

I tried to shake them off me, but they wouldn't let go.

"Are you okay?" Stacy asked Amber, who was lying on the ground, tears falling from her eyes. Dee and Tina were trying to pull the girls away from me.

"She broke my nose!" Amber yelled. She stood up and glared at me, blood dripping down her lips. She gave a yell like she was about to head into battle and ran at me.

Before she could reach me, Dee slammed into her. Amber stumbled to the side and into a stall door. The door opened and Amber fell, her head barely missing the toilet.

Stacy shoved me and went for Dee, taking a few swings at her. I tried to squirm away from Tiffy so I could go help Dee, but Tiffy held on tight. As I twisted my arm to get free of Tiffy, she dug her fingernails into my skin, the sting of the long scratch forcing me to take a quick gulp of air.

Tina jumped onto Tiffy and threw her arm around her neck, making Tiffy release me. Scrambling over to Stacy, I put my arms around her waist, pulling her away from Dee. I looked at Dee, who was lying on the ground. A small cut ran down her lip, blood streaming down her chin.

"Dee!" I went to her side, but as soon as I got to her, Stacy came up behind me, took me by my hair and pulled me away. "Let go!" I twisted my body so I could face Stacy and punched her in the stomach. She grunted but didn't let go. I grabbed her free arm and bit down, making her scream.

"She bit me!" Stacy yelled, shaking her arm out. "The brat actually bit me!"

"You wouldn't let go!" I yelled back at her.

Back up on her feet, Amber took the opportunity to jump on me, sending me to the ground, knocking the wind out of me. I banged the back of my head on the tile, causing spots to appear in my vision. Amber punched me over and over again in the stomach, making it harder for me to breathe and causing me to gasp for air. Dee tried to get back up to help, but Stacy jumped on her and pinned her down. I could hear Tiffy and Tina still going at it, but I couldn't see what was happening.

I put my hands around Amber's wrist, trying to stop her from hitting me, but the lack of oxygen made me weak.

A few moments later, the bathroom door opened. The next thing I knew, Amber was being pulled off me. I looked up to see DL Jen holding onto her, trying to keep her from coming at me again. A few other group leaders came in, breaking up the other fights. I just lay there on the ground trying to get my breath back.

"Let go of me!" Amber screamed.

"Stop squirming and I will," DL Jen said. For someone so petite, she held onto Amber quite well.

I closed my eyes, feeling a slight throb in the back of my head where it had hit the ground. I put my hand on the spot and immediately noticed it was wet. When I pulled my hand in front of my face, it was covered in blood.

CHAPTER 22

"Will you stop moving if I let you go?" DL Jen asked Amber.

"Yes!" Amber whined. "Just let go!"

DL Jen sighed and finally let go of Amber but kept herself braced in case she needed to grab her again. Thankfully, she didn't. Instead, Amber went off. The crack in her personality grew bigger by the day.

Amber pointed to her face. "Do you see what she did to my nose?! She and her stupid friends …"

DL Jen held up her hand to silence her. "Enough. I'm not listening this time. It's out of my hands." She looked around at all of us and shook her head. "This was really stupid of all of you. You're in Recruitment. Since RH Johnson has had limited supervision, it'll be President Randall you'll have to answer to. Stupid, stupid girls."

"But—" Amber said.

"No," DL Jen said, her voice not inviting any more interruptions. "Just shut up. I don't want to hear another word out of any of you. Follow me." DL Jen turned and stormed out of the bathroom.

I slowly stood and went to Dee, putting my arm around her waist.

"Are you okay?" I whispered to Dee, as we hobbled out of the bathroom. We stayed far back from DL Jen so she wouldn't hear us talking.

Dee forced a smile. "Couldn't be better." She wiped some blood off her chin.

The bathroom door opened, the other girls stepping out.

"Oh, Emmie, your head!" Tina came up to the other side of me. "That doesn't look good."

I grunted. "It doesn't feel good either." I looked at her face. She had a couple of scratches and her left eye was a little swollen. "That's going to be a nice shiner tomorrow."

Tina grimaced. "You should see Tiffy."

A laugh almost escaped my mouth when I got a good look at Tiffy. Her nose was bleeding, her left eye swollen, her lip cut, I think she was missing a patch of hair on her head and when she opened her mouth ... "Is she missing a tooth?" I looked wide-eyed at Tina.

Tina rubbed the back of her neck. "I didn't mean for it to happen. I was trying to stop her, but she's so feisty. I used a little too much force trying to push her off me and she landed against one of the sinks."

I took my free arm and pulled Tina close to me. "I'm just glad you're okay."

Tina sighed and leaned the side of her head gently against mine. "Me too."

"I'm so sorry you both got involved in this," I said to them.

Dee put on a real smile. "Emmie, we'll always be here for you, no matter what."

We moved down the hall, heading toward the exit. Complete silence filled the Recruitment Center, which meant everyone had already been evacuated.

The minute we stepped outside, hundreds of heads turned to look at us to see what had happened. The Recruits had all been gathered around outside, probably talking about the evacuation. The noise stopped abruptly when they saw us.

The cold air stung against the scratch on my arm. I pulled my arm away from Tina so I could look, turning my head too quickly, causing my world to spin. As I rocked a little where I stood, someone took my hands to steady me.

"Easy there," Eric said, holding onto my hands tightly. Luke and Tim stood near us. Eric looked at my scratched arm and then at my face. "What happened in there?"

"Exactly what it looks like." I could tell by the look in his eyes that he wanted to hug me, but he didn't, probably because we had a big audience. It made me happy and sad at the same time. Stupid Recruitment rules.

"Does that hurt?" Tim asked Dee, pointing at her lip.

"A little," Dee said.

Tim lifted his hand to her chin and almost touched it, but he pulled back at the last second. "You have some blood on your chin." His face was bright red.

Dee blushed, wiping her mouth and chin. "Oh, thanks."

"What about you, Tina? Are you okay?" Luke asked.

"Much better than Tiffy," Tina said, pointing over at her.

Luke looked over at Tiffy and then back at Tina, his eyes wide and his mouth slightly agape. "You did that?"

Tina shrugged. "Most of it was on accident."

I sucked in my breath, letting go of one of Eric's hands and putting my hand up to my head, my world dizzy.

Eric saw the blood on his hands and looked me in the eye. "Emmie, are you okay?"

"I'm just lightheaded. I knocked my head on the tile." I didn't care anymore who was watching. I was about to fall over, so I leaned the good side of my head against Eric's chest.

He put his arms around me. "I've got you." His embrace immediately filled me with warmth.

Footsteps approached from behind me. A few seconds later, President Randall spoke. "Dean, get everyone back to the dorms."

"Of course," RH Johnson said.

"As for the six of you," President Randall said, stepping so I could see him, "we need to talk." He looked at Eric, Tim, and Luke. "The three of you may leave."

Tim and Luke said goodbye and walked away.

Eric squeezed me tight. "See you tomorrow." His lips brushed across my forehead, causing my world to spin for an entirely different reason.

"Um hmm," I said in response. I didn't want to let go.

Eric turned his head to Tina. "Can you take her from here?"

"Sure." Tina put her arms around me and pulled me toward her.

Eric gave me one last look and then walked away, joining up with Tim and Luke.

"I think we need to be taken to the infirmary," Dee said to the president. When he gave her a stern look she added, "Please, sir."

President Randall eyed all of us and sighed. "Fine. Follow me."

We walked slowly to the infirmary in silence. When we got there, a few nurses came and led us to a big, white room with lots of beds. They sat each of us down at a bed and so they could clean us up.

My nurse was about my height, but much thinner. She had short brown hair, cut in an a-line. She had a pretty face and when she leaned in to check my pupils, I noticed she had long, curly eyelashes. "How are you feeling?"

"Dizzy," I said.

"That's expected with a head wound like yours," the nurse said. "You have a small abrasion, but you won't need stitches. I'll put some glue on it which will seal it up. You may have a slight concussion, but it's nothing to worry yourself about. Just take it easy the next few days."

I laughed. "That's easier said than done in Recruitment. You never know what's going to happen."

The nurse smiled. "True."

When we were all checked out, President Randall stood in the middle of the room and waited for the nurses to leave. He cleared his throat. "I shouldn't have to tell you how serious this situation is. You broke a rule. And a very important one at that. You should be taken out of Recruitment, for starters."

The fact that he used the word *should* was a good sign.

One of the nurses came back in the room. "Sir, Dean Johnson and Janice Woodard are outside demanding to come in."

I tensed at the mention of my mom. How upset would she be when she saw me like this?

"Tell them they'll have to wait outside!" President Randall barked at her.

"Yes, sir," the nurse said, her voice quivering. She put her head down and stepped out of the room.

President Randall's breathing was heavy, his face livid. He looked like he didn't know where to begin. "All the rules in Recruitment were created for a reason. I don't know how to stress that they're rules, not guidelines. They must be followed. This little girl squabble of yours has already created an upheaval among the Recruits. They saw all of you and how you look." He clenched his jaw tight.

"Sir," Amber said, putting out her lower lip, her eyes innocent. "Tiffy, Stacy, and I only went in there to tell them to evacuate. The three of them turned against us and forced us to defend ourselves."

What? Was she serious? He couldn't really buy that.

President Randall glared at her, but his eyes softened at her expression. Maybe he did buy it. "Please don't interrupt me again." He took a deep breath. "With all that said, I need to take into consideration your families. Most of you are children from predominant members of our city. If this were to spread, it could hurt us tremendously. But I can't sweep this under the rug, either. It needs to be known that this cannot and will not happen again. We can't have Recruits creating havoc. We need order around here."

He took another deep breath, rubbing his temples. "Emelia and Tina, since this is your second broken rule, you're suspended from Recruitment for three days. You'll be kept at the dorms and won't have contact with anyone. Your meals will be brought to you. You'll not speak of what happened tonight with anyone. This includes close friends and family. Once the nurses clear you, you'll both report to SO Clark every night for a week for workouts. I shouldn't have to mention this, but this will affect the outcome of your Recruitment status. If this happens again, you'll be removed from Recruitment. Do I make myself clear?"

"Yes, sir," we said in unison.

President Randall looked at the other girls. "Amber, Stacy, and Tiffy, you'll also be taken out of Recruitment for three days, but it will not count against you. This will give you time to heal and recover from your serious injuries. Dee, you'll be taken out for one day and then report to SO Clark for two nights."

I gasped. "What? They're just as much at fault as us, if not more. Amber's the one who started it all!" Hadn't she? She'd physically assaulted me and had thrown the first punch.

"I said to not interrupt me!" President Randall yelled. "This is my decision, not yours! From the look of the three of them compared to the three of you, we can tell who's to blame. Emelia, you need to learn to control that temper of yours. If you wouldn't be such a smart mouth, none of this would've happened." He paused for a moment. "This behavior will not be tolerated during Recruitment or at Infinity Corp. And to be so selfish to drag your friends into this." He shook his head as he took another pause. "I hope you understand the position you've put me in. If you'll excuse me, I have to go create a story I can tell the other Recruits." He gave me one last glaring look and left the room.

Furious didn't begin to describe how I felt. How could all of it be put on me? The whole situation was purely insane. Amber batted her eyelashes and had everyone wrapped around her finger. Why couldn't he see that she was crazy? She was, right? Or had I made it all up in my head? Maybe I really was the crazy one.

"Emmie!" I turned to see my mom headed for me. She pulled me into a hug when she got to me, stroking my hair. I should've been excited to see her, but for some reason, I wasn't.

She pulled back and put her hands on my face. "What on earth were you thinking?" The disappointment in her eyes was painfully obvious.

I sighed. "Does it matter?"

She furrowed her eyebrows together in confusion. "Of course, it does. What would possess you to do something like this?"

I looked behind her at Amber. Dean, scratch that, RH Johnson was coddling her like a baby. He must have sensed me looking at him because he turned and shot me a look of death.

I turned my attention back to Mom. "It's a long story."

"Well, from what I hear, you'll have a lot of time on your hands for the next few days." Mom brushed my hair behind my ear.

"How did you already find that out?"

Mom's mouth turned up at the side into a small, mischievous smile. "I may or may not have listened at the door. It's a bad habit of mine. Plus, Whit has a voice that can carry." Whit? Did she not have to address him as President Randall?

"Well, time or not, I'm not allowed to talk to anyone about this."

Mom pouted. "Even your mother? I thought I could come by tomorrow for lunch."

"President Randall said we couldn't talk about it to anyone, including family."

"How would he know what we talked about?"

It was Recruitment. There seemed to be eyes and ears everywhere, even in the places you thought were safe.

"I just ..." I looked at Mom, who stared at me, her face hopeful. "I just don't want to talk about it."

Mom's face fell. "Well, okay, if that's what you want. But know that I'm always here for you." She pulled me into another hug. "Em, I don't know what's going on with you, but you need to straighten yourself out. I know it's hard. Trust me, I went through the same teenage rebellion phase. But it's not worth it."

Teenage rebellion phase? She couldn't have been more far off on what was happening. I was being cornered. I felt like I had a big fat X on my body that stated, take your best shot.

CHAPTER 23

The next three days were incredibly boring. They made us stay in our dorm rooms the whole time, except to go to the bathroom. Even then, we were chaperoned. I felt bad for Dee. At least I had Tina to talk to. Dee had Amber to put up with. According to Dee, Amber whimpered and whined the whole time she was in the room with her.

My head wound had been healing nicely. The first day I became a little dizzy a few times when I stood, but after that, I felt fine. My abdomen was a little sore from the beating it took. Lying down on my stomach seemed to be the best position for me for the first two days.

Surprisingly, the one that bothered me the most was the scratch. It was deeper than I originally thought. Tiffy had daggers for nails. My arm stung every time I took a shower. Also, when the air touched it. Or if I looked at it. Or thought about it.

Day two just happened to fall on family day. I didn't think President Randall would let us see our families, but he allowed each of us a brief visit in a room located on the first floor of the dorms.

Only my dad and brother were there.

"Where's Mom?" I asked.

Dad's smile he'd had since he first walked in the room faltered. "She's busy with work."

Derek leaned forward, resting his arms on the table we were sitting at. "You're suspended? Man, you're lucky they didn't kick you out."

A frown appeared on Dad's face. I preferred the smile. "What happened, Emmie?"

"Amber." I sighed, rubbing my temples. "She's crazy."

"You know," Derek said, "you keep on saying that. I'm thinking you might be delusional."

I dropped my hands and glared at him. "I'm not delusional. There's something wrong with her. You know I wouldn't start a fight for kicks and giggles."

Derek raised his eyebrows. "You do with me all the time."

"That's different," I said, rolling my eyes. "You're my brother. We're supposed to fight."

"It would make my life easier if you didn't." Dad's smile returned. "I thought you said you'd be on your best behavior."

I never intended to let my dad down. He meant the world to me and I wanted to make him happy. He was the main reason I'd signed the Recruitment contract. Well, that and Eric's smile.

"I'm sorry, Dad. I'm trying." I looked at Derek. "Can you get access to the Recruitment files?"

He leaned back, stretching out his arms and legs. Derek

clasped his hands behind his head. "How do you think I found out what happened with you?"

"Derek." Dad shook his head. "Are you allowed to look at those documents?"

Derek shrugged. "No one has tried to stop me."

Tina and Dee were talking with their families at other tables in the room. RL Steven and DL Jen stood in the corner, watching us. Leaning in, I kept my voice low so only my family could hear me. "Can you look up Amber's file for me? I need to prove that I'm not delusional."

"No." Dad's voice was firm. "You can't violate her privacy like that."

I turned to him. "Did you know the Johnson's have another daughter?"

"What?" Confusion crossed Derek's face. "No, they don't. It's just Amber."

"Not according to Dee," I said. "Amber let slip that she had a sister."

"Two minutes." RL Steven's eyes were on mine as he said it.

I looked at Derek. "Please? Just look into it."

Dad reached out and took my hand. "Emmie, drop it. Forget about Amber. You need to focus on passing Recruitment."

Forgetting Amber wouldn't be an easy task. Because of her, my breaking point hovered right around the corner. If Dad wanted me to succeed, I needed to put an end to all of this. I needed closure.

With the way he looked at me, I couldn't say no though. I

sighed. “Fine, Dad. I'll drop it.”

His smile came back. “Good.”

Derek made sure Dad wasn't looking and mouthed, “I'll do it.”

Smiling on the inside, I stood and hugged my dad. I knew Derek would do it. The whole thing would entice him enough that he wouldn't be able to let go, either. We were different in a lot of ways, but we had the same sense of curiosity and an overwhelming desire to be right. Some may say that those were terrible traits to have.

I said it made me a fighter.

CHAPTER 24

I was thrilled when we were finally allowed to go back to the world of the living again. Well, until I stepped into the dining hall and all eyes turned to us. No matter what story they heard, they still knew we fought. Everyone I passed whispered and pointed at us. Some looked like they were waiting for another fight to break out.

The moment I sat down next to Eric, he took my hand under the table. "Where have you been? They wouldn't tell us anything." His knee bounced anxiously.

Before I could say anything, RL Steven sat down on the other side of me. I hoped it wasn't going to be a permanent situation, but I wasn't about to hold my breath.

I sighed and let go of Eric's hand. "Hello, RL Steven."

"Nice to see you, too, Emmie," RL Steven said.

None of us knew what to talk about, so we sat in silence for the rest of breakfast. Once we stepped on the bus, RL Steven stopped me and Tina.

"You'll sit up front from here on out," RL Steven said to

the two of us.

I saluted him. "Yes, sir."

After a long, silent bus ride, we stopped outside a big gray building. There were no windows, just one door in the front. When we got inside, we squeezed into a tiny foyer. The lighting was dim, making it dreary.

RL Steven finally stepped away from me so he could address everyone. The second he did, Eric stood at my side.

A small cardboard box sat on the ground. RL Steven picked it up and held it out in front of him. "Take off your watches and place them in here."

"Why?" Thunder Thighs asked.

RL Steven glared at her for a second. "Because you don't need them during this challenge."

A collective sigh filled the room. We all went up and one by one placed our Recruitment watches in the box. When we were all done and settled back into our spots, RL Steven pulled the box in and wrapped his arms around it, holding it close.

"I hope you all slept well last night," RL Steven said, freeing one of his arms and rubbing his head, "because this will be your most trying challenge to date. It will test your mental toughness, your fear, and basically your sanity. Just sit tight; it will begin momentarily."

"What are we supposed to accomplish during this challenge?" Luke asked, standing behind me. "What are the rules?"

"I have no further instructions for you," RL Steven said. "Good luck." He looked at me and then pushed his way through the crowd and out the front door.

When it shut, all of us stood there not knowing what to do. Will, the guy from my high school, tried to open the door, but it wouldn't budge.

"Can't you open a door?" Thunder Thighs asked him.

"It's locked," Will said.

We stood there for what seemed like ages. In reality, probably only ten minutes passed, but when you're cramped in a small area, not knowing what was going to happen or when, the seconds ticked by like hours. I started to fidget.

Eric put his hand on my arm. "Please stop moving. You're making me nervous."

"Sorry," I said, standing still. "I just hate not knowing what's going to happen. How much longer can they make us wait here?" That was why they took our watches.

"All day," Tina said.

Luke rocked back and forth. He looked at Tina. "This is getting ridiculous. They have to …"

Suddenly, the lights flickered on and off. A screeching sound came from all around the room, making me cover my ears. The lights went completely out a few seconds later. I could feel a few people pushed up against me, but I didn't know who. It was too loud to talk, and I wasn't about to remove my hands.

The next thing I knew, someone took me by my waist. I screamed, but they clamped their gloved hand over my mouth. Someone grabbed my shirt, trying to pull me back, but whoever held me was strong.

Keeping my hands pressed to my ears, I kicked my legs and squirmed. No matter what I did, I wasn't going to be let go. I finally gave up and let them carry me to wherever I was being taken.

They dragged me down a few halls. We finally came to a stop, but my captor didn't release me. We just stood there. The floor jerked and then we were moving. I couldn't tell if we were going up or down. A minute later, we stopped.

My captor took me down a few more halls. At least, I assumed we were going down halls. We kept making turns. The lights were still out, so I had no idea how the person holding me could see where they were going.

Without warning, I was thrown onto the ground. The sound hadn't stopped, and the lights hadn't come back on. I pulled myself up as best as I could without taking my hands off my ears. I stood there, not moving. I wasn't sure what I was supposed to do. There was no sense in trying to walk around in the dark.

A few minutes later, someone bumped into me. Their back pressed up against mine. They didn't move away from me and I didn't attempt to move either. I closed my eyes, trying to focus my mind. Even though I couldn't see with my eyes open, for some reason it helped to have them closed. I focused on my breathing, keeping it steady and even. I relaxed my body, letting go of the tension.

Someone tapped my shoulder. There was no one pressed up against me anymore. I opened my eyes and saw Luke standing there. He didn't have his ears covered, so I moved my hands down, only to hear silence. I looked around me, taking in my surroundings. We were in a small room, probably ten by ten feet. The walls, floor, and ceiling were concrete. Besides me and Luke, the only other people in the room were Skinny, aka Angela, Will, and a guy I didn't know.

Luke looked at me expectantly. I raised my eyebrows. "What?"

"What should we do?" Luke asked.

I shrugged. "I don't know." I turned to the other Recruits. "Um, I'm Emmie, if you didn't know."

"Will." He stuck out his hand and I gave it a shake. "I know we went to school together, but we've never met."

The other boy stuck out his hand to me. "David." When I shook his hand, he had a flimsy grip. He was a short, scrawny guy.

Skinny looked at me with her eyes narrowed. "We've met."

"You don't need to remind me," I said under my breath.

"Well, now that we're all acquainted with each other, shouldn't we do something?" Luke asked, anxious like always.

"Maybe we should try the door?" I suggested, walking toward it. When I turned the knob, nothing happened. "Locked."

David snorted. "Not surprising."

"We're just supposed to stand around in here?" Skinny asked.

I looked at the ceiling, only to see one light and a speaker. A table sat in the corner of the room. A box sat in the center, filled with electrical wires, a black box, a screwdriver, and some other tools.

Luke picked up a piece of paper sitting near the box. "Instructions."

"For what?" Will joined us at the table.

Luke read the top part of the paper. "'If you want to keep your sanity intact, assemble a stop button that will keep the lights from flickering and the screeching from deafening your ears.'"

Skinny looked at the paper, pushing her glasses up on her nose. "I don't like the sound of that. It seems annoying and complicated."

I glanced over at her. "Have a better idea?"

Skinny went to the door and banged on it. "Hey! Let us out!"

David joined in with her, banging and shouting.

Will looked over at me. "How long do you think it'll take until they stop?"

I laughed. "An hour? Maybe two?"

"They wouldn't leave us in here that long," Luke said, standing in the middle of me and Will. He put the paper down and stuffed his hands in his pockets, probably to keep himself from playing with them.

"Are you kidding? This is Recruitment. They do crazy things." I looked at Luke. "Let's try to assemble this thing before …"

The lights went off as the screeching began. I covered my ears and waited for it to end. It lasted a few minutes.

"I hope that doesn't happen again," Luke said, tapping his foot on the ground.

I put my hand on his arm. "I wouldn't get your hopes up." I looked at Will. "You want to read the instructions while Luke and I try to put it together?"

Will adjusted his glasses. "Sure …"

The flickering and screeching happened again, only it went on for twice as long. When it stopped, Skinny looked like she was going to pull out her hair. She and David had continued to randomly kick the door and scream, but of course, no one came.

I furrowed my eyebrows. We needed to start. I pointed to the paper. "Read."

Luke and I pulled everything out of the box as Will read. We worked as fast as we could, but not knowing when the havoc would start again had us all on edge, making it hard to concentrate.

The screeching was louder the next time, the lights flickering faster. I kept my eyes closed and focused on controlling my breath. It went on even longer.

I had my hands over my ears, but I could feel Luke shaking next to me. All the noise and flickering lights were getting to him. Even though the noise was the loudest it had ever been and making my head ache, I took my right hand off of my ear and scooted up next to Luke, putting my arm around him.

Using his shoulder as an earmuff, I leaned my ear against it. He was rocking back and forth, so I rocked with him, rubbing his arm with my hand. I wanted to talk to him and tell him it was going to be okay, but all the noise prevented me from doing so.

It went on for at least fifteen minutes. When it stopped, my head was ringing. It took a few seconds for my hearing to adjust. Luke had his head down, his hands on his eyes. It sounded like he was crying.

"What's wrong with you?" Skinny screamed at the ceiling. "Stop it!" She looked at me, her eyes wild and frantic. "Finish already!"

"We're trying." I didn't know what more I could add to that.

Will looked at our almost finished button. He read down the instructions one more time, grabbed the screwdriver, and tightened the knobs.

I pulled Luke's forehead down, so it rested on mine. "We're almost done. Let's just get this over with and then it will all stop."

I expected Luke to pull away from me. It never seemed like he was very fond of me. But he surprised me by leaning into me. I hugged him. "It's going to be okay." At least I hoped it was.

Hope.

I held onto that word like my life depended on it.

CHAPTER 25

After we finished the button, I let Skinny press it. There were no more interruptions after that.

We sat in that room for probably another hour. We were all getting hungry, a couple of us needed to use the bathroom—including me—and we were restless.

Luke had finally regained his composure, but I still sat close with my arm around him and he didn't protest. David and Skinny kept eyeing us, probably surprised by all the physical contact. Being in those kinds of situations pulled people close together.

Will stood and paced the room. David and Skinny had given up shouting about an hour before. Every ten minutes, Skinny would go try the lock, but it never opened.

"If they keep us here much longer, and one of us can't hold it anymore, what should we do?" David asked, looking at the ground.

"Hold it," Will said.

"But I have a weak bladder," David said, still looking at

the ground, his cheeks red.

"You still have to hold it, man," Will said. "I'm not listening to or smelling that."

David danced anxiously around the room. I hadn't noticed my leg was shaking until Luke put his hand on it.

"Sorry," I said. "I'm in the same boat as David."

"Well, stay in that boat," Luke said with a small smile. "There will be no going overboard."

I laughed and then squeezed his arm. "How are you holding up?"

Luke shrugged. "This whole thing is just getting to me. I want to do well in this and not let my dad down. But it gets to you mentally. Not being in control of what's happening to you, it's just hard, you know?"

I did know. All too well. I knew what it was like having a parent who constantly looked over your shoulder and was hard to please. "Luke, believe me, you're not going to let your dad down. You're one of the hardest workers here. He'll be proud of you. And no matter how much I tease you, I respect you and your dedication."

Luke looked at me. "Really?"

"Really, really." I smiled at him. "You were amazing in the paintball challenge. You're a natural-born leader."

A click caught our attention, and we all turned and looked at the door. Maybe we were expecting it to just open on its own, but we all sat there for a minute, staring. Skinny inched her way to the door and turned the knob. It opened. She looked at us, her eyes wide. Luke and I glanced at each other and then went and joined her near the door. For some reason, none of us wanted to be the first one to step out. I took a deep breath and looked outside.

The hallway was empty and only a few lights were on the ceiling, making it barely lit. I turned to the others. “It’s clear.”

The room we had been in was at one end of the hallway, so we headed down to the other end. There were a few doors along the way, but all were locked.

The other end of the hallway came to a T. I glanced both ways, but they looked the same. The silence seemed eerie compared to all the screeching we had previously heard.

“Left or right?” I asked everyone.

Luke said, “Right,” just as Will said, “Left.”

I chuckled. “Well, that settles it.”

“Right,” David said from behind me.

“Right it is,” I said, turning in that direction. When we were halfway down the hall, the lights began to flicker.

“Please, not again!” Skinny whined.

Luckily, no screeching came. The lights kept flickering until they went out. With no windows, pitch black cloaked the hallway. I couldn’t even see my hand in front of me. I moved my hand around until I found a hand next to me and took it.

“Who is that?” I asked.

“Luke,” he said.

Someone grabbed my other hand. “It’s Will.”

“David, where are you?” I asked.

“Here,” David said, right behind me.

“Can you grab Will’s other hand, and then Angela grab David’s other hand?” I asked.

After a few seconds, David said, “Done.”

"Let's just continue down the hall," I said. "Luke, you lead the way."

Luke walked, keeping his pace slow, with the rest of us trailing behind. When he got to the first door, he tried to turn the knob, but it was locked. We continued until the end of the hall, where one last door awaited us. You could hear Luke turn the knob, followed by the relieving sound of it creaking open.

Something brushed past my head. "What was that?"

"What was what?" Luke asked.

"Something touched my head," I said.

A second later, it happened again.

"I felt something," Will said.

"Me, too," Luke said.

Suddenly a bunch of squeals filled the hallway as a whoosh of air passed over us. There was fluttering all around me, something bumping into my head and pulling on my hair. We were under attack by something that could fly. I was grateful for the dark so I couldn't see what they were.

"What are these things?" Will screamed next to me. We had let go of each other hands to swat them away, but they kept coming. David and Skinny's wails echoed down the hall.

A sharp prick on my ear made me flinch. "One of them bit me!" My pulse rose as fear crept in. I swatted the air, hoping to keep them away. As quickly as it had started, it ended.

"Finally," Skinny said.

"That was creepy," Luke said.

"Tell me about it," Will said.

Someone touched my arm. "How's your ear?" Luke asked.

"It stings," I said. "But I'll live."

"Do you hear that?" Luke asked.

"Hear what?" I asked.

"Shhh," Luke whispered.

A faint whoosh came from the other end of the hall. As it got closer, it became louder. The distinct sound of the flapping of wings made my hair stand on end. It sounded like there were hundreds of them.

"Run!" Luke shouted.

He took my hand and pulled me along. I reached out behind me and took hold of Will's arm. We ran as fast as we could down the hall, but they were catching up. The lights flickered on a little and I turned to see what they were. Bats. And there were tons of them.

We got to the end of the hall and turned right down another one. The lights continued to flicker on and off. The bats were screeching, making me cringe.

Luke reached for the knob to the door at the end of the hall, but it wouldn't open. He threw his body against the door, but it wouldn't budge. Will and I joined in, throwing ourselves at the mercy of the door.

"Open the door!" Skinny screamed.

"We can't!" I screamed back.

I froze when I looked behind Skinny. The bats were almost on us, coming full speed. My heart pounded in my ears, my breathing so heavy that my lungs stung. We stood there hopelessly and watched the lights go out.

A couple of seconds later, Luke grabbed my body and threw me on the ground, using his body as a shield to protect me. Will fell next to us, covering any part of me that Luke couldn't. I couldn't see Skinny or David, but their deafening cries filled the hallway.

Both Luke and Will were twitching, trying to shake off any bat that touched them. Will let out a yelp.

After a few minutes, the flittering of wings started to fade. "I think they're leaving," Luke said into my ear. Soon there was complete silence. We lay there, afraid to move. Will finally pulled away from me.

"I think we're in the clear," Will said.

Luke backed away from me a little. "Are you okay?"

I turned to look at him, our faces only a few inches away from each other. "I think I'm okay, thanks to you. How are you?" I backed away, looking him over. His clothes were disheveled, and there were a couple of scratches on his head, but other than that he looked okay.

"I'm alive," Luke said.

He stood, reaching his hand out to me. I took it and he helped me up. Turning to look at Will, I noticed he looked a little worse than Luke. His ear had been bitten and his glasses were skewed. I reached up and straightened them out.

"Thanks," I said to him.

Will smoothed out his clothes. "Uh, sure, no problem." His eyes skittered all around.

I glanced behind me at Skinny and David. Their hair was all over the place, their clothes ruffled, and their wild eyes said it all. I couldn't help but laugh.

Skinny looked at me in horror. "How could you be laughing right now?"

My laughter was uncontrollable. "I'm sorry." I snorted

loudly. "You just look so crazy! This whole thing is crazy! It's just completely insane." I never expected a challenge like this in Recruitment. They were pushing us and finding our breaking points.

"I think you're going insane," David said to me.

I took deep breaths, trying to calm myself down. "I think I am, too."

"Maybe we should continue down the hall?" Luke offered, looking at me.

"Yeah, we probably should." I wiped a few tears from my eyes. Something was definitely wrong with me. I had laughed to the verge of tears. Maybe it was my lack of sleep. Or I was joining Amber on the crazy train.

We had only made it a few steps down the hall when one of the doors in the middle of the hall slid open. Luke turned to me. "You ready for this?"

"Nope, but let's go," I said.

CHAPTER 26

When we got to the door, Luke, Will, and I looked in to see a small opening.

"What's in there?" Skinny asked from behind me.

"It's an elevator," Luke said.

As soon as we piled in, the doors closed. There were no buttons to push, so we just went where it took us, which by the way the elevator jolted, we were going down. Once it stopped, the doors opened, revealing yet another bleak hallway. This time, there were only two doors; one at the other end, and one in the middle on the right.

We walked slowly down the hall, afraid of what might happen. We glanced around nervously as if something else might attack.

Once we neared the middle door, both doors swung open. Darkness came from the door on the right. The door at the end of the hall revealed the most beautiful thing I had seen all day: natural light. The way out.

"Thank you!" Skinny said, pushing past us and heading

toward freedom.

As I passed the middle door, I thought I heard a shout come from inside the room. I looked at Luke and Will. "Did you hear something?"

They both shook their heads. Curiosity got the best of me, so I peeked inside, only to see darkness. When I stepped inside the room, a light flickered on.

Inside, there was a desk covered in buttons and knobs. On the wall to the right was a large window, but I couldn't see what was on the other side.

"Are you going to leave with us?" Luke asked from the doorway.

Will stood behind him, looking back and forth between me and the door to freedom.

I sighed. "Yes, I was just seeing what was in here."

I had only taken a couple of steps when someone yelled. "Did you hear that?" I asked, looking at Luke and Will.

"Yeah, what was that?" Luke asked as he stepped into the room. The yell came again.

"It sounds like someone saying help," I said, looking around the room.

"HELP US!" The scream came from behind the window. I went to it and cupped my hands over my eyes, trying to see what was on the other side.

"HELP!"

"Maybe one of these switches does something," Luke said, looking at the table.

Will peeked his head out the door and shouted for David and Skinny to come back. Skinny whimpered down the hall.

Will came back inside, went up next to Luke and scanned all the buttons.

"This one says, 'interrogation room light'," Luke said. He pressed down on the button. As soon as he did, a light came on behind the window.

I gasped. "Eric! Tina!" I ran to the window and banged on it.

Eric, Tina, Thunder Thighs, and two guys who I took to be Will and David's partners, were in the room. There were rats everywhere, climbing all over them. All five of them were bleeding from bites and scratches.

"Is there a way to get them out of there?" I asked, going over to the table and scanning it.

Luke looked frantically at all the buttons. "I don't see anything."

"There's no door," Will said, staring through the window.

"What?" I asked, turning to him.

"There's no door in the room. How could they get out?" Will asked.

"They had to get in," I said, walking to the window. My stomach lurched, watching them squirm, with rats all over the place.

"Maybe there's a trap door," Luke said.

Will went to the door again and looked outside. "Angela, David! Come here!"

They both grunted, but a minute later they were in the room. Their eyes widened in horror when they saw our partners being mauled by rats.

Thunder Thighs had come up to the window and banged. "HELP!"

"There has to be a way to get them out!" Luke yelled, running his hands over his head.

A loud groan rippled in the air and movement started in the other room. I looked closely. "Are the walls moving?"

"They're moving in," Will said.

He was right; the walls were closing in on our partners. If we didn't stop them, they'd be squished. I shuddered at the thought.

Another loud groan came from outside our room. David walked to the door and looked to the left. He gasped. "Uh, guys, the elevator's gone, and it looks like the wall's moving in."

Skinny ran to the door. "That's impossible!"

"But it's happening," David said. "If we don't get out of here soon, we'll be trapped."

"We can't just leave our partners in there!" I said, tears coming to my eyes. "They'll die!"

"So will we if we stay here!" David yelled. "What's better, five or ten deaths?"

I couldn't believe what I was hearing. "I'm not leaving them." I ran to the table and hit all the buttons, turned the knobs, and pulled the levers.

"Stop!" Luke yelled. "The walls are going faster now!"

Sure enough, the walls were moving in faster, the rats going wild, and our partners screaming in pain and fear.

"There has to be a way!" I shouted.

A chair sat under the table, so I pulled it out and ran at the window full speed, thrusting the chair at it. The window vibrated but didn't even crack.

"The wall out in the hall is moving faster now, too," David said. "I'm sorry, but I'm out of here."

"Me, too," Skinny said, taking off with David.

I couldn't believe they would just leave like that.

Will and Luke looked as frantic as I felt. We stood there, trying to think of something, but there was nothing to do. I tried to block out the screams so I could concentrate, but they were too piercing.

"Up there!" Luke shouted, pointing at the ceiling. A vent was right above him. I grabbed the chair and put it directly under the vent. Luke stood on the chair and reached up, touching the vent cover. He pushed it up and lifted the cover, shifting it to the right.

"They have a vent cover, too!" Will yelled. "It's right in the middle of the room."

"Emmie, come here. I'll lift you." Luke held out his hand to me.

I took it and he lifted me onto the chair with him. He clasped his hands together. Resting my palm on his shoulder, I put my foot on his hands and pushed up. He lifted me into the air, and I grabbed the edge of the vent, pulling myself in. I crawled down the vent and turned left, going to their opening. I tried to take off the cover, but it wouldn't budge.

"Luke!" I yelled as loud as I could. I turned back around and headed toward the way I came in. Luke was just being hoisted up. "I can't open it," I said to him.

"Let me squeeze by and I'll see what I can do." Luke inched past me. It was a tight squeeze, but he moved ahead of me.

"It's almost closed off!" Will yelled from below. "I'm sorry, but I can't stay here any longer. The wall has already reached the door. Only a few more feet and we'll be trapped." He paused. "And our partners don't have much room now. Even if you got them out of that room, there wouldn't be time to get them out of this room. I'm so sorry."

With that, he was gone.

We were left alone, with no hope of saving them.

"I can't open it," Luke said, his voice filled with despair. The screams below were getting louder. I scooted myself next to him, trying to see if we could combine our strength to open it. We pushed and pulled, but nothing worked.

"It's welded shut," Luke said.

"Why would they do this?" I asked, tears filling my eyes again. "They're just going to kill them? Kill us? Why?" It didn't make sense.

Luke eyes were watery. "I don't know."

My body shook, the emotions too much for me. I couldn't believe they were capable of this. Luke wrapped his arms around me, squeezing tight.

"We need to go, Emmie," Luke said, his voice barely a whisper.

"I can't just leave them," I whispered back.

"It's too late," Luke said. He choked on a sob. He was right. Their screams had stopped. The sudden silence cut me to the core. "We need to go."

It took every ounce of strength I had left in me, but I scooted back toward the opening. Luke followed behind me. When I got to the vent opening, I threw my body over the edge and jumped down. Luke hopped down a second later. My eyes landed on the door, but the wall had already covered the opening.

"We're too late," I said.

I turned to the window, but the lights were out, making me grateful. I didn't want to see what lay on the other side.

I didn't know if they were listening, but I was done playing their games. They couldn't do this and get away with it. "What is wrong with you people?" I shouted as loud as I could. "Killing innocent kids! What for? Power? Control? Instilling fear in everyone? That's not how you run a corporation or city. That's not how you gain trust or support. This is on your head, Randall! I hate you! I hate River Springs and everything it stands for! Screw you all! I hope you rot in hell!"

I fell to the floor, screaming out my sadness and frustration. Luke sat down next to me, holding me close.

I shook my head. "They can't do this!" I buried my head into his neck. "They just can't do this."

"I know." Luke's tears fell on my head. My whole body shook in anger. In hatred.

A groan made me look up. Our walls started moving in. We stood, looking around the room as if we could find a way to stop it. I didn't want to die like that. Squished to death. All because they trapped my friends; the people I loved and cared about.

I turned to Luke. "I couldn't leave them, Luke. I couldn't live with myself knowing I lived, and they died. I had to try and save them. I'm sorry."

Luke grabbed my arms and looked me in the eye. "This

isn't your fault, Emmie. You did the right thing. You did everything you could to save them."

I shook my head. "But I didn't. They're dead. And we . . . we will be soon." I fell against Luke's chest, more tears coming. He held me tight, resting his head on mine.

We stood there in the middle of the room, listening to the groans of the walls as they moved in and to the sounds of the table snapping, breaking into pieces. The walls were getting closer, the seconds left in my life ticking away.

I don't know why, but I pulled back and looked at Luke. He pulled my head close, resting his forehead against mine. The whole experience had bonded us in a way I couldn't explain. I cared deeply about Eric. We had bonded in a way I didn't think was possible. I was starting to fall for him. And I know Luke loved Tina. It was so obvious.

But we were alone in that room after a day of terror together. We connected on a whole other level. Maybe it was the exhaustion, maybe it was the thought that my life was almost over, or maybe it was the way Luke looked at me, but when he pressed his lips to mine, I didn't stop him.

Instead, I put my hand on the back of his head, pulling him closer, pressing my body up against his, and kissed him back with everything I had. I concentrated on the warmth of his lips as the wall pressed against my back.

CHAPTER 27

When the walls started moving back, I pulled away from Luke. We stood there in silence, not knowing what to do. My heart raced, my breathing fast. I stared at Luke, trying to comprehend what had just happened.

When we finally broke eye contact, I looked around the room. Shards from the busted table lay scattered on the ground. What astonished me more was that the door wasn't blocked any more.

I was frozen in place, unable to make myself move toward the door. It took me a moment to realize Luke had his hand on my arm. He must have noticed it at the same time because he pulled it away fast and his face flushed.

I cleared my throat. "Should we go out there?"

Luke nodded. "Yes."

But we both stood there, not wanting to move. When we walked out that door, we had to face reality. I wasn't sure what that reality was going to be, but I wasn't ready to stare it in the face. We were alive, but our friends were dead. President

Randall had to have heard every word I had said. I didn't know what I would do if he was out there waiting for me. How would I explain? How could I continue in Recruitment?

"Emmie, we should probably leave," Luke said, his voice quiet.

I nodded and forced myself to move toward the door, Luke walking right behind me. When we stepped out of the room, I looked down the hall to the left and saw that the elevator was back. Then I looked to the right and saw the door leading outside stood open, beckoning to us.

I looked back at Luke. He gave me a small smile and then nodded toward the door. I took a deep breath and moved toward freedom, away from the crazy building. I paused at the door, not wanting to step out.

"We have to go out there at some point," Luke said from behind me.

"I know, I just don't know if I'm ready," I said, turning to him.

"You really want to stay in this place?" Luke asked, his eyebrows raised.

I gave a small laugh. "Not really. It's just once we step out there, I have to face the facts of what happened today."

Luke nodded. "I understand. It's a lot to take in."

"But everything I said, I'm sure they heard."

"Probably, but we'll just have to take it one step at a time." He reached his hand out to touch my arm, but then pulled it back.

I tucked my hair behind my ear. "You're not the one who shouted out back there." What were they going to do with me?

"But I didn't stop you." Luke looked me in the eye. "It's going to be okay. We'll get through this together. I'll be right there next to you."

I nodded slowly. "Okay, here goes nothing." I stepped outside, my eyes adjusting to the outside light. From the sky, it looked like it was late afternoon. The cold air made me shiver.

"They should've given us jackets to take today," Luke said, standing close to me. "Winter seems to be coming fast this year."

"I know," I said, rubbing my arms. There was no one in sight. "Where is everyone? There has to be some people left. At least Will, David, and Angela should be out here."

"Maybe they're around the corner," Luke said.

We started walking, staying close together. When we rounded the corner, there was a small cluster of Recruits standing near the bus. Among them were Will, David, and Angela. Will ran to us when he saw us coming.

"What happened in there? I for sure thought you two were dead." Will bounced on the balls of his feet.

"The walls moved back, letting us leave," Luke said, his voice clipped.

Will looked behind us. "Just you two? The others … you couldn't …?"

I shook my head and buried my face in my hands. Luke pulled me into his arms. "We did everything we could," he said, holding me tight.

"Wow, this is just crazy." Will shook his head and ran his fingers through his hair. "How could they do this? None of it makes sense."

"Are these the only Recruits left?" Luke asked Will.

Theo came over to us and for the first time since I'd met him, he wasn't smiling. He looked at me sympathetically.

"They're the only ones that have come out," Will said. "I haven't seen RL Steven or the bus driver."

"Have you done a headcount?" Luke asked.

"With you two, it's twenty-two," Theo said.

"So only half survived? Did you ask everyone what happened to them?" Luke rubbed my back, trying to console me, but there was nothing that could make me feel better at that moment.

"Sounds like they went through everything we did," Will said. "Groups of three to five Recruits locked in a room, then the bats, and then the room with their partners." Will shook his head. "You two were the only ones who stayed back."

I couldn't believe out of twenty-two Recruits, only two were willing to do anything to try to save their partners. I guess no one had bonded like Tina and I had, or Eric and I had. I was pretty sure Luke had stayed for Tina, not Eric. But I couldn't be sure of that and I wasn't about to ask.

Theo bounced where he stood. "You don't think they killed them, do you?"

"Who knows," Luke said. "I would think not, but it all seemed so real."

"It felt real," Will said.

It had to be fake. Why would they just kill half of the Recruits? I thought back to the tree "accidentally" falling and swallowed. Nothing made sense. Worry sat in my core, making me question everything.

We stood there for another twenty minutes with no sign of anyone else. I had finally regained my composure, but I didn't want to leave Luke's arms just yet. Only hours before it had been me comforting him, but now the tables had turned.

"Hey, look, it's RL Steven!" Theo shouted.

I pulled away from Luke and turned to see RL Steven walking toward us. All my emotions from the day flared and I ran toward RL Steven, stopping only inches away from him.

"Would you like to tell me what's going on here?" I screamed at him.

RL Steven shook his head. "I had nothing to do with this challenge, Emmie. I just do as I'm told."

My laugh bordered on hysterical. "Really? You do as you're told? So, they tell you to lead us all into a death trap, and you say, 'okay, everyone follow me?'"

"I didn't know what they were doing!" RL Steven yelled back at me. "They don't tell me what exactly is going to happen in a challenge. They just tell me when and where to show up and what to say to you. That's all."

I shoved him in the chest out of frustration.

RL Steven held up his hands. "Considering what you just went through, I'm going to pretend you didn't do that and I'm not going hold it against you." He walked away.

Luke came up beside me and put his arm around me. "It's not his fault."

"I know that. I'm just so upset I don't know what to do with myself. I've never felt these kinds of emotions before, so I have no idea how to handle them." I leaned into Luke and he pulled me into a hug.

"Are we leaving?" Will asked.

"Not yet," RL Steven said. "They just told me to come out here and watch you."

A couple of minutes later, someone gasped. I looked over at everyone and they were staring behind me, their jaws practically on the ground. I turned around and my heart leaped. There were a bunch of Recruits walking toward us. I scanned them and saw Thunder Thighs, Simon, Will's partner, and David's partner.

"Emmie!" I looked toward the source and saw Tina pushing her way through the Recruits. She broke free and ran toward me. My eyes filled with tears when I saw Eric right behind her. Tina reached me in no time, pulling me into a hug.

"You're alive!" she said into my hair.

"Me? You're alive!" I said, squeezing her tight.

"That was the scariest thing I've ever been through," Tina said through her sobs. "I thought you'd been squished to death!"

My mind whirled. What was she talking about? I saw her in the room. She was the one who had been squished.

"I don't mean to end this reunion so fast, but you're killing me and Luke," Eric said, his voice anxious. "We need hugs, too."

I laughed out of excitement and pulled away from Tina, throwing myself into Eric's arms. He held me tight, rocking me back and forth. He was alive. I didn't know how, but he was there in my arms.

"I thought I lost you, Emmie," Eric said.

Tina and Luke talked next to me, I'm sure hugging like

Eric and I were.

I pulled back from Eric just enough so I could see his face. I put my hands on his cheeks. "You're really here." I scanned his whole body, just to make sure everything was intact. "And in one piece." I hugged him again, crying and laughing at the same time.

"Can I have everyone's attention?" I reluctantly pulled away from Eric's warm embrace and saw RH Johnson standing there. He scanned the Recruits. "I'm sure you're all confused right now and have a lot of questions. As you all know, you were split up into groups. You were all locked in rooms, all let loose, and all had to escape a bunch of bats.

"The final test, though, was when you saw your partners trapped in a room with no escape. Or, at least you thought your partners were trapped. What you saw then was an optical illusion. There's a lot of technology involved that cannot be explained to you, but it wasn't real. You were just led to believe that it was real. There were a lot of reasons for what we did, but to sum it up, we wanted to see how you react in stressful situations. We also wanted to test your loyalty to your partner and River Springs." He looked at me when he said that last part. "But as you can all see, everyone is alive and well. RL Steven, you may take them back to the dorms now." RH Johnson turned around and left us there, baffled at what we had heard.

"Everyone on the bus," RL Steven said. "The box with your watches is at the front, so stop and pick yours up before you sit down."

The minute we were settled on the bus, the four of us

talked frantically about what happened. Tina and Eric were also the only ones in their group to stay back and try to save their partners. They weren't put in the same group, so they were by themselves in the end. When we got to the end of our story, Luke and I looked at each other. We couldn't tell Tina and Eric what had happened. There was no way to explain it.

My heart sped through a roller coaster of emotions. I had thought earlier that I had lost two people I held dear to my heart, only to find out they were still alive. I also shared a moment with Luke that I didn't dare tell anyone about. I didn't think I could even tell Dee. I also had my first kiss, but it wasn't with the person I had thought it would be. I felt like I had betrayed Tina and Eric. I knew that sounded silly, seeing as Eric and I weren't together, and Luke and Tina weren't together. But I knew our feelings for each other. I was sure it would break Tina's heart to know I kissed the boy she liked.

I looked at Eric across the aisle. He stared at me, smiling. I could see relief in his eyes from me being alive. I didn't know his true feelings for me, but it seemed like he cared for me more than just as a friend. He wouldn't want to know that I kissed Luke. My eyes wandered over to Luke, who stared at the ground. I had a feeling it was going to be uncomfortable around him for a long time.

CHAPTER 28

When we got back, we still had an hour before dinner. Tina and I decided to take a small nap, exhausted from the day. We woke up a few minutes before dinner and headed out.

"I need to use the bathroom," Tina said to me.

"Okay," I said. "I'm going to head down and see if I can find Eric or Luke. I'd like to tell them about my meeting with VP Oliver."

Tina nodded. "Sounds good. See you down there."

As I went down the stairs, I realized I hadn't seen Dante since the tree incident. I wondered if he had found anything out.

When I reached the bottom of the stairs, RL Steven came out of the room I'd met my family in the other night. He looked frustrated and thankfully didn't notice me as he stormed down the hall.

I went over to the room and leaned in.

"I've had enough of this," President Randall said. "We

need to end this. She's broken one too many rules already, and now it seems she's getting others to break the rules with her. She's a threat."

"Whit, do you think there's any chance that it could be referring to any of the others?" It was RH Johnson.

"I've thought about it, but no," President Randall said. "I've had a feeling it was Emelia since she was little. There's something about her that screams traitor. I've watched the others their wholes lives, and all through Recruitment, and not once did they step out of line. It has to be her. What she said today, and the way she addressed me and River Springs, it's unacceptable."

"What do you want me to do?" RH Johnson asked.

"We need to eliminate her from Recruitment. I want her out, and I want her out soon. This can't be put on Infinity Corp. We need it to look like it's Emelia's mistake. Do you understand me, Dean?"

"Yes, Whit, I do. The next few days are just classes for them, followed by a couple of days of written tests. Should we make it look like she cheated, or should I wait until the next physical challenge?"

There was a pause before President Randall answered. "I think waiting until the physical challenge would be the only plausible way to do it. This will give you a few days to prepare."

"Do you want me to let you know of my plans?"

"No, I know you'll get it done."

"I won't let you down." RH Johnson's voice sounded anxious, like he couldn't wait for the chance to remove me from Recruitment.

The question was, how would they do it? My life would be forever altered. Would I end up in the bad part of town with no job, no money, and no hope? The thought made me queasy. He had used the word *traitor*.

I backed away from the door, putting my hands on my head. How could they think that of me? I said some harsh words, but a traitor? I made it halfway down the hall before I became lightheaded.

Leaning my back against the wall, I slowly slid down until I was sitting on the floor. None of it made sense. For the second time that day, I was truly scared. The word eliminated kept running through my head. I had a sick feeling that my punishment wasn't going to be a strenuous workout with SO Clark. It would be far worse.

"Emmie?" The voice sounded far away. "Emmie?" A hand on my arm brought me back to reality. I looked up to find Tina, concern in her eyes. "Emmie, are you okay?" She brought her hand to my face and wiped away my tears.

When had I started crying?

"Emmie, what's wrong? What happened?" Tina asked, sitting down beside me. "Is it about earlier?"

"No. I, uh …" I couldn't find the words to express what I was feeling or what I had just heard. I wanted to run away and never look back.

"Let me go find someone. You look sick." Tina started to stand, but I pulled her back down.

"No. Don't tell anyone, Tina. I'm fine. Let's just go eat."

"You don't look fine." Tina gave me a small smile. "Although, it's nice to know you feel comfortable enough with me to break a rule right in front of me without worrying that I'd rat you out."

I looked at her, confused. "What?"

"You're lying, Emmie. You're a big, fat liar." Tina placed her hand on mine.

"Are you calling me fat?"

Tina laughed. "There's the Emmie I know and love." She squeezed my hand. "We should go find Eric, Luke, and Dee and go talk."

"We should probably eat first. It'll be more noticeable if we show up late to eat than if we take a little while getting back to the dorms after."

"True." Tina stood and offered me her hand. "Let's go eat."

I took her hand and she helped me up. She linked her arm through mine as we walked. "It's bad, isn't it? Whatever you're upset about?"

"You have no idea," I said, my voice coming out in barely a whisper.

We entered the dining hall and placed ourselves at the end of the line. After we got our food, we went and sat by Eric and Luke. I looked around the hall for Dee and found her on the other side. Her eyebrows drew close together like they always did when something was wrong. She knew me too well. I gave her a small smile before I started eating.

"I'm not looking forward to this week," Eric said beside me.

"I am," Luke said in response. He was sitting across the table next to Tina. "I know everyone thinks it'll be boring, but this part is just as crucial as the physical testing. This is the first time they'll see us perform individually."

"Only you would like listening to lectures and taking tests," Eric said, making Tina and I laugh.

"Laugh all you want, but you'll soon see that I'm right." Luke fidgeted in his seat. He wouldn't look at me, which was understandable. We had kissed only a couple hours before and now we were sitting there all together and all alive, pretending as if nothing had happened. RL Steven had insisted on the bus that everyone try to push everything aside and focus on the fact that everyone was okay. If only it were that easy.

"You're right, Luke," Tina said. "It will be important, but that doesn't change the fact that it'll be boring."

All I could think was that it didn't matter to me. No matter how I performed during the next week, I would be eliminated. There was no point to me sticking around.

Eric nudged me. "Are you okay? You've seemed a little off recently. Like something's on your mind." He said it quietly, but we were still close enough for Tina and Luke to hear. All three of them were staring at me, waiting for a response.

"It was just an intense day," I said.

Eric nodded. "It was. But we're all fine." From the way Eric and Tina had described their situations during the challenge, it was clear they didn't experience the same intensity that Luke and I had. Eric stared at me. "There's more, isn't there?"

"I don't want to talk about it here," I said, looking down at my food. I squished a couple of peas with my fork. After my elimination, I was swearing off peas.

"Where do you want to talk about it?" Eric asked, eying my dead peas. I shouldn't have taken my anger out on the peas, but I was ornery, and they were gross.

I looked at RL Steven a couple of tables away, but he wasn't looking our way. I was glad he had chosen not to sit with us at dinner. He was a little ornery, too, but luckily for his peas, he wasn't taking it out on them. His potatoes were the unfortunate ones.

"There's a room at the bottom of the stairs that lead to the girl's dorms. Will you meet Tina and me there after dinner?" I asked, looking at Eric and then Luke.

At the same time Eric answered, "Yes," Luke answered, "No." We all looked at Luke, a little shocked.

"What? This is Recruitment. I don't think we should be talking secretly in a room. What if we get caught?" Luke looked at Tina and Eric, waiting for them to agree. But they didn't. I was sure the events of the day were another reason he didn't want to talk.

"You seriously need to grow a pair," Eric said to Luke.

I had taken that inopportune time to take a drink of water and ended up having it spray from my mouth across the table.

"Oh, thanks a lot, Emmie!" Tina said, laughing while wiping off her face. "So gross!"

"Sorry," I mumbled.

"What did you say to me?" Luke asked Eric, putting his fork down.

"You heard me, Luke, and I'm pretty sure you don't want me to repeat it. It's not a big deal. Besides, Emmie says she needs to talk to us and as her friends, I think we can do her the courtesy of listening."

"Friends or not, I don't want to get in trouble. No offense, Emmie." Luke said my name quietly as if it hurt him to say it.

"None taken. I totally understand. Just forget I mentioned it." I finally set my fork down, giving my peas a break.

Eric didn't want to drop it. "No matter what your dad says, Luke, you don't always have to be perfect. Sometimes you need to bend the rules to do the right thing."

Luke's face turned red and he balled his hands into fists. But he closed his eyes and took a few breaths. I had a feeling he was more upset with himself than with Eric or any of us. "Do what you want. But I'm following the rules. I'll see you all tomorrow." Without looking at us, he got up and left.

Only hours before, I had seen a side of Luke I had never seen before. Someone who was compassionate and didn't give up. Someone who let me scream things he wouldn't dream of and didn't try to stop me.

Now it seemed the old Luke had come back. The rigid Luke. Always too afraid to make the wrong step. But maybe what he thought was the wrong step was the right one.

CHAPTER 29

I thought our little argument might have attracted RL Steven's attention, but it hadn't. His mashed potatoes were still getting slaughtered. I didn't know what President Randall had said to him, but he didn't feel the need to keep his eyes on me all the time. Maybe President Randall had told him to stop.

"Want to go talk?" Eric asked me. He put his hand on mine underneath the table. It warmed my heart knowing that I had at least some people that truly cared for me.

"Sure." I sought out Dee in the crowd. After a second, she looked at me and I gave her a small nod, pointing toward the exit. She nodded in return.

Eric, Tina, and I left the dining hall, waiting for Dee to come out. The second she stepped out the door, Dee pulled me into a bear hug. I could barely breathe. "Dee, I love you, but I still need to breathe."

She loosened up a little. "I'm sorry, I'm just so worried. What's wrong, Emmie?" She pulled back and looked me in the eye. “I know something's majorly wrong. So, spill it!” I loved that even though she was so much smaller than me, and three months younger, she always felt the need to act like my mom.

“I don’t even know where to begin,” I said.

We walked down to the room. After a quick sweep, we saw the room was empty, so we went in and sat down at one of the tables.

“Start at the beginning,” Tina said. “Eric doesn’t know anything.”

“In general, or about what you’re talking about?” Eric joked.

“I’ll sum it up since I don’t know how much time we have,” I said, turning to Eric, who sat next to me. Tina and Dee were sitting across from us. “I talked with VP Oliver the other day. For whatever reason, the president is having me watched. He wanted RL Steven to report every move I make to him.”

Eric narrowed his eyes. “Wait, what? Why?”

I shrugged. “I’ve been trying to figure it out for days. VP Oliver couldn't tell me much. He's watching all of you, too.”

“They’ve been watching us, too?” Eric asked. “And Steven just told him everything? That arrogant …”

“We don't know if he had a choice.” I closed my eyes and took a deep breath. RL Steven couldn't have just ignored the president's wishes. Who knows how much fallout would come from that? I opened my eyes. “He also seemed interested in the fact that you and I, well, that we spend a lot of time around each other. That we’re friends.”

Eric’s face turned pale. “This is my fault.”

"What?" Tina, Dee and I all asked at the same time. How could it possibly be his fault?

"It's because of my dad," Eric said.

I reached out and touched his arm. "It's not because of your dad, Eric. It's because of me. The president seems to think I'm a threat. Me. Not you. Not your dad. Me." Eric didn't look convinced, so I continued. "He talked about something that he read. That whatever it was, it referred to me. I'm not sure what, though."

Suddenly I remembered that Dante had talked about the prophecy. They couldn't possibly think it was me, could they? My eyes went to Eric. What if he would be the one to start the revolution? If his dad really was a traitor, then maybe Eric was, too. That could be why VP Oliver wanted me to stay away from him.

"What?" Eric asked.

My face flushed a little. I'd been staring at him. "Sorry. My mind has a habit of wandering." I took my hand off Eric's arm. I didn't want to bring up the prophecy until I knew more. That pesky word trust came into my mind. Could I trust Eric? I needed to change the subject before I let my mind wander again. "Have any of you seen Dante lately?"

"No." Eric's eyes fell on his arm where my hand had been. "Who is that guy, anyway? He's been following you around like a lost puppy."

"He's visiting from Kingsland." I glanced over at Tina and Dee, who were both holding back smiles. "VP Oliver said that he came to find out more about Recruitment."

"You don't believe that?" Eric scooted a hair closer to me.

Our legs were suddenly touching.

Tina shook her head. "No. There has to be more behind it."

I hadn't talked to anyone about my near-death experience. Now seemed like a good time to bring it up. It had rattled me more than I'd thought, but I kept pushing it out of my mind. "Something happened during the paintball challenge."

"What?" Dee asked.

"It was when I went back to get Simon." Pausing, I took a deep breath. Had it been on purpose? Eric must have noticed my hesitancy because he reached under the table and took my hand.

Tina sat forward. "When the tree fell?"

Dee's eyes went wide. "A tree fell?"

"Yes," I said, nodding. "Dante and I examined it. It had been cut."

Silence filled the room. Eric, Dee, and Tina looked at me, then at each other, and then back at me. Eric's grip around my hand tightened.

Dee broke the silence first. "Are you sure?"

"Positive." My voice came out quiet. "We saw someone running away. Dante went to go check it out and I haven't seen him since."

"Wow." Tina rubbed her forehead with her hands. "Have you talked with VP Oliver?"

I shook my head. "No. I haven't had a chance."

"No wonder you looked so worried out in the hall." Tina's gaze went to the frown forming on my lips. "It was something else? What scared you so bad?"

Butterflies settled in my stomach. "I heard President Randall and RH Johnson talking. Randall was mad, I think because of the fighting, of the challenge the other day and today's challenge. The other day we all worked together in the maze, which I orchestrated. I shouldn't have…" My voice caught. If I couldn't get through talking about the maze, there was no way I could tell them what I said today. Not that I wanted to right then. I was glad Luke wasn't with us at the moment. Besides him, no one else knew what happened in that room. Well, besides the people that were watching.

"You couldn't have known, Emmie," Eric said. "Besides, how were we supposed to know we couldn't work together? They never mentioned it."

None of us had received a punishment for breaking that rule, so maybe they hadn't seen what happened. I always assumed they saw everything in Recruitment.

"Seriously? Did none of you read the book?" Dee asked.

Oh, the Recruitment Guidelines Manual. I meant to read it, but I got too tired and fell asleep. From the look on Eric and Tina's faces, they did the same thing.

Dee rolled her eyes. "Honestly, it wasn't that long. But it says in there that groups can't work together during any part of Recruitment unless they're instructed to."

Luke came to my mind. "Wouldn't Luke have read it?"

"You'd think so," Tina said. "And I'd think he would've read it fifty times."

"Yeah, fifty times a day for a few weeks leading up to Recruitment," Eric said.

That made me laugh a little. And then I remembered the

rest of the conversation between Randall and Dean.

I closed my eyes, trying to stop the tears. I couldn't cry. Not in front of Eric. But those stupid tears came.

Eric rubbed my arm with his free hand. "What is it, Emmie? What else happened?"

My heart raced as the tears fell. I looked up at my three friends. My only friends in the world.

"I'm being eliminated from Recruitment."

CHAPTER 30

The three of them sat there, stunned. I couldn't continue. The whole thing had overwhelmed me. How could I face my family after this? My mom? How would I explain it? I had completely let them down. I'd let myself down.

Eric had stood, so Dee came over, sat next to me, and put her arm around me.

Tina was the first to speak. "When?" She reached across the table and took my hand. "Are they coming tonight?"

I took deep breaths, trying to calm myself. When I finally got it together, I pulled my head up but continued to lean on Dee. Eric stayed standing, resting both of his hands on the wall next to us.

"After all the testing this week," I said.

"Why are they waiting?" Tina asked.

"He wants me taken out during a physical challenge," I said. "He said he didn't want it falling on River Springs. The only thing I can think of is that they want to make it look like I did something wrong and needed to be taken out of

Recruitment. They want a scene." Maybe they intended to make me an example. The thought sickened me.

"I guess that makes sense," Tina said. "Of course they wouldn't want it to look like they had anything to do with it."

"We need to find a way to talk with VP Oliver," Dee said as she stroked my hair. "There has to be some mistake. We need to fix this."

I laughed and sat up to look at her. "Dee, there's no fixing this. Once President Randall has made up his mind, it's done. There's no changing it."

"Can't we just be really careful during the challenges?" Tina asked. "They need something plausible to be able to pull you from Recruitment."

"RH Johnson's the one on top of it. He'll find a way. He'll *make* a way. There will be no right or wrong way for me to perform." I wiped the tears off my face. At least they had stopped coming.

"So, you're just going to give up?" Tina let go of my hand and scooted back. "Just like that, you're going to let it go and let them do this to you?"

"It's not that simple, Tina."

She swore, taking me by surprise. "It is simple. You're a fighter, Emmie, so fight."

I sighed. "I broke the rules. I signed the contract. They have every right to eliminate me."

The fact that they weren't going off what I'd already done and were planning something bigger and better worried me. Why? So many questions and no answers.

"Tina's right," Dee said with a nod. "You can't give up.

We'll find a way to talk to your mom, or VP Oliver, or someone."

They were right. I didn't want to give up. It wouldn't be easy to fight. But I wasn't one to back down to a challenge. There had to be a way to stay.

My heart jumped as a loud bang erupted in the room. Eric had slammed his fist into the wall, shaking his hand out afterward. Until then, I had forgotten he was even in there. He hadn't said a word since I told them I was going to be eliminated.

"What are you trying to do, Eric? Scare us half to death?" Tina placed her hand on her chest. "What if someone heard that?"

Eric breathed heavily. I had never seen him so upset.

"Dee, Tina, would you mind leaving Eric and me alone for a minute?" I asked, standing. Tina and Dee both stood as well.

"We'll figure this out, Emmie. It's going to be okay." Dee gave me a tight hug. "Love you."

"Love you, too," I said.

Tina hugged me. "I'll see you back at the dorm."

Once they had left, I went up to Eric and tried to place my hand on his arm, but he shook it away. He looked me in the eye. "They can't …" His jaw was pulled tight and the veins on his neck became visible. "They can't do this to you."

"They can, Eric. What can I do to stop them?"

"VP Oliver. I can tell you trust the guy. Let's go talk to him." Eric turned toward the door.

I hurried and got there before him, blocking him from

leaving. "What are you going to do? Walk up to his office? Demand to talk to him?"

"Yes." His eyes were determined.

I shook my head. "Are you crazy? They would never let you. You would get stopped as soon as you leave this building. You can't just walk around this town, you know. Not as a Recruit. And you can't sneak your way there, seeing as there are cameras all over the place."

"You've left to talk to him before." Eric ran his fingers through his hair. "He just needs to stop them. We'll tell him what you heard, and he'll stop it."

"He's the vice president, Eric, not the president. He'll be overruled."

"But they can't …" Eric leaned into me, placing his forehead against mine. "They can't just take you away. I can't lose you, too."

I hated to bring it up right then, but it seemed like the only time I would be able to. "Eric, what happened to your dad?"

Sighing, he pulled away. "My dad was a researcher for River Springs. He kept track of everything that happened so they could check for patterns in our society. He had access to all the events that happened in the past, before the divide. Most of what he did was top secret. Two years ago, my dad changed. He came home every night flustered. You could tell he had a lot on his mind. He kept mumbling to himself, which he hadn't done since we lost Mom."

My breath caught for a second. "You lost your mom?"

Eric nodded slowly. "Five years ago. Cancer."

"But I thought they had cured every cancer."

At least, they had always claimed that. It seemed fishy to me since we'd lost so much technology and supplies after the divide. But that was their main focus during the rebuild of the city. Medical research and technology became the two biggest focuses, before running water or other necessities. With so many people gone, the number of diseases had dropped dramatically. They put the best scientists and doctors on the issue to stop anything before it spread or became serious.

"That's what they say, but there are still a couple of rare forms they haven't cured. We weren't allowed to tell anyone how she died. They didn't want to alarm anyone." Eric rubbed his temples. "One night I overheard my dad on our house phone. He sounded upset. He kept talking about his 'findings' and that something needed to be done or the city would be in trouble. Whomever he was talking to didn't want to listen. They told him to drop it." He laughed. "My dad never drops anything."

"So that's where you get it from," I said, smiling a little.

"I guess so." Eric leaned against the wall. "My dad kept making phone calls. He came home with stacks of paper and would keep them locked up in his room. One night he came home, completely out of sorts. He was going around the house like a mad man. I tried to ask him what was going on, but he wouldn't acknowledge me. He finally snapped out of it for a second when there was a knock at the door. He told me to go to my room and keep the door closed. He told me not to come out, no matter what I heard."

He closed his eyes. "There was so much shouting. I heard doors slamming over and over again. It went on for a good half hour. Dad yelled at them, telling them to stop and that they wouldn't get away with it. Then suddenly it went quiet. I sat in my room, unable to move. After two hours, I decided to go out. When I opened the door, I couldn't believe what I saw. The house was a mess. Everything was scattered about. I went into my dad's room and noticed everything had been taken but the bed and dresser. The place where he kept stuff locked up was empty. I went out into the front room and there …" He stopped. His eyes were wet.

I walked up to him and took his hand in mine. He squeezed my hand tight.

He opened his eyes. "There was blood on the floor. My dad was gone."

"Is he …?" I didn't want to finish the question.

Eric looked into my eyes. "I don't know. I haven't seen him since. Two guys came to my house the next morning and took me away. They gave me to a couple who had only been able to have one child but wanted more."

"So, what did they tell you about your dad?"

"To forget about him. They made up this horrible lie that he was a traitor. That he'd stolen stuff from River Springs and couldn't be trusted. They even accused him of killing my mom."

"Just to cover up cancer?" I couldn't believe it. I had doubts about River Springs growing up, but I never thought it was that bad.

"Just to cover their backs. They don't want anything pointing to them. Not everyone knows about my dad. The people in my precinct know he's gone, but they were never told why. The only people who think he's a traitor are the people President Randall wanted to know so they would trust him and be on his side."

"What does Luke's dad do for the company?" I asked. Tina always brought up how brainwashed Luke had been.

"He's the head of research and development, so he worked closely with the researchers, my dad being one of them. Of course, plenty of rumors have gone around, but none of them are confirmed. Just Tina and Luke's families think they know the actual truth."

I shook my head. "I'm not sure Tina believes it. I think she has her suspicions about Randall. So, you don't know for sure that your dad's dead, right? Where would they take him?"

Eric let out a sigh. "I've thought about that for the past two years. I've thought about him being dead, being locked up in the infirmary, but my cousin Richie has an idea, too."

"What?"

He rubbed my hand with his thumb. "He thinks that maybe he was banished from the city."

Banished? Would they do that to a person? And if so, could someone survive? Could they live in another city? "If he was banished, do you think he's still alive?"

"That's what I hope. He was a brave guy, but I don't have any idea what's out there. I've tried many times to escape, but they always stop me. I've tried being reckless in the hopes that they would banish me, too."

"No wonder you've been willing to break the rules." It all made sense now. "You didn't care if you got caught."

Eric chuckled. "Nope."

"And here I thought you were breaking the rules just to impress me." I gave him a playful smile.

"That played into it. It would have been easier to say no if you weren't so hot." He pulled me into him, and I leaned my head against his chest.

"So, what am I going to do?"

Eric sighed. "I have no idea. But there has to be something we can do." He squeezed me tight. "We'll figure it out."

"I hope you're right. We should probably go. We've been gone a while."

"True. Emmie," Eric said, pulling away from me to look me in the eye, "I'm not going to let anything happen to you, I promise."

I bit my lip. I needed to know how much faith I could put in him. "Eric, can I trust you?"

He kissed me on the forehead. "Yes." That was all I needed to hear. Eric took my hand and went to the door. He opened it slowly and looked out. "Coast is clear."

We stopped near the bottom of the stairs that led to the girls' dorms.

"See you tomorrow." Eric squeezed my hand, let go, and started down the hall.

"Hold it right there." RH Johnson came down the stairs and stopped, his arms folded making his muscles look more threatening than they usually did. Behind him, smiling big, was his evil brat of a daughter, Amber.

"Where were you two?" RH Johnson asked.

"What?" I asked.

"Don't play dumb with me, Emelia," RH Johnson said. "Where were you?"

"We were in the dining hall, eating," I said.

"That's a lie, daddy," Amber said, using a baby voice. "They left a half-hour ago."

"It took you a half-hour to walk down the hall?" Dean asked, his eyes drilling into mine. I could tell he was looking for some reaction, waiting for me to be flustered.

"We were just down the hall," I said, as calmly as I could.

"Doing what?" Dean asked.

My thoughts raced as I tried to think of a plausible answer. What took a half-hour?

"We were making out," Eric said from behind me.

I turned around to look at him, my eyes wide. Had he really just said that?

He came up next to me, putting one arm around me and putting his other hand in his pocket. He shrugged. "We were just down the hall, making out." He really had said it. And now he had said it twice, making it hard to say he had just misspoken the first time.

"Ewww!" Amber's face scrunched. "You were making out? With her? How desperate are you?"

I threw out my arms. "Hey!" Why wouldn't he want to make out with me? He had said I was hot. Although, that probably wasn't a good thing to use as an argument.

"Quiet, Amber," RH Johnson said, making her pout. It also made me smile a little. But the smile quickly faded when RH Johnson turned his glare to me.

"Do you need to be reminded of the rules?" RH Johnson

asked. "You aren't allowed to date during Recruitment." He watched us, waiting to see our response. If he wanted me to feel guilty, that wasn't about to happen. I, for one, would rather have been making out than talking about me being eliminated.

"We aren't dating, sir," Eric said. "We were just kissing."

"Well, that's still not allowed," RH Johnson said. "Eric, you can join Emmie, Tina, and Dee tonight for their workout with SO Clark. I'll make sure to let him know to make the two of you stay later. I never want to hear of you kissing again. Do I make myself clear?"

"Yes, sir," Eric said.

RH Johnson looked at me, waiting for my response. After a couple of seconds, Eric nudged me.

I cleared my throat. "Yes, sir."

"Good. And the touching," RH Johnson said, pointing to Eric's arm that was still wrapped around me, "has to stop, too. Now, you two had better get back to your dorms immediately."

Eric slid his arm away, brushing my back with his hand, sending a shiver through me. He was lucky RH Johnson had just said no touching because otherwise, I would have slapped him upside the head since he did that on purpose.

"Goodnight, sir. Goodnight, Amber. Goodnight, Emmie." Eric turned around and marched down the hall.

"That's it?" Amber's voice squeaked. "Daddy! That's unfair! They broke a rule! They should have a bigger punishment! She should be taken out of Recruitment!"

I flinched. She would have her way in just a week when they eliminated me.

"Stop it, Amber," RH Johnson said to her, his voice laced

with annoyance. "This is just a minor infraction and I will handle it how I see fit. They agreed to not do it again, right Emelia?"

"Yes, of course, sir. Never again." I smiled on the inside.

"No harm, no foul," RH Johnson said. "Don't let us keep you, Emelia. Good luck tonight during your workout."

"Thank you, sir." I walked past them, ignoring Amber and her ever-annoying pout.

I knew he kept the punishment light because he was going to have me taken out of Recruitment in just a few days and probably because President Randall wasn't there to overrule him, but I didn't care. It still felt like a small victory in my book.

CHAPTER 31

Over the next week, I tried on multiple occasions to sneak out so I could find VP Oliver, my mom, or my dad, but there were too many security officers everywhere. No way my leaders wouldn't give me a pass to leave the Recruitment dorms.

I only had one day left, so I had to find a way out. If I got caught, would it matter anyway? It would just push up my elimination from Recruitment, which could be a good or bad thing.

I waited until Tina fell asleep and then snuck out of my dorm. I'd put on my black top and pants, hoping to blend in with the darkness. I couldn't hide my blonde hair, though. The only thing I could do was pull it back in a ponytail.

At the bottom of the stairs, two dorm leaders stood near the door that led outside. I couldn't sneak past them without being seen.

Crouching down, I leaned against the stairwell trying to come up with a plan. A few minutes later, a loud bang came from the other end of the hall.

“What was that?” One of the dorm leaders had spoken.

“I don't know,” the other one said. “Let's check it out.”

Knowing I'd be seen if I stood and ran back up the stairs, I made myself as small as I could and kept still. The two dorm leaders were too focused on the other end of the hall to notice me. Once they were far enough away, I crept to the front door and snuck out. How convenient for me.

The cool fall air hit me right when I stepped out. I welcomed it. I'd been so nervous that I'd made my temperature skyrocket. When I got to the end of the sidewalk, I started to cross the street, but someone pulled on my arm.

“Ah!” I clamped my hand over my mouth, hoping I didn't draw too much attention to me. Luckily, it seemed empty out on the street.

“Emmie?”

When I turned to see the source, Richie stood there. He pulled me down the alley where we first met after I'd ridden on his motorcycle with Eric.

Richie smiled at me. “Sorry, I didn't mean to scare you. I was expecting Eric.”

“Eric?”

“Someone call my name?”

The sudden voice behind me made me jump. Both Eric and Richie let out quiet laughs.

“She's jumpy tonight,” Richie said.

I frowned at them. “Of course, I am. I just snuck out of Recruitment, I'm going to be eliminated tomorrow and a guy grabbed me in the middle of a dark street. Then Eric creeps up behind me." I shivered, the cold finally getting to me.

Eric stepped up close, putting his arm around me and rubbing it for warmth. My heat suddenly came back.

"Sorry," Eric said.

"What are you two doing?" I suddenly wondered if Eric had been the source of the commotion that caused the dorm leaders to leave the front entrance.

Richie looked at Eric then back at me. "Eric asked me to meet him here. He mentioned it the other day in the mechanics class." He scratched the back of his neck. "I don't know why, though."

I glanced at Eric. "Did you make that ruckus in the hall?"

"Richie had a friend create a distraction," Eric said. "He let some mice loose near the dining hall. I'm sure they'll be busy for a while trying to round them all up."

Richie had been looking at me with surprise. He waited until Eric finished talking before he spoke. "You're getting eliminated?"

I nodded. "Yes. Tomorrow."

"Unless we can stop it," Eric said.

"How are you planning on doing that?" Richie asked.

"I was heading to talk to VP Oliver," I said.

Richie shook his head. "He's not here."

I stiffened. Not here? "Where is he?"

"Don't know," Richie said with a shrug. "I just overheard my dad talking about it. He said something about Oliver leaving for business."

"Business outside of River Springs?" Eric asked.

I had been about to ask the same thing. Had he headed to

Kingsland with Wallace and Dante?

"I think so." Richie smiled at me apologetically. "I guess talking to him is out."

Eric rubbed my arm, only now it seemed like it was meant to console me. "Can you talk to your dad?" Eric asked Richie. "They're kicking Emmie out because she broke a couple of rules, but so did others. They're only targeting her. Plus, it seems like there's more behind it than rule-breaking. Something suspicious is going on."

"Like what?" Richie rested against the wall and folded his arms.

Leaning into Eric, I sighed. "I don't know. That's why I wanted to talk with VP Oliver. He knows much more about what's going on than I do. All I know is that President Randall and RH Johnson are out to get me." Why had VP Oliver left? I needed him.

"Can your dad find a loophole in the contracts?" Eric asked Richie. "Maybe something that gets Emmie off the hook."

Richie looked up at the dark sky, thinking it over. Clouds had rolled in, covering up the moon and stars. The streetlamps were the only thing giving out light, and there weren't many of them. Richie finally looked at Eric. "He's just a clerk. I'm not sure how many strings he could pull."

"He doesn't need to pull any strings," Eric said. "He just needs to find a loophole in the contract. That's all." He looked at me. "Emmie's last day is tomorrow so this is our only chance."

"Wait a minute," Richie said, his eyes confused. "Why

haven't they kicked her out yet? Why tomorrow?"

I looked down at the ground, trying to control my emotions. Anger bubbled to the surface, but it wouldn't help me out. "They want to do it in a challenge. I think they want to make this a big deal and get me in a lot of trouble."

"Something's not right." Eric pulled me closer. "This all feels so … wrong. I can't pinpoint what it is, though."

A nervous laugh escaped my mouth. "You're telling me. It's been driving me crazy all week. I keep racking my brain trying to figure this all out, but nothing's coming to mind. None of it makes sense."

"We just need time," Eric said. "If we can extend Emmie's time in Recruitment, maybe we can find a way to talk to VP Oliver when he gets back. Or even talk to her mom or dad. They've been keeping a strict eye on us, so we haven't been able to do anything."

Richie pulled away from the wall and faced us. "Well, I know now. I'll look into it and talk to everyone I can." He looked at me. "Woodard, right? That's your last name?"

I nodded. "Yes. My mom's name is Janice and my dad's name is Philip. I have a brother, too. Derek."

"Okay," Richie said. "I'll see if I can contact any of them tonight."

Eric let out a breath of relief. "Thanks, Richie."

He held up his hands. "I'm not promising anything will come of this, but I'll try." He glanced around the quiet street, making sure we were still alone. "I find Randall an overbearing jerk and Johnson even worse. I'd be glad to stick it to them." He slapped Eric on the arm. "Take it easy and good luck tomorrow." Richie smiled at me and then left the alley, leaving Eric and me alone.

Eric pulled me into a hug. "I hope he can find something." He drew back and looked at me, rubbing his thumb along my cheek. "This isn't over yet. We'll fight until it gets put back right. You don't deserve to be eliminated."

I didn't, but I never wanted to be there in the first place. The only reason I wanted to stay now was to tick off Randall, Dean, and Amber. "Thanks, Eric, for everything. You've been an amazing friend."

He leaned in closer, giving me a playful smile. "I hope you'd consider me more than a friend by now." His thumb brushed across my lips. "Would it be too forward to ask for a kiss?"

"No." I'd wanted a kiss from him for a while. I still needed to erase Luke's kiss from my mind, and kissing Eric seemed like the best way to do it.

His lips were soft, gentle, and so delicious. I finally knew what it was to be truly kissed. To feel the want and need on his end, but not have it be forceful or eager. From the way he held me and the way his lips moved on mine, I could tell how much he respected me. How much he cared for me.

I never wanted that moment to end.

I held onto the hope in my heart, the desire in his kiss, and the trust between us as we stood in that alley. It could get me through the night.

It could get me through anything.

CHAPTER 32

The next morning as Tina and I headed down to breakfast, a small butterfly fluttered above me at the bottom of the stairs.

"How did that get in here?" Tina asked.

Standing on my tiptoes, I looked at it closer. "Is it real?"

Tina squinted her eyes at it. "Why wouldn't it be real?"

The butterfly took off, heading toward the door where I'd met my family in and had my conversation with Eric, Tina, and Dee. I followed it, wanting to get a better look. When I entered the room, Derek was sitting on top of one of the tables with a remote control in his hands. The butterfly landed on his shoulder.

"Pretty cool, right?" Derek smiled at me. "I made it myself. It has a camera and a microphone in it." He looked at Tina. "So, no, it's not real."

"You heard us?" Tina asked.

Derek nodded, taking an earpiece out of his ear and slipping it in his pocket. He took the butterfly off his shoulder and handed it to me. "It's just a prototype. It still has a few bugs to work out." He laughed at his pun.

I was in too much awe to roll my eyes at him. "This is so cool, Derek." Turning it over in my hand, I examined it closer. It looked like an ordinary butterfly. Even up close, I couldn't see a camera on it.

Derek pointed to the eyes. "One is a camera, the other a microphone." He took it back carefully. "You can't keep it, though. No one knows about it."

"What are you doing here?" I asked, leaning against a chair. Tina took a seat at the table.

"You said you wanted information about Amber," Derek said.

My eyes widened. "Did you check out her files?"

"Uh." Tina looked back and forth between me and Derek. "You had him look into Amber? Is that allowed?"

Derek laughed. "No, sweetheart, it's not. So, I'd appreciate it if you didn't say anything."

"And I'd appreciate it if you didn't call me sweetheart," Tina said with a glare.

Derek's face colored. "Sorry." He cleared his throat. "Dee was right. She did have a little sister. She died when she was only three."

"What?" I took a seat in the chair I had been leaning on. "How?"

"Mysterious circumstances." Derek had used air quotes. "That's all the file said. Well, it also mentioned that Amber was the only one with her at the time."

Tina's jaw dropped. "Oh, wow." She looked at me. "Do

you think she had something to do with it?"

I shrugged. "Who knows? I wouldn't be too surprised. She definitely seems off."

Amber seemed capable of anything. She gave me the creeps multiple times growing up. It was just something in her manners and the way she looked at people. There was something lacking, like emotion or empathy. I could never pin down the problem.

Derek nodded, a slight hint of fear in his eyes. "She is. I checked out her psych evaluation. I'm not sure how she got accepted into Recruitment." He licked his lips. "Most of it had been redacted, but I was able to use my magical programming skills to undo it." His face went pale.

I reached out and touched his arm. "What is it?"

"She's insane, Em." Derek turned his finger in a circle around his ear, motioning that she was crazy. "Certifiably."

"What do you mean?" I asked. "She's actually been certified as crazy?"

"A psychopath is the more appropriate term." Derek scooted off the table and took a seat next to me. "She shows no remorse, no empathy, and has no regard for human life." He drummed his fingers along the table.

I reached out and placed my hand on his to stop it. "What's bothering you?"

"Seriously?" Tina asked, looking at me in surprise. "That's not enough? That would bother the crap out of me."

"Of course, it would," I said. "But I know my brother well enough to know there's more. He's not one to get this nervous unless it's bad."

Tina shook her head. “Call me crazy but knowing she's a psychopath and that she may have been involved with her sister's death is what I would consider bad.”

A nervous laugh escaped Derek's mouth. “It is bad, but Em's right. There's more.” He stared at me for a moment, concern on his face. I'd never seen my brother look at me with such worry. It frightened me.

“Just tell me, Derek.” I rubbed his hand, hoping that would help.

He sighed. “When she had just turned sixteen, her mom found a list in her bedroom. A list of names.” He looked at me. “You were the first one on the list.”

“What was the list for?” I didn't know if I wanted to hear the answer. Derek's face told me enough to make me wary.

Derek swallowed. “It was a hit list.”

Tina looked at me, complete and utter horror on her face. “Oh, that is bad. Way bad.”

A hit list? Amber wanted to kill me? Why hadn't she? Not that I wanted her to, but she hadn't made an attempt on my life before. Then I thought about the tree. She couldn't have been behind that, could she? I shivered. She had all the right connections. Had that been her running away? Someone she'd asked to do it? My mouth went dry. Dante. Was he still alive?

Derek snapped his fingers in front of my face. “Em, you still with us?”

“What?” I looked at him. “Yes, sorry.” I rubbed my free palm over my eye. “Who else was on the list?”

Derek scratched the back of his neck. “Uh, you see, well …” He placed his other hand on top of mine. “Emmie, you were numbers one, two, three, four, five, and all the way down to one-hundred."

"Oh." I could feel the blood drain from my face.

Tina just stared at me from across the table.

"And then they flipped the paper over and found your name one hundred more times." Derek smiled at me sheepishly. "Apparently she really, really, really, times two hundred wants you dead."

I snapped my hand out from under his. "Yeah, I got that." Dante entered my mind again. "Derek, have you seen Dante or Wallace Brown? The two men from Kingsland who came to visit."

Derek shook his head. "Not for a couple of days."

"Will you look into that, too?" I asked. "Check for any footage of them in River Springs? I'm worried something may have happened to Dante."

Tina finally spoke. "Do you think Amber had something to do with the tree?"

"What tree?" Derek asked, looking at me.

"A tree fell during one of the challenges," I said. "Dante and I looked at it and it seemed to have been cut."

Derek swore under his breath. "There's no mention of that in any of the reports." When I looked at him with raised eyebrows, he continued. "I've been checking all your challenge reports. I wanted to make sure you weren't embarrassing the family." He gave me a twisted smile. "That challenge when you were trapped, towards the end …"

I stomped my foot on his. If he was about to mention the kiss, I needed to put a stop to it. I didn't want Tina finding out like this. I didn't want her finding out about it at all.

"Ow!" Derek swore again. "What was that for?"

"I just don't want to talk about that challenge." I gave him an apologetic smile.

Luckily, Tina took my outburst as something else. "That challenge was really draining on Emmie. I don't think she's ready to talk about it."

"I'm not," I said. "Can you please look into Dante for me? Make sure he's still alive?"

Derek frowned at me for a minute but then nodded. "Yeah, sure." He stood. "I need to get back to work. Oh, and a guy named Richie called last night and told us what's going on. We're working on something, Em, but I'm not sure if we'll be able to do anything."

"At least you're trying," I said. "That's all that matters to me."

When I stood, Derek reached out and gave me an awkward pat on the shoulder. "Just be careful, sis. While I'd love to turn your bedroom into an office for me, I might actually miss you if something happened."

"Aw, thanks, bro." I slapped him on the shoulder. "You're too sweet."

He rubbed his shoulder where I'd hit him. "Yeah, I know. I shouldn't be." He looked at Tina. "Keep an eye on this one."

"Will do," Tina said.

We all forced ourselves to eat at breakfast knowing we would need our strength. Dee was able to escape the vicious Amber to eat with us. After breakfast, Dee squeezed the life out of me and kissed my cheek.

"Love you," Dee said to me. She turned to Tina and Eric. "I'm counting on you two."

"You can count on us," Eric said.

"Good." Dee quickly hugged Tina and then squeezed Eric's arm. "Good luck today."

"You too," I said.

As we walked to the bus, I looked up at the sky. Even though it was cold, it was a beautiful day. The sun shined bright and the sky was perfectly blue. Not a cloud in sight. At least there was something positive about that day.

"Green's a good color on you," Eric said as we sat down in the bus.

We had made our way to the back and RL Steven didn't try to stop us. Eric and I sat on one bench, and Tina and Luke sat across from us. Most people sat by their partners, but Eric wanted to sit by me. Luke would have protested if it wasn't Tina he got to sit by. In fact, I was pretty sure she was the reason he sat with us at every meal. Otherwise, I don't think he'd put up with Eric.

"It brings out the color of your eyes," Eric said to me.

I looked down at my green shirt and black pants, our wardrobe colors for the day. Wearing my regular clothes again would be nice. The conformity had seemed so restricting and stripped us of our individuality. That should have been River Springs's motto.

Eric held my hand, apparently not worried that cameras were watching.

I turned to look at him. "My favorite color on you is blue."

He batted his eyelashes. "Because of my eyes?"

I smiled. "Of course."

I rested my head on his shoulder, not a care in the world. If it was my last day of Recruitment, I wanted to enjoy it.

CHAPTER 33

An hour later, we arrived at our destination. Eric leaned over me and looked out the window. "The lake," he said with a smile.

The sun reflected off the rippling water, the sight beautiful. I'd never been there before. My parents always said they would take us one day, but they never got around to it. Too busy, I guess.

We all got off the bus and followed RL Steven to the edge of the lake. The lake seemed to be in the middle of the town. About a quarter mile out from the lake, homes surrounded the area.

Two men were waiting for us, dressed in all black. They were tall, muscular men, their faces all business. I immediately recognized one of them as SO Clark.

Despite turning out to be a nice guy, I'd seen too much of him recently. My muscles screamed out in pain just at the sight of him. A faint, amused smile touched his lips when he made eye contact with me.

"This seems like a nice place to live," I said.

Eric stood on my right, Tina on my left, with Luke on the other side of her.

"It is," Tina said. "I've always loved this area."

Pebbles covered the shore around the lake. I wanted to take off my shoes and walk around. I had never stepped on pebbles before. We had grass along the river in our precinct.

"Listen up!" SO Clark shouted. The red in his hair and beard stood out in the sunlight. "I'm Security Officer Mack Clark. Today you'll be performing an underwater challenge. You'll be changing into water suits in those changing rooms over there." He pointed to a couple of makeshift rooms made of tarps. "After that, I, along with Security Officer Pierce Martin," he pointed to the other man, "will help you get your breathing equipment on. Let's have the first four teams get changed and then we'll go from there."

They had arranged it so three to four teams would go at a time in six different groups. RL Steven listed off what teams would go in each group. Eric and Luke were going in the third group. Not surprisingly, Tina and I were in the last group. So, I had to anxiously await my removal.

Once the first group was changed, they lined up on the edge of the lake. There were four areas of entrance created for that challenge, with a flag marking the spot. RL Steven told each team which entrance they would be taking.

"This challenge has to do with patrol and salvaging," SO Clark said. "It will test your memory, your teamwork, and your ability to stay calm." He had a naturally loud and commanding voice that carried outside. "Each team will be given a map showing the coordinates of three large keys and three pieces of equipment that have been placed on the bottom of the lake. Your key colors will correspond with the flag color you are assigned to. The map will also show you the coordinates of a box, which will also be the same color. You will be given a waterproof digital compass that lists the longitude and latitude on it, which you can take with you. If you can memorize the coordinates listed on your map, then it should go easy. Once you retrieve all three keys and artifacts, you must go find the box which will be inside a clear container. To retrieve the box, each partner must use one key to release the latch holding down the container. Then you'll use the third key to unlock the box. Inside you will find these." SO Clark held up a tiny set of keys.

"What are those for?" Will asked, standing near the entrance with the orange flag. Lucky guy. He got to go first.

"They unlock these," SO Martin said, holding up a pair of cuffs. He looked similar to SO Clark in his strong and tough build. The only differences were that he had brown hair, his eyes were a darker shade of blue, and he was cleanly shaven.

"Wait, we have to wear cuffs, too?" Will asked.

"Yes," SO Martin said, his tone not inviting more questions.

"Once your cuffs are unlocked," SO Clark said, "remove them, clip them onto your shoulder strap, and return to the surface."

RL Steven handed out the maps and compasses to the teams who were at the flags.

"There's one more thing." SO Clark paused, waiting for

everyone's attention. "Each tank only has thirty minutes of oxygen in them. Although, this time can be lessened if you breathe too fast. Make sure you breathe calmly and evenly, so you may get your full thirty minutes out of it. If at any point you want to remove yourself from the challenge, there's a red button on the back of your compass. If you press it, it will alert us, and we'll immediately come get you."

"Any questions?" SO Martin asked. If anyone had a question, it didn't matter. The look on his face told us not to ask.

As the first group of teams were looking at their maps, a vehicle pulled up towing a trailer with a few small motorboats on them. It stopped close to the shore.

Six guys, who looked as every bit as intimidating as SO Clark and SO Martin, jumped out, unloaded the boats, and put them on the edge of the lake. Two guys got in the first boat, two in the second, and two in the third. Apparently, they were our search and rescue team.

Luke, Tina, Eric, and I sat on the ground and watched the teams go. After the first group finished, the men out on the boats jumped in the water to replace all the keys. As Will walked past us after he had changed, I stopped him.

"How was it?" I asked Will.

He smiled at me. "Pretty nice, actually. It's beautiful down there."

"Was it easy?" Luke asked.

Will shrugged. "If you can memorize the coordinates, you'll do fine."

"That seems easier said than done," Eric said with a small laugh.

"You guys will do great," Will said. "Good luck!"

I laughed on the inside. "Thanks." I had a feeling that I needed a lot more than luck.

Theo and Simon went in the second group and ended up having to press their button during the challenge. SO Clark and SO Martin didn't look too happy about it and neither did Simon when they came back to shore. Theo, of course, still had a smile on his face.

With his shoulders slouched and his face defeated, Simon wandered over to RL Steven and wanted to look over the coordinates again. Even though they couldn't go back out, he wanted to see where he'd gone wrong. Theo stood by him the whole time, giving him words of encouragement and support. It didn't look like Simon noticed, though.

Then it was group three's turn. Eric and Luke made it in record time. For how much they didn't like each other, they sure worked well together. Thunder Thighs and Skinny were also in their group. They came out fighting, but they still finished. I caught part of their conversation as they passed by us.

"Did you need to swim so fast?" Skinny asked, tugging at her hair.

Thunder Thighs glared at her. "I had to make up for lost time since you took so long to remember your coordinates! It was only a couple of numbers, Angela!"

"I couldn't think straight with your piercing gaze on me, *Rachel*!" Skinny started to hyperventilate.

"I wouldn't have to look at you like that if you'd just do something right for once!" Thunder Thighs kicked at the pebbles on the ground, sending them flying in the air. A few of them hit Skinny in the legs.

"Ouch!" Skinny shoved Thunder Thighs with all her might, which wasn't much. It ended up being more of a gentle prod.

Thunder Thighs opened her mouth to say something but then saw RL Steven staring at them. She snapped her mouth shut and walked as far away from Skinny as she could go.

Once group five entered the water, everything started to sink in. I lay down on the ground and closed my eyes, a bunch of questions forming in my head. How were they going to do it? Say I cheated? Would I be able to prove I didn't?

Someone lay down next to me on my right. I turned my head and opened my eyes to see Eric lying beside me.

"How are you doing?" Eric asked, taking my hand.

"Anxious. I just want this over with." I sighed and tried my best to keep calm.

Tina lay down on the other side of me. "I wish there was something we could do. But what?"

"We could make a big scene and try to get us eliminated, too," Eric said.

"What's the point of that?" I asked. "We don't know what they're going to do with me. You guys don't need to be sentenced to a crappy life, too."

Eric squeezed my hand. "You don't deserve it either, Emmie."

"Maybe it won't be that bad," Tina said. "Maybe VP Oliver and your mom will be able to help in some way."

I laughed a little. "Yeah, maybe. But once President

Randall has his mind set, there's no changing it."

"What are you guys talking about down there?" Luke asked. He stood over us, looking down at us like we were crazy.

"Our dreams in life," Tina said.

Luke narrowed his eyebrows. "I highly doubt that. Unless you have horrible dreams. You all look like someone died."

Something could potentially die. My hopes and dreams of one day being in management and trying to fix River Springs. I needed to make sure that didn't happen.

"Group six!" SO Clark shouted. "You're up!"

"Here goes nothing," I said, standing up.

After we changed, Tina and I went to SO Clark to get our breathing equipment on. We both held onto our goggles and flippers, waiting to put them on until right before we entered the water.

"Steven, I need two more tanks," SO Clark said to him.

RL Steven had to hustle to bring over the tanks. By the look in his eyes, he was trying to impress the men. But by the sweat on his brow and the tightness in his jaw, it was a struggle for him. He handed a tank to SO Clark and he strapped it on Tina's back. Then RL Steven handed him the other one and SO Clark strapped it to my back. It didn't feel as uncomfortable as I thought it would.

SO Clark held up the mouthpiece. "This is a mouthpiece. Stick it in your mouth and breathe." He held up a gauge that was attached to the tank. "This will tell you how much air you have left. As you can see, the arrows are pointed at full. If it gets in the red zone, you only have a few minutes left, so I would suggest getting out of the water."

After SO Clark's instructions, RL Steven assigned us to the purple flag. We went over to our flag and waited.

RL Steven finally came over and handed us our map and compass. "Key number one will be for Tina to retrieve and key number two will be for Emmie. Either of you can retrieve the third key, which opens the container. Tina, your key will be purple with a green dot, and Emmie your key will be purple with a blue dot. When you get to the container, you'll notice a keyhole on each side of it. There will be a green dot above one and a blue dot above the other, letting you know which one you need to use. Do you understand your instructions?"

"Yes," Tina and I both answered.

RL Steven tied a pouch around each of our waists. "Put the artifacts you find in these. Each one should be near a key, so keep your eyes peeled." He looked at me, his expression serious. "Good luck."

"Uh, thanks," I said.

It made me wonder if he knew that this could be my last challenge in Recruitment. I hoped my family and VP Oliver would pull through.

If not, I'd find my own way. I always did.

CHAPTER 34

Tina and I studied our map. I memorized the coordinates to my key and the box and Tina memorized the coordinates to her key and the third key.

"Ready for some flippers and goggles?" Tina asked, holding hers up.

"You know it," I said, putting my flippers on.

As Tina did the same, I looked over at Eric. He gave me a small smile and a wave. I smiled in return, but my heart hurt. In mere moments I would start my last challenge as a Recruit. Surprisingly, the thought made me sad. It also made me more determined.

A couple of minutes later, SO Clark came over and strapped on our cuffs, and then signaled that we could start. Tina and I put on our goggles, put in our mouthpieces, and entered the water.

As we dove, warm water surrounded me. The crystal-clear water made it easy to see where we were going. Unfortunately, we were wearing cuffs, making it difficult to swim. It was all leg work.

We swam over to the first key. An anchor was propped up against a rock, the key attached with a rope. Tina handed me the compass and pulled at the rope, trying to untie it. As she worked, I searched around for the first artifact. A cluster of rocks sat nearby, so I swam over, moving them around. No luck.

Out of the corner of my eye, I saw something barely sticking out from the mud below. I dove deeper and dug around the object. It turned out to be an old radio that you would find on a boat. Opening my pouch, I pushed the radio in and sealed it back up.

Tina had finally got the key undone. She held up her purple key with the green dot and gave me a thumbs up.

I used the compass to get us to my key. The anchor lay flat on the ground, so some of the rope was underneath it. I tried to pull the anchor up to make it easier to untie, but it was too heavy. No matter how hard I worked at the rope, it wouldn't budge. I took out my mouthpiece and used my teeth to loosen it enough for me to use my fingers.

Tina had looked around while I undid the key. When she came back, I couldn't tell what she'd retrieved, but the only thing that mattered to me was that she had it.

With my key in hand, Tina steered us toward the last key. Luckily, this key was tied to an anchor leaning against a rock like Tina's first one had been. We both took turns working at the rope until it finally broke free. Tina grabbed the key and we searched for another artifact.

Wreckage from a ship sat a few yards away. Tina and I

moved the debris around, trying to find our last object. As I pulled up some old, wooden boards, I saw a sextant. Smiling, I picked it up and showed it to Tina. The only reason I even remembered the name of it was because of a boy in my class who kept laughing every time our teacher said the word. Placing it in my bag, we set off for the box.

We were almost to the coordinates when I noticed a ship on the bottom of the lake. From the rust covering the exterior, it had been down there for ages. I pointed at it, trying to indicate to Tina that the box should be inside. She nodded in understanding. As we got to the top of the ship, there was an opening that would take us down inside.

I went through the hole first and followed the stairs down. They led us into a hall. Still using the compass as my guide, I went down the hall, passing a few rooms. When I got to the third door on the left, the coordinates indicated that was the room we needed.

The clear container sat in the middle of the room. A piece of metal lay on top of the container to keep it from floating away.

Rectangular in shape, the metal had an arm on the left and right side of it. The arms connected to the floor of the ship. I examined it and noticed that the arms were being held by a latch. There was a lock inserted through the latch so you couldn't lift it. The bottom of the lock had a green dot. I pointed at Tina and then pointed at the lock, telling her it was hers.

The lock on the other side had the blue dot. Tina gave me a nod and we both inserted our keys, turning them at the same time.

A metal cuff shot up from the ground and clamped my wrist down. I tried to wriggle my hand through it, but my other cuffs stopped me. I looked over at Tina, trying to tell her with my eyes that we had a problem. She swam over and noticed the metal cuff. She tried to pull my hand out, but the other cuffs stopped me.

Tina surprised me by her quick thinking, giving me another reason I was so grateful I had her as my partner. She immediately removed the lock and lifted the latch. She had already done that on her side, so the piece of metal drifted up, letting her remove the clear container. She grabbed the purple box inside and used the third key to unlock it.

Taking the smaller key, she unlocked my cuffs. I tried again to pull my hand out, but it still wouldn't fit through. Tina grabbed my arm and yanked, but nothing worked. I motioned for her to give me the key so I could unlock her cuffs.

As I took them off, Tina glanced around the room, trying to find something that could help. The room was empty besides the piece of metal and the container. She motioned for me to stay put and left the room. Sure, I would stay put. It wasn't like I had a choice. A low throb developed in my wrist from all the pulling.

While I waited for Tina to come back, my chest tightened. My stomach churned and my world closed in on me. Now that I had stopped swimming, claustrophobia set in. I closed my eyes and tried not to think about the fact that water surrounded me, my life out of my control.

A minute later someone's hand landed on my shoulder. Tina was back in the room and for the first time, panic filled in her eyes. She pointed up and shook her head. She must have noticed the confusion on my face, so she tried to elaborate. She held up her two index fingers and made an outline of a square. Then she took out her mouthpiece and mouthed something to me. It took me a moment before I realized she was saying 'closed.' Closed? What was she talking about? A square? Closed? Oh. The entrance that led us down into the ship was closed. We were trapped.

I reached for my gauge to see how much air I had left. My heart sank when I saw it had entered the red zone. Tina came over and looked at my gauge, her eyes widening. When she looked at her own gauge, her eyebrows pulled together in confusion. She held it up for me to see. She still had at least a quarter of a tank in there.

So, I had a couple minutes left of oxygen, I was clamped down by a metal cuff, and the only way out of there was closed, making it so Tina couldn't leave to get someone.

We were screwed.

CHAPTER 35

Apparently, when your life was on the line, the ability to think logically went out the door. I scolded myself when I finally remembered the red button on the compass. I had let go of it when I went to unlock the latch. It lay on the floor nearby.

With my free hand, I tried to reach out and grab it, but it had floated too far away. Tina saw what I was trying to do and hurried to go get it. She turned it over and pressed down on the red button. She pressed it over and over again, getting more determined with each push. She finally came over and handed it to me. I took it with my free hand and tried to press the button. Nothing happened. The button wouldn't go in. It must have been stuck. I pressed repeatedly, but it didn't work.

When I went to take my next breath, no air came out of my mouthpiece. All gone. I took out my mouthpiece, signaling to Tina that it was out. She took hers out of her mouth and put it in mine, letting me take a breath. She looked around the room, trying to figure something out. I saw a spark of hope in her eyes as she looked at the wall of the ship. There were a couple of round windows, leading out to the lake. I couldn't believe I hadn't noticed them before. She let me take another breath and then she went over to a window. Taking off one of her flippers, she kicked the window continually with her foot, but it didn't budge.

Tina put her flipper back on, came over to give me another breath, and then went and took hold of one of the metal arms attached to the piece of metal that had held down the container. She pushed the metal square down onto the floor of the ship, held it with her foot and worked one of the arms back and forth. She kept going until finally the arm broke off from the piece of metal. She swam over again, giving me another breath of life.

Watching Tina work, the determination in her eyes, and the ability to act quickly, made me admire her. At that moment, I wished we could've talked to each other. Not to make it easier to communicate with her, although that would've been helpful, but just so I could tell her how amazing she was. To give her some words of encouragement. If I were the leader of a city, a military unit, or even a precinct, Tina would be the one person I would want by my side.

Tina took the metal arm and thrust it as hard as she could at the window. After a couple of thrusts, a small crack formed. She continued hitting the window, coming over to give me some oxygen now and then.

Finally, the window broke open, leaving a hole big enough for Tina to get through, but only without her equipment on. She unstrapped her tank and brought it over to me. I wrapped my legs around the tank, holding on tight.

Tina took one last breath, hugged me, and then swam out the window. I put her mouthpiece in my mouth and checked her gauge. Her tank had just entered the red zone. All I could do was sit there and hope someone reached me before the air ran out.

The next couple of minutes were the worst minutes of my life. Each breath took me closer to my death. The gauge sat in my free hand, the dial getting lower and lower while I waited around for help. I had never felt so hopeless, so alone. The realization of everything hit me like a huge wave.

I was going to die. Underwater, trapped in an old rusty ship.

I also realized that President Randall and I had two very different ideas of the word eliminated. I thought he was just going to eliminate me from Recruitment. Apparently, he meant he wanted me eliminated from life, and it seemed like he was about to get his wish.

If I did survive this ordeal, I needed to fight back, whatever it took. I didn't want a terrible life. I wanted to make a difference. I wanted my life to matter. If working at Infinity Corp wasn't in my future, then I would have to make my own destiny. Carve my own path.

I'd been so lost in thought that I hadn't noticed when someone came into the room. Someone touched my arm, bringing me back to reality.

SO Clark floated next to me, trying to pull my hand out of the cuff that held me down. He finally gave me a look that said he was sorry. Sorry for what? That my life was over? That there was nothing he could do to save me?

Pain shot through my trapped hand, making me scream, bubbles shooting out from my mouth. As my mouthpiece fell away from my lips, I swallowed some water, making me choke a little. SO Clark had broken my thumb so he could pull my hand through.

I put the mouthpiece back in with my good hand and held onto Tina's tank as if my life depended on it. Which of course, it did.

As SO Clark pulled me through the ship and out the opening that had been busted open, the last of Tina's tank went out. I spit out the mouthpiece having no more use for it. SO Clark was too busy pulling me up to notice I had run out of air. I looked up and watched the sky come closer and closer.

We were almost to the surface. My throat stung from the water I had swallowed making me want to cough, which I knew I couldn't. All I could feel was the pain in my hand and the hope in my heart when everything went black.

CHAPTER 36

I stood on a rock located on a tall mountain. Fresh snow covered the ground, the air bitter cold. Behind me were hundreds of trees; tall pine and aspen trees thick with a blanket of snow. Down below me sat a vast open field of white. The mountain circled the field, enclosing it from the outside world.

I hopped off the rock and looked down at my feet to see a small, blue flower rising from the snow. Picking it up with my right hand, I pulled it to my nose and took in the scent. It smelled wonderful. It smelled like hope.

Suddenly someone took my left hand. I looked up to see Eric, smiling at me, making his blue eyes flash. A rustle sounded behind me. When I turned around, Tina, with her beautiful red hair, and Dee, with her amazing brown curls, were standing there, their eyes excited.

To the left of Tina stood my dad. His expression confused me. He looked sad but happy at the same time. It didn't make sense.

SO Mack Clark stood to the right of Dee. His shoulders

were square, his face determined. He looked confident as he scanned the valley below us. Next to Mack stood two others, but their faces were blurry. I tried to focus my eyes, but it was no use.

A cough came from the right of me. I turned to see VP Oliver. He smiled at me as he took the flower from my hand. He held it up, sniffed it, then put it in the palm of his hand and blew.

We watched it float down to the valley until it landed on the ground. As soon as the flower touched the snow, the snow melted away, exposing a field of the same blue flowers. It was the most beautiful thing I had ever seen.

Smiling, I turned back to look at VP Oliver, but he was no longer there.

"Emmie," Eric said. He sounded far away.

I turned to my left, looking for Eric, but my world went black. I tried to reach out, but no one was there.

"Emmie," Tina said.

Again, I tried to reach out, but emptiness surrounded me.

"Come on, Emmie!" Mack said, his voice fierce.

Suddenly, my lungs were on fire. I couldn't breathe. I tried to gasp for air, but nothing happened.

"Please, Emmie!" Tina sounded scared and desperate.

At that moment, I knew I could let go and end it all. It would all be over. No more worries. No more rules. No more Amber. No more President Randall.

My left hand warmed. It comforted me, making me want to hold on. I focused on that warmth, trying to expand it. It spread to my arms, then my legs. I held on tighter, pushing it all around me.

"Emmie, please, come back to me." Eric's voice was in my ear.

My lungs were still on fire, but I held onto the warmth and pushed it up the middle of my body. The fire went out, leaving my chest and my heart warm. I didn't want to leave. Not yet.

I needed to stay. There was so much to do. So much to fix. So much change that needed to happen.

"Emmie." Eric's voice was barely a whisper.

My eyes shot open and water escaped from my mouth, pouring down my neck. I coughed, gasping for air. My right hand throbbed, the pain unbearable.

"I thought we lost you." I focused my eyes to see SO Clark leaning over me. "Welcome back."

"Oh, Emmie!" Tina kneeled on the other side, tears streaming down her cheeks.

Right next to her was Eric, holding my good hand. He was my warmth. My hope. He had also been crying, his shirt wet from all the tears that had fallen. He laughed when I looked into his eyes. "You're alive." He kissed me on my forehead. "You're alive."

"Was I dead?" I choked out. My throat and lungs burned a little.

"For a few minutes," SO Clark said. He turned to SO Martin. "Let's get her to the infirmary."

"Sure thing," SO Martin said.

SO Clark and Eric helped me up. I wobbled a little, but Eric held on tight. "I've got you," he said, his voice soft. I held my right hand close to my chest, clenching my jaw to hold in the screams from the pain.

As we walked over to a security vehicle, I noticed RL Steven sitting down on the pebbles. He rocked back and forth, staring straight ahead. His face was pale, and his eyes were wide. I thought he might throw up.

Will ran up next to us, keeping pace with me and Eric. "Emmie, are you alright?"

I forced a smile. "I think so." Inside, I felt far from alright. Will's eyes told me he was still worried, so I forced a bigger smile. "I'll be fine, Will. Thank you for checking."

Will nodded slowly. "Yeah, sure. I just wanted to make sure you were okay. You had us all worried." He straightened his glasses. "I never knew Recruitment was going to be this intense."

Eric gave a small laugh, but I could hear the strain in his voice. "I don't think any of us thought that. This is far from what I imagined."

"Well, take care of yourself, Emmie," Will said. "I'm not sure if they'll let me, but I'll try to come visit you in the infirmary later."

They wouldn't let him. "Thanks, Will. That means a lot." And it truly did. Our city had some terrible people in it, but there were still a lot of good people.

Will gave me a small smile and stopped walking, letting us continue our own.

Luke stood off to the side. He looked like he wanted to come over, but he didn't. We made eye contact for a few seconds. Worry and pain consumed his eyes. I wanted to tell him to come over so I could let him know I was okay, but I wasn't sure if I should. He ran his hand over his head and turned away. It looked like his eyes were wet, but I couldn't tell for sure.

"Pierce, drive Emmie to the infirmary," SO Clark said. "I need to go talk to the president and report this." He glared at his hands.

"This isn't your fault, Mack," SO Martin said to him. "You couldn't have known this was going to happen. Plus, she's alive. You saved her."

"It was on my watch, Pierce, therefore I'm responsible for what happens." SO Clark's jaw tightened.

I wanted to say something to him, to thank him for saving my life, but the words wouldn't come. Besides, he had turned away too fast.

"Steven!" SO Clark yelled. "Get the rest of the Recruits on the bus now!"

RL Steven looked up, snapping back to reality. He slowly got up and nodded at SO Clark. "Everyone on the bus," RL Steven said to all the Recruits sitting on the ground. I noticed them for the first time since I came to. Most were staring at me and a lot of them looked scared.

"Let's go, Emmie," SO Martin said to me, opening the back door of the vehicle. Eric still held onto me.

Eric helped me into the vehicle and then moved to get in himself.

"What do you think you're doing?" SO Martin asked.

Eric stopped and turned to SO Martin. "I'm going with you."

"No, you're not," SO Martin said, his voice flat.

"The only way you can stop me is to knock me out and drag my body back to the bus. I'd like to see you try." Eric didn't bother waiting for an answer. He just got in the vehicle next to me and shut the door. Now that was the Eric I had come to know and care about.

A small smile came to SO Martin's mouth, but it was gone just as quick. Tina went around to the other side of the vehicle and opened the door.

"What about you?" SO Martin asked her.

Tina nodded toward Eric. "Same as him."

"Okay then," SO Martin said as he got into the driver's seat.

The whole ride to the infirmary, I leaned my head on Eric's shoulder. He held on tightly to my left hand, caressing my hand with his thumb. I set my right hand in my lap and tried not to think about the pain.

I was alive. Whatever President Randall, well, RH Johnson had rigged to eliminate me didn't work. But that wasn't the last try they would make.

So now I had to decide what I was going to do. I couldn't go back to Recruitment because they would keep trying to kill me until they did. But if I didn't go back, where would I go? I needed to figure out a plan, and I needed to figure it out soon.

CHAPTER 37

As soon as they got me to the infirmary, they took me to a room and had me change into the mandatory white short-sleeve shirt and white pants.

The same nurse that had helped me after my fight with Amber was the one helping me. She hooked me up to tons of equipment. She tried to explain what it all did, but my head was spinning from everything that had happened that I couldn't pay attention. She wrapped up my broken thumb and gave me some medicine for the pain.

Unlike the last time I was in the infirmary, they put me in my own room. The small, square room had plain white walls and no windows. Just the bed, the medical equipment, and two chairs took up the space.

Once the nurse left, Eric pulled his chair up next to me and intertwined his fingers with mine. Tina dragged her chair to the other side of the bed. We sat in silence for a few minutes. I hadn't the slightest idea where to start. I guess with the main issue.

"So, I guess Whit Randall wants me dead." I figured I could drop the titles. Recruitment was over and I would never work for Infinity Corp.

Eric shook his head. "This is crazy, Emmie. I can't believe this. What happened down there? All I saw was the boat speeding toward the shore and when it came to a stop, SO Clark carried your lifeless body out and set you down. By the time I had run over, he was already performing CPR trying to bring you back to life. Seeing you lying there, not breathing . . ." Eric choked up and couldn't finish.

I squeezed his hand. "They had rigged it so that as soon as I turned my key a metal cuff came up and clamped my right wrist down. They also had messed with my tank so there wasn't as much air in there. It ran out while we were down there."

"They also locked the entrance to the ship once we were inside," Tina said. "When we went in, it must have triggered it so it would close."

"A ship? You went in a ship?" Eric asked.

"Yeah, that's where the box was," Tina said.

"Weird, our container was just sitting on the lake floor," Eric said. "And how did they know that was the key you would use? What if Tina had turned that side?"

"Steven assigned our keys," I said. "Didn't he do the same with you?"

"No," Eric said, shaking his head. "That means Steven was in on it."

"Well, haven't we always known that?" Tina asked.

"Not that he was willing to kill Emmie," Eric said, his voice sharp.

I looked at Eric. "We don't know if he knew that was going to happen. After I woke up, I noticed him sitting by himself on the ground. He looked sick like he couldn't believe what happened. He could've just thought it was a way to eliminate me from Recruitment, not kill me."

Eric nodded. "That could be true. So, if you ran out of air down in the ship, what did you do?"

"Tina gave me some of hers. You should have seen her, Eric. She was awesome. I couldn't believe how quickly she assessed the situation and tried to think of solutions." I smiled at Tina.

"All I could think about was that I needed to save you," Tina said. "I needed a way out so I could get someone to help."

"What about the button on the compass?" Eric asked. "Why didn't you just press that?"

Tina and I both laughed a little. It was kind of sad that it took us so long to think of that.

"We finally remembered that but when I tried to push it, it didn't work," Tina said. "The button was stuck and couldn't be pressed in."

"How did you get out?" Eric asked Tina.

Tina leaned back in her chair. "I used one of the arms from the piece of metal holding down the container to break open a porthole in the side of the ship."

"I'm impressed, Tina," Eric said, "that you got that open. Nice work."

"Thanks," Tina said. "It wasn't easy, that's for sure. But when your adrenaline's pumping like that, it's amazing the amount of strength you get. Plus, all those workouts made me stronger. I left my tank with Emmie and went up to get help. When I surfaced, a boat was nearby. SO Clark and another guy were in it and I told them that Emmie was stuck. SO Clark immediately jumped into the water and went to get her. The other guy pulled me into the boat, and we waited, which was agonizing." She rubbed my arm. "That's all I know."

I smiled at her. "Mack broke open the door into the ship and came down to where I was. He assessed my situation and thought the best possible solution was to break my thumb." I held up my poor hand.

"Are we dropping the titles?" Tina asked.

"Oh, yes," I said with a nod.

Tina let out a sigh of relief. "Thank goodness."

Eric looked at my hand. "I wondered what happened. That must've hurt a lot."

"Oh, you have no idea," I said. "I'm sure if I wasn't under water the scream that came out of my mouth might have made some people go deaf. But it got the job done. Mack was able to pull my hand out and he took me out of the room. Right when we got out of the ship, I ran out of air. I blacked out before we surfaced. I was having a crazy dream and then I felt Eric's hand."

"You felt that?" Eric asked.

"Yeah." I looked at Eric. "It was the one thing that pulled me back to reality and made me hang on. I could hear you both saying my name. It was the warmth of your hand that woke me up."

Eric looked at Tina. "Can you close your eyes for a second?"

"Sure thing," Tina said, covering up her eyes with her hand.

Eric reached over and pressed his lips to mine. It felt as good as the first kiss and I hoped I would always have that warm, butterfly sensation whenever he kissed me. I sighed when he pulled away.

"You can open your eyes now, Tina," Eric said.

Tina pulled down her hand. "So, what do we do now?"

"We?" I asked, looking at her.

"Of course, we," Tina said. "You think we're going to go back to Recruitment and pretend as if none of this happened?"

"We all can't drop out," I said. They had already risked so much for me. They still had a chance to live a normal life. "Who knows what they'll do to us."

Eric looked at me. "Emmie, they're trying to kill you, and I'm pretty sure they'll keep trying. I'm not going to work for a corporation that sits back and lets that happen."

"Me either," Tina said, shaking her head.

"Well, we can't just leave. Where would we go?"

We all sat quietly for a while, trying to think. Really, what could we do? We were seventeen.

While I was thinking, another thought came to my head. "Why was Mack out on the boat? He was on the shore when we left."

"A couple of minutes after you two went under, one of the boats came back," Eric said. "One of the guys was sick and had been throwing up. Mack took his place on the boat and went out there."

"Ewww," Tina said. "He threw up in the water that we

swam in?"

"I'm sure that happens now and then," Eric said with a laugh.

"Well, it's still gross to think about," Tina said with a shiver.

I rested my head against the pillow and let out a sigh.

"We're going to figure this out, Emmie," Eric said.

"I sure hope so," I said. "I need to talk to Frank Oliver. Maybe he can help us some way." My head started to feel a little dizzy. "I think those pain pills are making me a little drowsy."

"Close your eyes and get some sleep," Eric said to me, rubbing my hand. "We'll be right here when you wake up."

"Good. I need the two of you." I let out a yawn. "I feel like I need a nice, warm shower, though."

"Well, get some rest and I'll help you take a shower when you wake up," Eric said.

I let go of his hand and pushed his shoulder. "Nice try, Eric. I just broke my thumb. I think I'm capable of still taking a shower on my own."

Eric laughed. "Hey, you can't blame a guy for trying."

Smiling, I closed my eyes, letting the drugs take me away to sleep.

CHAPTER 38

My sleep was restless. I dreamed of being trapped down in the ship, but instead of Mack coming to my rescue, a shark came into the room and attacked. Right as the shark opened its enormous jaws to have me for dinner, I shot up in bed, screaming.

It took Eric a couple of minutes to calm me down and let me know I was safe. Well, at least for the moment. It wouldn't be long before a shark of a different kind was trying to eat me whole.

When I finally regained my composure, two arms threw themselves around me, squeezing tight. From the brown curls covering my face, it was Dee. I hugged her back, not wanting to let go.

Eric and Tina had thrown a fit until the nurse finally gave in to their demands and had someone go and fetch Dee.

Dee pulled back and took my good hand in hers. She was sitting on my bed next to me. "How are you feeling?" She brushed some hair off my face and tucked it behind my ear.

I had to take a second to evaluate how I felt since waking up. My hand ached a little and my head was a little dizzy, but other than that I felt fine. "Much better."

Someone cleared their throat, catching my attention. Standing near the door was my father. "Dad!" I was so happy to see him. Dee moved out of the way when he came over to the bed.

Dad stroked my cheek with his hand and kissed me on the forehead. I could tell from his eyes that he had been crying. "My little girl," he said, pulling me in for a hug. "You're okay."

I squeezed him tight. "I am, Dad. I'm just fine."

He pulled back, looked into my eyes, and squeezed my arms. "I'm glad. I was so worried when the nurse called to tell me what happened. I got over here as soon as I could, but you were asleep. I didn't want to wake you. You looked so peaceful." He chuckled. "Well, at least until you woke up. Bad dream?"

A vision of the shark with its jaws wide open, his huge teeth calling my name, came into my mind, making me shiver. "Very bad."

"Well, it's just a dream. You're here and you're alive. That's all that matters." Dad pulled out a handkerchief and wiped his nose.

As I watched his face, so relieved that I was okay, it made my heart ache. How did you tell a father that their little girl has someone trying to kill her?

"I found another chair," Eric said, pulling a chair right up next to the bed.

"Thank you, son," Dad said, patting Eric on the shoulder

and taking a seat. He looked at me and pointed to Eric. "This guy really cares about you."

I smiled at Eric. "Yes, he does."

Eric smiled in return and went and sat in his chair on the other side of the bed. Tina had moved her chair next to Eric. Dee took the opportunity to reclaim her seat on my bed. I scooted over so she could sit next to me.

Dad smiled at me, his eyes a little red and puffy. "What happened in the water? All they said is that you got stuck down there, lost some oxygen and they had to revive you. What did you get stuck on?"

I had no idea how to respond. Would my dad believe me when I said that Whit Randall was trying to kill me?

A knock on the door interrupted the uncomfortable pause.

"Is it okay if I come in?" Mack asked.

"Of course," I said.

Mack walked into the room and stood at the foot of the bed. "I just wanted to make sure you were okay."

"I'm doing well," I said. "I still have a little bit of pain in my hand, but it's much better."

Mack cleared his throat. "I'm sorry about that. I didn't think there was another way when there was so little time."

Dad leaned over Dee and grabbed my wrist, examining my wrapped-up hand. "What happened?"

Mack, Tina, Eric, and I all shared an awkward look. From Dee's expression, Eric and Tina must have filled her in on what happened before Dad arrived.

"I'm sorry, sir," Mack said, "but the way your daughter's

hand was caught, the only way I could get it out was to break her thumb."

Dad's eyes widened in horror. "You broke my daughter's thumb?"

"Dad, it's okay. It was necessary," I said, trying to reassure him. "Mack saved my life. If he hadn't gotten there when he did, I'd be dead."

Dad's shoulders relaxed.

"Well, it shouldn't have happened in the first place," Mack said, his voice filled with frustration. "I've never had anything like that happen on my watch. I take full responsibility for what happened."

"There's no way you could've known that was going to happen," Eric said.

Well, if he was in on it, he would have. But by Mack's behavior, Whit hadn't filled him in on the 'eliminate Emmie' mission.

"Well, it won't happen again," Mack said with a confident voice. "You can be sure of that."

Oh, it would happen again, and it would keep happening until I was good and dead.

"She's alive, right?" Dad said, smiling at me. "Everything's fine."

The nurse showed up at the door. "I hate to break this up, but I need everyone out for a little bit. I just need to run some tests on Emmie. I had some food brought up for all of you since I'm assuming none of you will leave. It's two doors down on the left." She looked at Mack. "I didn't get anything for you, though."

Mack stepped back from the bed. "That's okay. I should probably get going. I just wanted to check on her. I would be grateful if you could keep me updated on your progress, Emmie." I just smiled and nodded, knowing that I probably wouldn't be able to.

After everyone left, the nurse checked my eyes, my blood pressure, and my temperature. When she was almost done, a small cough came from near the door. I looked over to see Luke standing in the doorway.

The nurse glanced at him and then turned back to me. "You're quite popular today."

"I guess that happens when you die and then come back to life," I said with a small smile.

"I guess so," the nurse said. She finished up and left the room.

Luke came in and stood next to the bed. He stuffed his hands in his pockets and rocked back and forth where he stood, something he did when he was nervous or uncomfortable.

"Do you want to sit down?" I asked him, motioning to the chair. Luke eyed it and then nodded, sitting down slowly.

He pulled the chair closer to the bed and looked me in the eye. "How are you feeling?"

"Alive, for one thing," I said. "I don't think I can handle many more near-death experiences. It drains you."

Luke reached his hand out and then pulled it back. "Seeing you there lifeless shook me up. It shook everyone up." His eyes watered. "I'm just glad you're okay. That's the second time I had to watch you almost die."

I reached out and took his hand. He started to pull away, but then ended up scooting closer to me. "I know I keep saying I'm okay over and over again, but I am." I looked him in the eye. "I'm fine, Luke. I promise."

He nodded his head, but I could tell he didn't fully believe me. He cleared his throat. "I'm sorry I've been so distant lately. It's just with everything that happened in that room, I'm not sure how to act."

I understood that. I'd been trying to figure that out ever since we'd kissed. How do you go from sharing a passionate kiss to being just friends? "I know how you feel. That was … intense."

Luke gave a small laugh. "Intense is almost an understatement. I don't know what to make of it. I've been so confused. I mean, we're friends. Just friends. You like Eric. I like Tina. We're just friends." He looked at me, scratching the back of his head. "Right?"

I nodded. "Yes, we're just friends. It was just one of those moments. We were about to die. We thought we had just seen the people we cared most about die. We had been through so much that day. I don't think we should make too much of it." I didn't want to make too much of it. A part of me still wanted to erase it. There were moments where I could still feel his lips on mine.

"But that kiss, it just felt like there was so much passion behind it." His face reddened.

"There was." I smiled. "Maybe you should kiss Tina. You'll see the difference. And feel it."

"Have you kissed Eric?" Luke asked.

It was weird talking to him like that. Luke and I normally didn't talk by ourselves, let alone about our feelings.

"A couple of times." I smiled on the inside, remembering each one. They were perfect.

"He's a better kisser than me?" Luke had a small smile, the softness of it touching his eyes.

"It's different. I care about you, Luke. But I like Eric a lot more. There's more of a spark between me and him." I let go of his hand. "Luke, I need to tell you something and I need you to really listen to me."

"Of course, I'll listen," he said, surprise in his eyes. "Why wouldn't I?"

"It goes against everything you believe." I took a deep breath. "The explanation and reasoning behind what I'm about to tell you is too long to go into right now, but President Randall is trying to have me killed." I looked at him, waiting for a response.

He just stared at me blankly. "What?" He shook his head. "That's impossible."

"It is possible. I overheard him talking to Dean Johnson. They're trying to kill me. They find me a threat."

"A threat?" Luke scratched his head. "You're a little bit of a rule-breaker and hardheaded, but I highly doubt you're a threat."

"Not according to them. I don't have a lot of time right now, but I just wanted to give you a heads up that things are changing. I might not be around here much longer. Whether I will be alive or dead, I don't know, but I have to try to leave. And I think Eric and Tina will be coming with me." The words surprised me as soon as they left my mouth. Leave? That sounded so ridiculous. Yet so right.

Luke scooted back. "You're crazy. This can't be true. And you can't just leave and take others with you."

"I have to, Luke. River Springs is corrupt, whether you want to face it or not." I tried to reach for his hand again, but he recoiled. "I know this is a lot to take in, but things are not what they seem. The leaders of this place are not good people. They're driving our city into the ground."

He stood. "Why are you telling me this?"

"Just so you would know. You have an option, Luke, to stay here with the evil people of this city, or to leave and stand up for something better. It's up to you, but I didn't want to leave without telling you." The more I spoke, the more I knew it was right. I had to leave River Springs.

His compassion and worry for me left. The stone-hard Luke was back. "No. No. This is not right, Emmie. You're wrong."

"I'm not wrong." Why wouldn't he just trust me? "How can you be part of a place this corrupt and willing to kill a teenager?"

His chest heaved in and out. I could tell he was trying to control his temper the best he could. "I've been a resident of River Springs as long as you, Emmie, and they've had a good reason behind everything they do."

His words stung. I couldn't believe he'd just said that. "You think I deserve to die?"

"I think President Randall wouldn't do anything this rash." He paused. "But if he did, it would only be because it's for the good of the city."

I felt like I'd been slapped.

Eric, Tina, Dee, and Dad walked back into the room. They stopped when they saw Luke and me staring at each other, with Luke fuming and me fighting back tears.

"What's going on?" Eric asked, walking up next to me. He looked at Luke. "Are you okay?"

Luke just responded by pushing past Eric and storming out of the room. I guess you couldn't undo years of brainwashing by your father in just a few minutes.

"What's with him?" Tina asked as everyone sat down.

I shook my head. The conversation wasn't helping with my dizziness.

"It's crowded in here," a voice said from the door. Frank Oliver. "How's our Em doing?"

Horrible. My life had just been forever altered. Two people wanted me dead—Whit and Amber. I felt betrayed by Luke. I had no home to go to. I was trapped in a prison and wasn't sure if I could escape.

Instead, though, I said, "Fine."

CHAPTER 39

Frank stepped into the room. "Good, good. I'm glad to hear that." He looked at me. "It shouldn't be too long before the president will be here to check on you, so I was wondering if I could have a moment alone with Em." He glanced around the room, his eyes pausing a second on Eric. Frank shot me a questioning look, but when I nodded, it seemed to satisfy him.

"The president?" Dad asked, his eyebrows furrowed. "I didn't know President Randall came to the infirmary to visit people."

Nope, he wanted to double check on the ones he was trying to take out to see if they were still alive before he made another attempt to kill them.

Frank smiled. "He doesn't all the time. Just on special occasions, like if a Recruit gets hurt."

Dad made a face I couldn't read. He seemed a little upset, which didn't make sense to me. Honestly, nothing had been making sense to me. Everyone got up to leave, but I spoke before they got too far.

"No." Everyone turned to look at me. "I mean, they don't need to leave. Whatever you have to say to me, I would like you to say it in front of my friends and family."

Frank shook his head. "I think it would be best if we talked alone, Em."

"It's okay. You can talk in front of them."

"Emmie," Dad said in a warning tone, "if VP Oliver wants to talk to you alone, you need to listen."

"Dad, I'm not trying to be rude. It's just that whatever he tells me, I'm pretty sure I'll just turn around and tell all of you. So why not have everyone listen so I don't have to repeat myself. I've been doing enough of that lately." I adjusted myself on my bed while Frank stood there contemplating the matter.

"Are you sure about this Em?" Frank asked. "It's very … sensitive material. The things I'm about to tell you could be hard to take in. You might want to let it soak in before you talk to others about it."

"What's going on?" Dad asked, sounding a little irritated.

Eric, Tina and Dee shifted uncomfortably where they stood.

I glanced at everyone in the room. They were all the people I cared deeply about. I loved them all and I wanted them by my side. Even if it was hard to hear, they needed to know, too. Dad needed to find out what was going on and who better to hear it from than the vice president of Infinity Corp?

"No, everyone stays," I said firmly. "Will someone please

shut the door?"

Frank was still closest to the door. He glanced outside to see if anyone was out there and then shut the door. Everyone went back to their seats.

"I'm having someone distract the president for a while, but I don't know how long they'll be able to. I need to be quick." Frank took a seat on the edge of the bed. He glanced at everyone in the room. "What I'm about to tell you is top secret. It also could have the ability to," he cleared his throat, "ruin some lives. Are you sure you want me to go on, Em?"

"Yes, I need to know." I reached out for Eric's hand for some comfort.

Frank gave me a small smile. "River Springs was created to stop the havoc going on in the world. It had gone to complete chaos. All the rules, all the structure, it was meant for good. Not long after the city started to get back on its feet, Lee Augustine had a vision of the future. He prophesied that River Springs would take a turn for the worst. He said greed and power would form in the hearts of those running the corporation and this city would self-destruct much faster than the world did from the beginning of time." Frank took a deep breath. "The prophecy states that the leaders will resort to violence, even death, to get what they want. It says that unless something is done, man as we know it will cease to exist."

"This prophecy, do you think it's true?" Eric asked Frank. Something in the tone of Eric's voice told me it wasn't all new information to him.

"Yes, Eric, I do." Frank sat up tall. "This is unknown to a lot of people, but the prophecy has manifested itself to others since then. Including me." That took me by surprise. It made me wonder who else had the prophecy.

"How come no one knows about it?" my dad asked.

"The president of Infinity Corp at the time didn't want to alarm anyone." Frank folded his hands in front of him. "He didn't think it was true. He said he wouldn't let River Springs come to that, so he sealed it up. All the other presidents have agreed with him, even Whit. Only a handful of people have known about it."

"So, what does this all have to do with me?" I asked. None of that answered any of the hundreds of questions floating around in my head.

"The last part of the prophecy states that there will be one among the city who will lead a revolution. One who will want to stop the leadership of this city and take it down piece by piece." Frank looked at me.

"A traitor," I said quietly.

Frank nodded. "If you want to use that term, I guess it could fit."

"That's the term Whit wants to use," I mumbled.

"Hold on a second, how could it be Emmie?" Eric asked, his eyebrows furrowed. "It's not possible."

"How is it not possible?" Dee asked, looking slightly offended. "It has to be someone in the city. Why not Emmie?"

Eric looked at Frank. "I saw it one time, the prophecy, when I was with my dad at work. It specifically states that the person would be a descendent of either the president or vice president of River Springs." Another reason why Whit would want to cover it up.

"It would have to be either Samantha or Austin Oliver, or Joshua or Tami Randall. One of yours or the president's kids," Tina said, looking at Frank. "If the leader of the revolution is from the current president and vice president."

Frank nodded in agreement. "Yes, that's true."

"I'm confused," I said. "How could it be me, then?" My confusion kept getting higher and higher by the minute.

"Em," Frank started, his eyes soft. Sympathetic even.

Dad stopped him. "No, Frank, let me be the one to tell her."

"Tell me what?" My pulse began to rise, and my cheeks warmed as I looked at my dad. He took a gentle hold of my arm, right above my bandaged hand.

"Emmie," Dad said, looking into my eyes. I stared back, not sure I wanted to hear what he was about to say. "Em, I'm not your real father." My heart dropped. Frank shifted uncomfortably at the edge of the bed.

"What?" My head felt dizzy. "What do you mean?"

Dad held firmly onto my arm even though he seemed to be shaking. He took a deep breath.

"President Randall is your real father."

CHAPTER 40

I couldn't breathe. I felt like I was underwater again, drowning with no one to save me. "No!" I pulled my arm away from Dad. "How? … It's impossible." I looked at Dad. "You're my dad."

"Yes, sweetie, I am in a sense," Dad said. "I'm the one who raised you and you'll always be my daughter in my eyes. But it was not me who … contributed to you being born."

"I don't understand. How did this happen?" My voice filled with panic. I didn't want to believe it. I couldn't be *that man's* daughter.

Dad kept his eyes down. "You know your mom works long hours with the president." Sadness consumed his voice.

"She cheated on you? With him?" I gripped the sheet tight. How could she? It was so disgusting.

"It was a long time ago. It's over now." The words came from Dad's mouth, but he didn't sound convinced of it. How could they have kept working all those years together and not have anything more happen?

"She did this to you and you stayed with her?" I couldn't look at him right then. "You let her keep her job? Working next to that sick, disgusting animal?"

"Emmie, I didn't feel like I had a choice," Dad said. "Divorce is frowned upon. And we still had you and Derek to raise."

"What about Derek?" I asked. "Is he …"

"He's mine." Dad sighed. "Although, most days I'd much rather claim you as my blood relative." That at least made me smile.

Dad reached out and took hold of my arm again. "Emmie, I know this is a lot to take in, but I want you to know that I love you. You are my daughter and you always will be."

"I love you, too, Dad," I said, smiling at him. "I'm not mad at you. I understand why you did what you did. It's just hard to digest, you know? And I can't believe mom's capable of doing something like this."

Dad turned to Frank. "I didn't know about this prophecy, though. Janice never mentioned it to me."

"I'm not sure that she knows," Frank said. "Unless Whit told her, I can't imagine how she would find out."

"They think Emmie's the one it's talking about?" Dad asked. "What does this mean? What does the president want to do with her?"

It took a moment for me to respond. Everyone was looking at me, waiting for me to answer. Obviously, none of them wanted to be the one to tell Dad the truth.

"Dad, today, with me getting caught underwater, it wasn't an accident." I stared at him, waiting to see his reaction.

Dad shook his head. "It was done on purpose? That can't be true."

I sighed. "It was a trap. President Randall did not intend for me to make it out of there. He didn't even care if Tina didn't make it out alive."

Dad's face turned pale. "He tried to …"

"He tried to kill me, Dad. And could've killed Tina, too, in the process."

Tina shifted in her seat. When I turned to look at her, her eyes were wide. With all the stress and chaos that followed the events, she probably hadn't stopped to think that he intended for her to die, too.

Whit probably saw it as a necessity to protect everyone from little ol' traitor me.

"Well, we need to stop him," Dad said. "Maybe I can talk to Janice and she could try to reason with him. Killing Emmie is not the solution."

"It is to him," Frank said. "He already feels threatened by her. If she's alive, she will continue to fight. She can expose everything he has done, everything that he's capable of."

"So can we," Eric said, indicating everyone in the room.

"Another reason he wants Emmie stopped," Frank said. "She has already convinced four others that the president is not the man we thought he was."

"Only four?" Dee asked, looking at Frank.

"Well, I was convinced a long time ago." Frank smiled. "But one man can't do much."

"But the six of us, we can at least do something, right?" I asked.

"What about Luke?" Dee asked. "Why did he leave? You told him, right?"

Tina and Eric looked at me.

"Luke is …" I started, but I got choked up.

"He isn't on our side," Eric finished for me, the tone of his voice closing the matter. He must've read my face to know Luke wasn't going to stand with us.

Suddenly a beep went off near Frank. He pulled a little device out of his pocket and looked at it. His eyes shot up to me. "We need to get you out of here, now."

"Why?" I asked.

"The president is on his way," Frank said. "He'll be here any minute."

"Where do I go?" I asked.

Eric took the heart monitor off my finger, slowly removed the needle the nurse had put in my arm, and helped me out of the bed.

Frank opened the door and headed out of the room. The five of us followed. As we were walking down the hall, which was a little too fast for my still woozy self, Frank talked.

"There's an underground system that a previous vice president had installed," Frank said. "He knew the president didn't believe the prophecy, so he wanted an escape route just in case something like this ever happened. The president doesn't know about it."

"Where does it lead?" Dad asked.

"Out of the city," Frank said.

Before anyone could comment, Frank opened a door at the end of the hall. He led us down a flight of stairs and out another door. As we made tons of twists and turns, he started talking again. "I had some supplies arranged for you. They should be waiting for you at the entrance of the underground tunnel. I wasn't sure if you were going alone or not, so I had some extra supplies put in."

"I'm going with her," Eric said.

"Me, too," Tina said.

"Me, three," Dee said.

"Me, four," Dad said.

My heart swelled. It comforted me knowing that no matter what happened, I had all of them with me. I looked at Dad as we walked. "Are you sure, Dad? What about Mom and Derek?"

"My relationship with your mother ended a long time ago and I haven't had any belief in River Springs for years. To have someone who runs a city not abide by their own rules is unacceptable. And Derek, well, he'll be fine. Frank will look out for him for now. Besides, I can't leave my baby girl alone out there in the wild. Let alone, three other teenagers. You'll need some adult supervision." Dad winked at me.

When Frank finally came to a stop in the middle of a hallway, a few totes were waiting on the floor. He turned to look at us. "When you go through the door, it will lead you down a few flights of stairs. Follow the tunnel all the way out. When it ends, it will open to a small cave. Drop down and head straight. The cave will take you out to the forest." He handed me a map. "Follow this map the best you can. It will take you to an area my predecessors scouted out years ago. I have some things to finish up here, but I'm hoping to leave here sometime in the next week."

"You're going to meet us?" I asked, making my heart hopeful.

"I hope to, Em," Frank said. "River Springs needs a change and I don't think anything can get done here. We need a fresh start. Besides, I'm pretty sure the president's on to me. It won't be long until I'm next on his hit list."

"What about your wife and kids?" I asked.

"As I said, I have some things left to do. Just follow this closely." Frank pointed to the map. "You need to get going."

Dante came to my mind. What had happened to him? Was he still alive? "Frank, where are Dante and Wallace? Did they leave?"

Frank nodded. "Yes, they left. There's not enough time to explain it all right now."

I breathed a sigh of relief. "So, they're alive. That's all I need to know."

"Uh, where's the door?" Tina asked.

I looked around, thinking the same thing. We were, after all, just standing in the middle of a hall.

Frank gave us a mischievous smile. He reached over and touched the wall. A green line went down, scanning his hand. The ground opened next to us.

"Cool," Dee said, looking down the opening.

"Grab the bags and get going," Frank said.

I threw my arms around him. "Thank you."

He kissed me on top of my head. "Be safe, Em. I have faith in you." When I pulled back, he had tears in his eyes. "Now, go."

Eric, Dad, and Tina all picked up a bag and the five of us went down the stairs. Once we reached the bottom of the stairs, the opening above closed, leaving us in the dark tunnel.

"They didn't think to install lights?" Tina asked. Right when she said that, a light flickered on above us. "Well, look at that, they did think to install them."

As we continued down the tunnel, the light behind us went off and another one in front went on. They continued to turn on and off as we made our way through the tunnel as fast as we could.

It took a couple of hours to get through the tunnel since I couldn't go so fast, but we finally reached the end. Just as Frank said, the tunnel opened into a cave. There was some natural light coming from the top of the cave, making it just light enough so we could see.

Dad and Eric jumped down first with their bags. Tina threw her bag to them and then jumped down. Dee and I were last. When I jumped down, Eric caught me as I stumbled a little.

"You okay?" he asked me, holding on to my waist.

"I'm still a little lightheaded, but okay," I said.

Right as we started walking, a noise came from the right. I turned to see a silhouette of a person standing there.

"You didn't really think things went on in River Springs without me knowing about it, did you?" The man stepped out from the shadows. President Randall.

A few more noises and more figures stepped out, including Dean, Mack, and Pierce. There were at least ten others I didn't recognize.

"It's a shame to see such talented young kids and a valued employee go to waste." Whit tsked. "But you all brought this on yourself, didn't you? If only you would've obeyed the rules, this never would've happened."

That made me laugh. "That's funny, Whit, because I was just thinking the same thing about you."

Whit's face tightened. He motioned for the men to grab us.

The next thing I knew, we were all being bound and taken away. That whole day I had been anxious, afraid, and in pain. At that moment, it all disappeared.

Now I was just pissed.

CHAPTER 41

They ended up having to gag and hogtie me, Eric, and Tina. We all put up a nasty fight. Dad and Dee went into a trance mode. Neither of them showed any emotion. It probably would've been smarter to go that way, but I wasn't one to go down without a fight.

Pierce was the one who grabbed me. I squirmed so much, he knocked me across the face, a ring on his finger scraping my cheek, leaving it bleeding.

They took us to an underground holding cell area. All the walls, ceiling, and floor were concrete. The frigid temperature made my hair stand on end and the dank air was so thick I could taste it. I wondered how often that area was even used.

Pierce pulled my gag out, then took me by my still bound feet and hands, and tossed me in a cell like a bean bag. I landed on my side, the sting of the cold concrete floor on my arms catching me by surprise. Pierce locked up my cell and stepped back.

Whit came forward, looking at me with a smug smile. His

face told me one thing: he'd just won. Well, that was what he thought. I was still alive, so I took that as a good thing.

"Oh, Emelia," Whit said, leaning against my cell door. "You've turned into such a problem. I wish it didn't have to come to this."

"Come to what, Whit?" I asked. "Killing me? Why haven't you yet, I wonder? I thought you wanted me eliminated right away?"

Whit smiled. "Oh, I want to, Emelia, and I will. But you have caused pandemonium and there needs to be a punishment for that. Before I kill you, I will make sure you see each one of your friends and family die before you. I want you to understand the consequences of your actions. And to think, all you needed to do was obey the rules."

"You keep saying that, but it's hard for someone to want to obey the rules when the president can't even do it." I scooted my body a little closer so I could see him better.

"I do what's necessary for River Springs," Whit said, folding his arms.

I tilted my head. "Really? That's interesting. And how is committing adultery helping the city, exactly?"

A flash of anger crossed his face, but he quickly changed it to a mischievous smile. "You heard the good news? I must say, the determination you get from me, and the fiery part you get from your mother." His smile twisted. "But this resisting authority, I just don't know where you get it from. It's rather unbecoming, Emelia."

I clenched my teeth. I wanted to hurt him so bad. Fortunately for both of us, I wasn't in a position to. "What you call resisting authority, I call using my brain and thinking for myself. And that, I know for a fact, I get from my *real* father."

Whit gripped his hands around the bars to my cell. "I am your real father, Emelia, and it's about time you show me some respect."

"You're not my father, Whit," I said, disdain filling my voice on the last word. "Philip Woodard is my real father. He's the one who raised me, the one who taught me everything I know, the one who showed me love. Just because you contributed your genetic material to have me doesn't make you my father. All it makes you is a sperm donor."

Whit narrowed his eyes at me. "I want you to sit here and think about everything you've done. I want it to sink in that you'll be responsible for five deaths besides your own. Once it has had time to settle, we'll start with VP Oliver and end with your boyfriend, Eric." He slammed one of his hands against the bar and left.

Pierce snarled at me before he followed him out.

Dean walked past my cell.

"You know this is partially your fault, too," I said to him.

He stopped and looked at me. "What did you say?"

"If you hadn't failed at your job in the first place, then none of this would've happened."

"Don't you dare talk to me like that." His eyebrows furrowed together making a small vein pop out from his massive forehead.

"Does it make you mad, Dean, that you were outwitted by a seventeen-year-old?" I asked, a small smile forming at the corner of my mouth.

Dean came up to my cell and looked me straight in the eye. "You deserve everything that's going to happen to you, you selfish, selfish brat."

Before I could respond, Dad spoke up from his cell. "Em, that's enough. Just let it go."

Dean smiled and then walked away. His footsteps faded down the hall and then the door closed, leaving us prisoners by ourselves.

"What now?" Tina asked from her cell.

"There isn't much we can do right now," I said. "Are you still bound?"

"Yes, I am," Tina said.

"Me, too," Eric said.

"No," both Dad and Dee said. Of course, they weren't. They were the good ones.

"Dee and Mr. Woodard, can you see any way out of your cells?" Eric asked.

"No," Dad said, "and you may call me Philip, Eric."

"I don't see anything in my cell that could get us out," Dee said. "Unless a miracle happens, we're stuck down here."

"Have any brilliant ideas this time around, Tina?" Eric asked.

There was a small cough down the hall. "Eric?" The voice was hoarse. "Eric, is that you?"

"Dad?" Eric's voice sounded hopeful.

He scooted closer to the opening of his cell, which was just to the left of me. It sounded like Tina was to my right and Dee and my dad were across the way.

"Son! It's you!"

Eric released a small laugh. "You're alive."

"Last time I checked, yes," Mr. Greene said. Or should I call him Alexander? No, Mr. Greene was the appropriate way to say it. And we all know how well I do at appropriate.

"I don't believe it," Eric said through sniffles. "All these years, I thought you were dead."

"I have been in a way," Mr. Greene said. "I've been down here this whole time."

"How come they've kept you down here, alive?" Eric asked.

"Information," Mr. Greene said. His voice shook with emotion. "There are still a lot of the historical documents they need help with and I'm the only one who knows it."

"Why did they take you?" Eric asked.

"It's a long story, Eric," Mr. Greene said. "It had to do with my research into your mom's condition."

"I thought mom had cancer?" Eric asked.

"That's what they originally thought, but after working with some of the medical staff and doing some tests, it was something else entirely. It was a disease they had never seen before. I kept looking into it and found some others who had died in different cities that had the same symptoms as your mother." Mr. Greene sighed. "After going back about fifty years, I noticed that the number of deaths from the disease was steadily increasing. Of course, they kept covering it up, making up all sorts of excuses. I told them a cure needed to be found and that something had to be done or it could end up being an epidemic."

"And they didn't care?" I asked. I didn't mean to butt into

the conversation, but I was curious.

"No," Mr. Greene said. "They told me to keep quiet. But I just couldn't let it go. Something had to be done."

"That's why they took you? So you wouldn't tell people about this disease?" Eric asked. That seemed so extreme to me.

"More or less. There was also the prophecy issue," Mr. Greene said.

"What prophecy issue?" I asked.

"Well, you see, there's a prophecy …" Mr. Greene started.

I laughed. "Oh, we know about the prophecy. That's all I've been hearing about lately."

"Oh, well, I had brought up that I hoped the prophecy would come true so then something could be done." Mr. Greene coughed, his throat dry and raspy. He probably hadn't talked this much in a long time. "I also said I'd be the first one to sign up to help the one who will lead the revolution."

"I'm sorry to tell you, Dad, but you aren't the first one to sign up," Eric said.

"What do you mean? Has the revolution already started?" Mr. Greene asked.

"Well, we're trying to get it started, but we keep getting stopped," Eric said. "But they have the one who they think the prophecy is talking about."

"Who?" Mr. Greene asked.

"Me," I said.

Mr. Greene sucked in a sharp breath. "Oh, well, that explains everything you were talking about with the president. You have quite the little fire in you, young lady."

"Thanks," I said, laughing. "It's too bad my fire isn't big

enough to get us out of here, though."

"I do have a question," Mr. Greene said. "I heard the president call Eric your boyfriend. Is that so?"

I smiled. "Uh …"

"Yes, it's so," came Eric's response. I could hear a smile in his voice.

"Well, then I need to be properly introduced," Mr. Greene said.

Eric laughed. "Okay, Dad, this is my girlfriend, Emmie, and Emmie, this is my father, Alexander."

"It's nice to meet you, Emmie," Mr. Greene said.

"You, too, Mr. Greene," I said. "I hope I get to see you in person before this is all said and done."

"That would be nice, Emmie. But I must insist on you calling me Alexander."

"Then Alexander it is," I said. Dad coughed. "Sorry, Dad. Alexander, this is my father, Philip Woodard, and Dad, this is Alexander."

"I hope my son has been a gentleman to your daughter," Alexander said, "even though they're probably too young to be dating."

I smiled. Of course, a dad would think seventeen was too young to date.

"He's been wonderful to my Emmie." Dad chuckled. "Well, at least for the few hours I've known him."

Alexander laughed at that. "Good to hear."

"Alexander," I said. "You should also know that my two best friends are down here, too. Dee and Tina."

"Hi," both Tina and Dee said.

"Hello," Alexander said.

"I think this is the weirdest conversation I've ever had," Eric said.

With that, we all laughed. It was strange to think that only a couple of weeks earlier the idea of a boyfriend was nonexistent. I'd never dated anyone before, and I didn't have any interest. It all seemed so complicated and not worth the trouble. And now here I was, sitting hogtied in a cell, with a boyfriend, meeting his dad who we originally thought was dead but was sitting in another cell, and soon we would all be executed.

Life never turns out the way you think it will.

CHAPTER 42

An hour later, the door to the holding cells opened. As footsteps came down the hall, a sudden pang of dread washed over me. This was it. In just a short while, I would watch everyone I love die, followed by my own death. I tried over and over again to tell myself that it had all been worth it, but now that the time had come, I wasn't so sure. At least I would never have to eat peas again.

Someone unlocked my cell. I looked up to see Dean Johnson. The corner of his mouth turned up, forming an evil smile. "You know, Pierce and I flipped for who got to be the one to take you out of here. I won."

I thought about responding, but I wanted to try a new method: keeping my mouth shut. Dean grabbed me around my waist and lifted me up, placing me on his hip. He carried me out of the cell and down the hall like it was nothing.

Tina was in front of me, being held by Mack. Pierce had Dad by the arm, and he didn't look too happy about it. I figured Eric and Dee were behind me.

All of us were quiet as they took us to another room. It was a large, concrete room. Seeing all the concrete brought me back to the room I was locked in with Luke, Will, David, and Skinny. The thought of Luke hurt my heart. I had wanted him to come with us and support what we were doing, but with my death only moments away, I realized he was going to be the lucky one in all of this. He was going to survive.

Whit was waiting for us when we came in. Dean cut the cord connecting my feet and hands and threw me down on my butt. Then he reconnected my feet and hands, only this time in front of me so I could at least sit up.

Frank lay unconscious on the floor on the other side of the room. They sat Tina down next to him, then Dee, then Dad, and then Eric. I assumed it was the order in which they would die. I shook the thought from my head.

Mack, Pierce, Dean, and five other security guys stood near the door, their arms folded across their chests. A big chair sat in the middle of the room. There were straps on the arms, which I figured were to hold our arms down. There were straps near the feet, too. A cord ran from the chair to the wall, where it had been plugged in. Straight above the plug was a small lever.

"Welcome to the electrocution room, everyone," Whit said with a smile. He stood next to the chair, resting his hand on the top of it. "I'm so glad all of you could make it here today for this historic event. It's been so long since we've been able to use the electric chair, so I was excited about this opportunity to make use of it. I hope you don't mind, but I got a historian to come today to make note of this unique experience." Whit turned his head toward the door and nodded at Dean.

Dean went out the door and came back in with an older man. From the intake of breath from Eric, I figured it must have been his dad, Alexander. He was tall like Eric, but he had long gray hair. I didn't know what he looked like before, but it seemed being down in the cell had aged him. His eyes were tired, and he moved slowly. Slouched over, he shuffled into the room, keeping his eyes on the ground. There were fresh bruises on his face. Dean sat him on the floor near the security guards, which gave him a good view of the electric chair.

"Thanks for joining us today, Alexander," Whit said to him. "I hope your reunion with your son was sufficient." He turned to me. "We all know why we're here. I don't want to drag this on since I have a lot of meetings today. Before we begin, do you have anything you would like to say, Emelia?"

I stared at him, willing myself to be quiet. There was nothing I could say to stop it. I needed to take action, but the odds were stacked against us. How could we get out of here alive? I couldn't go down without a fight, though. For the moment, all I could do was look at Whit with all the hatred in the world as I tried to think things through.

Whit laughed. "Well, if that isn't a first!"

Dean and Pierce gave out a small laugh. I looked at Mack, but he stared straight ahead, no emotion behind his eyes.

"Since you have nothing to say, let's get started." Whit turned to Dean. "Let's start with Frank."

Dean grabbed Frank, dragging him to the electric chair. He sat him in the chair, strapping down his wrists and ankles. He took a strap from behind the chair and wrapped it around

Frank's chest. Dean opened a vial and put it below Frank's nose, waking him from his unconscious stupor. Frank looked around, bewildered.

Whit placed his hand on Frank's shoulder. “It’s a real shame to have to mark this down in the Oliver family legacy. To think of all the things your ancestors did for this city and this is how you repay them? With betrayal?”

Frank looked up at Whit and said something, but his voice was hoarse. Whit leaned his ear in close to him. “What was that, Frank? I can't hear you.” Whit turned to Dean. “Let's get the man some water, please. I would love to hear what he has to say.”

Dean left the room and returned a minute later with a bucket of water. He went up to Frank, throwing the water all over his body. “Refreshing, isn't it?” Dean said, shaking out the remaining drops of water over Frank's head.

Frank shook his head back and forth, trying to get some of the water out of his eyes. He looked up at Whit and cleared his throat.

“You always say that everything you do is for River Springs,” Frank said, anger in his voice, “but you do the exact opposite. Everything you do is for the benefit of you and only you. The people of this city deserve better.” He practically spat those last words out. I had never seen Frank so fired up. It made my respect for him go up more.

Whit backhanded Frank across the face and then leaned in close. “You’re pathetic, you know that, Frank? You’ve never had the courage and backbone it takes to run a city. You’re too soft. I’m really surprised it isn’t one of your kids the prophecy talks about. I'm just hoping that Austin will be a better leader than you."

"My son will never, ever be like you, Whit. I raised him better than that."

Whit raised his hand to strike Frank again, but there was a sound at the door.

"Am I late?" Amber pushed her way into the room and glanced around, panicked. Relief washed over her when her eyes settled on me. "Oh, good, I didn't miss it."

Dean smiled, though it seemed strained. I wondered if he knew that his daughter was a psychopath. "Amber, sweetie, what are you doing here?"

"I came to watch the execution," Amber said, looking baffled by the question.

Whit grimaced. "How did you find out about this?" His eyes went over to Dean.

"It's not my dad's fault," Amber said quickly. "I overheard him talking with the security guards."

Whit looked at Pierce. "Get her out of here."

When Pierce stepped toward her, Amber jumped back. "No! I want to watch."

"Amber," Dean said, stepping toward her, "you need to leave." By the expression on his face, I could have sworn he was frightened by his daughter.

She glared at him, her eyes full of hate. "No! I want to watch her die!"

Pierce took her by the arms and dragged her toward the door. Amber kicked and thrashed, yelling the whole time. "No! I want to see Emmie die! I want to pull the lever!"

"Get her out!" Whit yelled.

Pierce threw her out of the room and slammed the door shut. Amber immediately pounded on the door, demanding to come back in.

Whit straightened his tie and continued like nothing had happened. "Now, Frank, do you have any last words?" He stepped back from the chair. Dean had moved over to the lever on the wall, his hand anxiously waiting for the go-ahead.

"You disgust me, Whit," Frank said. "I'm ashamed that I stood so many years next to you and didn't do anything to stop you. You won't get what you want in the end. You'll lose, Whit. I'm just sad I won't be there to witness it."

Whit stood there for a moment before he said anything. "Dean, you may begin." He didn't take his eyes off Frank.

Dean smiled and tightened his grip on the lever. He was about to pull it down when I couldn't take it anymore.

"STOP!" I yelled. Everyone turned to me. "Please, stop. Don't do this. This is crazy. No one needs to die." I needed to stall. We had to get out of here. I didn't want to die like this. I didn't want my family and friends to die like this.

"You need to be punished for your actions, Emelia," Whit said.

"I'll do whatever you want," I said, desperate to save the ones I loved. "Please, just tell me what you want me to do and I'll do it. I'll be on my best behavior from now on. I'll go along with all your rules and won't put up a fight."

"It's too late for that, Emelia. You had your chance and you blew it." Whit's face was stone cold.

"But this isn't their fault," I said, looking at my friends and family. It had all been my doing. They didn't need to be punished for my stubbornness. I got up on my knees and scooted closer to him.

"It is their fault," Whit said. "They all had a choice and they chose to disrespect me and everything River Springs stands for." Whit's hands balled into fists. "Dean, pull the lever!"

With that, Dean slammed the lever down, springing the electric chair into action. I threw my body forward but ended up falling since I was tied up.

A blur of motion came from the right of me. Eric and Tina had both jumped forward too, as if our small action could stop it.

All I could hear was Frank's screams. I looked away, not wanting to watch. I squirmed, trying to make my way toward the chair, but Dean pulled me back. A burning smell filled the air, making my stomach churn. I did this. Because of me, Frank was going to be dead in a matter of seconds. And I still had four more to listen to.

Suddenly the lights flickered. There were a few popping sounds and then the lights went out, shutting down the chair. I would've had some hope for Frank's life, but he had stopped screaming before the lights went out.

CHAPTER 43

I sat in the dark, stunned by what had just happened. My heart hammered through my chest and my thoughts raced so fast, I couldn't pin any of them down. Shouting and loud thuds surrounded me, but I wasn't paying close attention. Frank Oliver was dead. He had risked so much to help and I would never be able to repay that debt.

I was so shaken up it took me a while to realize someone was trying to pull me up. Somehow, my hands and feet had been freed. I tried to concentrate on what was happening when I heard a voice.

"Emmie, we need to leave, now." It was Mack. He pulled me up onto my feet. "Can you walk on your own?"

I nodded, but then realized he couldn't see me since the lights were still out. "Yes," I said, my voice barely a whisper. He took my arm, guiding me through the room. "Wait. What about the vice president?"

"He's dead, Emmie," Mack said. "We need to get out of here."

"Not without Frank. Dead or not, I'm not leaving his body here with these monsters." I couldn't imagine how they would dispose of his body.

Mack hesitated a second before responding. "Stay right here, I'll get him."

As I stood there waiting in the dark, some footsteps came behind me. Someone bumped into me, making me stumble forward.

"Sorry!" Dee said.

"It's okay, Dee, it's Emmie. Is everyone else free?"

Voices replied, first Eric, then Tina, and then my dad.

"Eric, where's your dad?" I asked.

"I'm right here," Alexander responded from the right of me.

"We need to leave! Now!" The voice came from a few feet away.

"Steven?" I was so surprised to hear his voice.

"Yes, it's Steven, and we need to leave before everyone regains consciousness. Get the lights back on now!"

"What?" I asked.

"Oh, sorry, I was talking to someone else," Steven said.

A few seconds later the lights came back on. Whit, Dean, Pierce, and three other guards were lying on the floor, unconscious. Two other guards were standing over them. By the way they were panting, they had been responsible for knocking everyone down. The door had been opened and Amber's unconscious body lay outside.

"Let's go," Mack said. He held Frank's body over his shoulder.

"Is he …?" I couldn't finish the sentence. Just looking at him confirmed it.

"Not yet," Mack said.

I didn't hide my surprise. "But he looks like he's dead."

"I felt a small pulse, but who knows how long it will stay," Mack said.

"We don't have time for small talk!" Steven yelled, rubbing his head, looking scared.

I didn't blame him. I would be scared if I had just participated in knocking out the president of River Springs and some of his security. He looked over the unconscious bodies on the floor, his eyes stopping when he saw Amber. He almost looked pained.

"Lead the way, Steven," Mack said. When Steven just kept staring at Amber, Mack cleared his throat and spoke louder. "Steven, lead the way."

Steven looked at Mack and snapped back to reality. He turned around and left the room. We all hurried toward the door, following Steven wherever he turned. He must have been talking to someone with a communication device, or he was just plain crazy and talking to himself. He had a bag slung across his back and he kept pulling at the strap as he walked.

"Now what?" Steven asked. He made a right, leading us to some stairs. He headed up and we all did the same. "When we get to the top, where do we go?" Steven paused, waiting for a response. "Yeah, okay. Have all the other security guards been distracted? Good. Okay. We should be out there soon. Is everything ready?"

When we got to the top of the stairs, Steven led us through

some more halls and then out a door. We stepped outside, the change in temperature startling. It was freezing and the clouds overhead threatened with snow.

"We're outside now. We'll meet you there," Steven said to his imaginary friend.

We continued to follow Steven, the frosty air stinging against my face and arms. I was still wearing my short sleeve shirt from being in the infirmary.

We soon arrived in front of the Recruitment Center. A bus waited near the front door of the Center with Eric's cousin, Richie, leaning against the bus. The nurse that had helped me out in the infirmary stood on the steps inside the bus. I think she had told me her name was Marie, but I was out of it when she treated me.

"It's about time!" Richie called out. "We need to get going. The change of guards around the outside fence will be changing in twenty minutes and we have nothing arranged with them."

"It's at least a half-hour to the gate from here," Dad said as we approached the bus.

Richie smiled. "But I'm driving."

Eric walked up to Richie, slapping him on the shoulder. "What are you doing here?"

"Marie approached me and told me you needed a way out of here," Richie said. "Of course, I couldn't say no when she told me you were one of the people leaving."

"How do you know Marie?" I asked.

"We were in Recruitment together," Marie said, smiling at me. "How are you feeling?"

I tucked my hair behind my ear. "I'll feel much better when we're out of here." I gave her a warm smile. "But overall I'm doing much better, thanks to you."

"Glad I could help," Marie said.

Marie went inside the bus so we could get in. Richie hopped on the bus and we all followed. As I walked past him, he winked at me. "Nice to see you again, Emmie."

"You, too, Richie," I said. Eric and I sat down on a bench in the front.

"Marie, we need your help," Mack said, taking Frank to her.

As Mack laid Frank on the floor of the bus, Marie's eyes became wide. "What happened to him?"

"The electric chair," Mack said.

As Marie went to work on Frank, everyone else sat down and Richie booked it toward the gate.

I looked at Mack. "Where are the other guards who helped us out?"

"They didn't want to leave their families," Mack said.

"What about your family?" I asked.

Mack shook his head. "I don't have one." He looked down at Frank, closing the conversation.

Eric put his arm around me and rubbed my cold arm for warmth. "How are you holding up?"

I looked at Frank unconscious on the floor. "Not too well." I buried my head in Eric's chest, not wanting to face the reality of what was happening.

"Come on, Frank," Mack yelled from the floor. He had kneeled next to him. "Come on!"

Eric hugged me tight, continuing to rub his hand up and down my arm.

Mack swore and then pound his fist against a bench. I turned and looked at Marie. Her face said it all.

"I'm sorry," she said, looking up at me. "I did everything I could, but it was too late."

I removed myself from Eric's warm embrace and knelt on the floor next to Frank. I took his cold hand in mine and hung my head down. "I'm so sorry, Frank," I whispered. I lay my head on his chest and sobbed.

I couldn't believe it had come down to this. We had lost a wonderful man, and for what? Control? Power? It was all Whit's fault. And I was going to make him pay for it if it was the last thing I did.

With Richie's fast driving, we arrived at the gate with only a couple minutes to spare.

Mack bent down next to me on the floor. "We need to leave, Emmie," he said as softly as he could.

"What about Frank? We can't just leave him here." I stared at his lifeless body on the floor.

"I'll take care of him," Richie said from the front of the bus.

"You aren't coming with us?" Eric asked.

"No," Richie said. "I have a pregnant wife to think of. As much as I agree with what you're doing, I can't risk their lives."

Eric nodded in understanding.

"Don't worry, Emmie, I'll make sure he gets a proper burial," Richie said to me.

"Thanks, Richie." I bent down and kissed Frank on the cheek and then stood. As we walked to the front of the bus, someone came up the steps.

"What's taking so long? The next guard is almost here." The person stopped at the top of the stairs. He smiled when he saw me. "Hey sister from another mister!"

"Derek?" I couldn't believe it. He had been the one helping that whole time? "So, I guess you heard."

"Yup. It explains so much about you," Derek said. "Now we need to get going." He counted our heads. "Where's VP Oliver?"

I looked down at the ground, unable to speak. Mack was standing right behind me.

"He didn't make it," Mack said.

Derek's face paled. "What?"

"He died before we could stop it," Mack said.

Derek looked like he might throw up. He clasped his hands on the top of his head. "I tried to shut off the power as soon as I could. There were so many security guards to get through and distract."

"It's not your fault," Mack said.

"I tried to do it in under twenty seconds," Derek said. He looked at Mack. "I thought you said that was the maximum amount of time I had from when the chair was turned on."

Mack looked down at Frank and swore. "It should've been. He could have survived it. But Dean ended up throwing water all over him before it started, which must have sped up the process."

"We don't have time for chit chat!" Steven yelled. He

rubbed his head so hard, I thought the small amount of hair that was there would fall off.

Mack pushed me from the back, making me walk forward. When we all stepped off the bus, Richie took off, going back a different way than we came. The gate guard came up to us.

"Everything you need has already been thrown over. We got together as many supplies as we could. There are winter jackets, gloves, and beanies for everyone over there." The guard pointed to a pile on the ground.

We all went over and got one of each, putting them on. It helped block the cold somewhat. It was going to be a long winter.

Mack turned to Eric. "You go first. I'll help everyone else up and then you can help them down." Mack handed Eric a blanket. "Put this over the barbed wire on top."

Eric nodded. "Sounds good." He climbed up the chain-link fence and put the blanket in place. He swung his body over and climbed down. I had a feeling it wasn't going to be as graceful for everyone else.

I looked beyond the gate and saw an endless number of trees. I had never been that close to the gate before. Once we got over, we would be alone in a forest, with absolutely no survival skills. I desperately hoped that we would all make it to our destination alive.

Dee and Tina followed, both making it easily over the fence. We had a harder time with my dad and especially Alexander. Eric ended up climbing back up so he could hold on to his dad as they climbed down.

Marie went over the fence next and then Steven. Derek

turned to me. "Illegitimate children first, of course."

"You're such a gentleman," I said, smacking him upside the head. To my surprise, Derek pulled me into a hug.

"I'm glad you're okay," Derek said quietly, so only I could hear. Not that there were many people left standing next to us. I squeezed him back and then pulled away.

"Don't go all soft on me now," I said. "The love/hate relationship, with more emphasis on the hate, has always worked so well for us."

Derek laughed. "Yeah, I guess you're right. Now get up there."

I climbed as quickly as I could, with Derek right behind me. My broken thumb slowed me down a little. Mack was the last one over. Right when he landed on the ground, a vehicle approached the gate. The next guard was coming.

"Everyone grab a bag and run into the forest!" Mack yelled. As we grabbed the bags, yelling sounded behind me.

"Stop!" It must have been the new guard who yelled at us, but we kept running, disappearing into the trees. A few loud shots rang out and I turned to see the guard who had helped us fall onto the ground.

"No!" I yelled, stopping. Mack took me by my waist and pulled me back.

"There's nothing you can do, Emmie," Mack said as he carried my body through the trees. The other guard continued to shoot at us. I stared into his eyes until we were swallowed up by the forest, hidden from his view.

We ran for a little while longer and then Mack halted us. He put me down on my feet. "Is anyone hit?"

"I think I got grazed by a bullet," Steven said, pointing to his left arm. His jacket had been torn, blood forming on the exposed area.

Mack went up to examine it. "It's just a flesh wound. You'll be fine. Marie, do you have something you can place on it?"

"Yes," Marie said, pulling out some bandages from her bag. She put some liquid on his arm, causing Steven to squirm a little. "Sorry, this stuff can sting." She placed a bandage over his wound.

"No kidding," Steven said. He looked over at me, his eyes full of sorrow. "Emmie, I … I …"

"Don't worry about it, Steven," I said. "You did what you had to do."

Steven clenched his jaw, sucking in his breath a little from the pain of his wound. "He threatened my family. Otherwise, I wouldn't have spied on you like that."

"Whit threatened them?" I asked. It didn't surprise me. The man had turned out to be more calculating than I'd originally thought.

"Whit?" Derek asked me, his eyebrows raised.

"He doesn't deserve the title of president." I looked at Steven. "How's your family?"

"Dead," Steven said, choking back tears. "He killed my parents and my sister. That's why I'm here. I couldn't stay one more day in that place."

I walked up to Steven, putting my hand on his arm. "Steven, I'm so sorry." When he started to cry, I pulled him into a hug. "You know none of this is your fault, right? It's all his fault. He did this to all of us."

"I know," Steven said, his head buried in my hair. "I know."

Mack cleared his throat. "Listen, I know this is hard for everyone, but we need to get as far away as we can today. They'll be sending search crews soon."

"He's right," Dad said.

I pulled back from Steven and looked him in the eye. "We're going to make him pay, Steven, for everything he has done to our families. I promise you."

Steven let out a little laugh and wiped away his tears. He took off his beanie and rubbed the top of his head. "I don't know why, but I believe you."

As we walked deeper into the forest, the cold became unbearable. We tried to go as fast as we could, but Alexander slowed us down. He was still weak from being held captive for so long.

At nightfall, Mack found a spot for us to sleep for the night. He didn't want to start a fire to alert anyone where we were, so we all slept huddled together, trying to keep warm through the night.

As I slept that night, I had the same dream I had when I was 'dead'. Only this time, the two blurry faces became clear. It was Alexander and Derek. At the end of the dream when Frank Oliver blew the flower out of his hand, he turned to me and smiled, gesturing to the valley below as he disappeared.

I woke up crying, thinking about Frank and all that he had sacrificed for us. Eric pulled me close and wrapped his arms around me. I hoped in the end it would all be worth it.

A thought came to my mind and I wasn't sure if I should be worried about it or not. Steven and Marie weren't in my dream, but they were there with us. They were the two people I knew the least, and one had betrayed me before.

As I lay there, curled up in Eric's arms, I said a silent prayer in my heart that everything would be okay. That I could trust Steven and Marie and that the only reason they weren't in my dream was because I never thought they'd be there to begin with.

All I could do was hope.

CHAPTER 44

The next few weeks were torturous. We had a small amount of food to feed the ten of us and most nights we couldn't find shelter, so we had to just sleep out in the open. It took ten days before Mack would let us light a fire. And even then, it was small.

Alexander was still weak and the climate and terrain weren't helping the situation. After twenty-five days, I was exhausted, dirty, and just plain ornery.

I think all of us were still digesting everything that had happened because we hardly spoke about River Springs during those weeks. We probably should've been coming up with a game plan, but when you're out in the wild, with nothing to look forward to, it was hard to be optimistic. We would soon run out of food. We had no promise of finding a permanent establishment. Even if we did, we didn't have the skills or tools to build one up.

I had noticed one thing along the way: Tina was very flirtatious with Steven, and even worse, my brother. So gross.

It wasn't until the fourteenth day that I got the chance to talk with her without any guys around.

We'd found a river, surprisingly not frozen through. It probably wasn't the best idea, but all the girls wanted to wash off. It had warmed up a little for a couple of days, so we took advantage of the opportunity.

We left the guys and found a highly covered place along the river. Stripping down to our underwear, we took the plunge. We didn't last in there very long, but it was enough to make me feel a little better. As we were trying to dry off and redress, I finally spoke up.

"So, Tina, you seem a little cozy with Steven and Derek," I said, looking at her.

Tina just shrugged. "There's nothing wrong with a little flirting." I could tell from her eyes that there was more behind it than just flirting.

"A little?" Dee laughed. "More like a lot." Marie nodded in agreement.

"It's no big deal," Tina said, wringing out her hair.

"I think it is," I said, doing the same with mine. "I guess I could understand Steven. But Derek? That's just wrong."

"Not all of us have lived with him our whole lives and have a biased view," Tina snapped. "He's actually quite nice."

"Now that's crazy talk," Dee said.

I looked at Tina. "I'm sorry."

"Sorry for what?" Tina asked.

I sighed. "Tina, I know this is about Luke. You can talk to us, you know. We'd understand. You've had a crush on the guy for years and now you may never see him again."

Tina sat down and leaned up against a tree. “I guess deep down inside I was hoping he would open his eyes and see what was going on around him. To see we were on the right side. He’s just so brainwashed by his father. Half of the time I don’t know if he's speaking his own mind, or what his father would want him to say.”

I sat down next to her, taking her hand. “I wish there was a way we could talk to him. To shake him until he understood River Springs is completely crazy and wrong.”

Tina’s mouth curled up a little. “Me, too. I know he’s a good guy. I just wish he were here.”

“He may not know everything that's going on, Tina,” Dee said. She and Marie had sat down next to us. “We never had the chance to talk to him, so anything he heard about what happened, he would’ve heard from his dad. And I’m sure that his dad would've gone out of his way to make us look like the bad guys.”

I didn't bring up the fact that I had talked with Luke. It wasn't in great length, but it was enough to get the point across. But I didn't think telling Tina right now was the best idea.

“It doesn’t make it easier,” Tina said, wiping tears from her eyes.

“I know. It’s going to be hard for a while. But we’re all here for you.” I stroked her hand with my thumb. “Just do me a favor and lay off my brother. We already have hardly anything to eat, I don’t want to be throwing up the tiny amount I’m allowed to have.”

“He’s not that bad,” Marie said. Dee and I turned to her and raised our eyebrows. Marie shrugged. “What? He isn’t.”

"In his defense, he is only mean to me," I said. "I guess when I look at him, all I see is all the teasing he's done to me throughout the years. The thought of someone liking him as a person is completely insane to me."

"He's good with technology, too," Marie said. "I got to work with him a little when we were trying to figure out how to get out of River Springs. He's quite the genius."

Dee and I laughed.

"Okay, now you're just pushing it," I said through my laughs. Once I got myself under control, I looked at Marie. "How did you get involved in all of this?"

Marie ran her fingers through her wet hair, trying to untangle and smooth it out. "Mack approached me after they captured all of you in the cave. He was upset about what happened and wanted to put a stop to it. He had already talked with Derek and Steven, telling them to find an escape route for all of us. He wanted me to come along, so you'd have a nurse."

"And you agreed that fast?" I asked.

Maybe I should've had Mack talk to Luke and then he would've been there with us.

Marie nodded. "I hate the president as much as you do. Mack and I lived next door to each other growing up. He's ten years older than me, but he always watched out for me like a little sister. I was the nurse Mack and the rest of security would come to when the president did something to cause harm or injury to one of our residents. I saw way more than I wanted to. When Mack told me there was a way out, I jumped at the opportunity."

"Well, I'm glad you did," I said. "Your skills will definitely come in handy." I was also glad to hear that Mack trusted her. It put my mind at ease about having her there with us.

Marie let out a sigh. "I'm a little worried about Mack. He's not one to show much emotion, but I know the death of the vice president is upsetting him. He holds himself responsible."

"Mack needs to realize he can't take responsibility for everything bad that happens," I said.

"That's the way he is," Marie said. "I know he wishes we could have stopped it faster, but we had so little warning. We were scrambling to come up with supplies and a way to get out. I know Derek and Steven tried to stop it as fast as they could, but the president is secretive. There were a lot of things he hadn't told Derek about yet since he is so new to the staff. Derek had to figure out himself where the controls were for the electrocution room and how to turn them off."

"Wow," Dee said. "Way to go, Derek."

Tina nudged me. "Told you he wasn't that bad."

"Just be grateful he stopped it when he did," Marie said. "It could've turned out a lot worse."

When we got back to the camp that we had made the night before, we found the guys packing everything back up.

"You girls have a good time?" Eric asked.

"Yes, we did," I said.

"How was the water?" Dad asked.

"So cold!" Dee said, rubbing her arms for warmth. "So, so cold!"

"But refreshing," Marie said.

"Now that you girls are back, we should talk," Mack said. He was sitting on a log next to the fire. When all of us sat down, he spoke. "We should only have about a week left until we reach our destination. We need to make sure we ration the food to last us until then."

"What are we going to do when we get there?" Derek asked.

"Yeah, what's even there?" Steven asked.

"I don't know much," Mack said. "Frank just told me it was a safe haven that was found. He said it would be a good starting place for a new city."

"There are only ten of us," Tina said as she warmed up her hands over the fire. "That isn't much of a city."

"It's a start," Alexander said. He hadn't talked much during the trip, but when he did, it came out slow and shaky. "Even the city we just came from had to start from nothing. It'll be a slow process, but it can be done."

"I'm hoping once we get settled there and the springtime comes, we can send a few of us to River Springs and round up some more people," Mack said. "I know there are others who would like to get away."

"The more people we can get, the better." Dad poked at the fire with a stick, causing the flames to flare. "I'm sure the president won't give up looking until he finds us. And the ten of us won't cause a threat and be able to fight back long."

"What if we do get attacked?" Marie asked. "What are we going to do?"

Mack glanced at a bag near him. He'd kept it close to him the whole trip. "I have a few weapons, but not much. I would like to teach everyone how to use them. I would also like to start doing self-defense training. I want you all to be able to fight back if you get attacked."

"I have some technical equipment I brought with me to get our new city started," Derek said, pointing to the bag next to him. "With it, we should be able to know in advance if we're about to be attacked. Of course, we would need power, so unless this place we're going to has electricity, it will be of no use to us."

I sighed. "This is going to be so much work. It seems so impossible."

"It's not impossible, Emmie," Mack said. "It will be hard, yes, but we can do it. We just need to get there in one piece." Mack stood and went over to the food supply. He pulled out some granola bars and tossed them to everyone. "Let's eat and then get going."

As we were eating our breakfast, there was a snap of a twig behind me. I turned around, the sight making my eyes go wide.

Someone stood there in the shadows with a bow and arrow pointed at us. There were a few more snaps and I looked all around us.

We were surrounded.

CHAPTER 45

All of us stood, backing into a circle. The person pulled his bow back more, ready to release it at any moment.

"Don't move!" another guy yelled. It came from behind me, so I couldn't turn to see who had said it, but he sounded older.

Instinctively, we all put up our arms, showing we had no weapons of our own and we meant no harm.

"Who are you?" It was the same voice as before.

"We should be asking you the same question," Mack said, his tone steady and confident.

The person in front of me stepped forward from the shadows, putting their bow and arrow away. I lowered my hands and smiled.

Running toward him, I threw my arms around his neck. "Dante. I'm so happy to see you." I pulled back. "You had me worried. You disappeared after the tree fell."

Dante smiled back at me. "It's good to see you, too." He looked past me at the others with him. "Lower your weapons.

I know Emmie."

"Emmie?" Wallace stepped into view. "Sorry, I didn't see you earlier." He looked at Dante. "You recognized her, yet still drew your weapon?"

Dante's smile twisted. "I wanted to scare her, that's all."

I punched him playfully in the arm. "Thanks a lot. It worked, by the way. I thought I might pee my pants." I folded my arms. "What happened?"

As everyone else sat down and started talking, Dante pulled me off to the side. "I ran after that person who was near the tree. Turns out it was a member of River Springs security. Someone else had been with him and together they rigged the tree to fall. When President Randall found out I knew, he ordered for me and my dad to be killed. Frank was able to help us escape."

Wallace came up to us. "Where's Frank, anyway? He contacted me weeks ago, telling me that we needed to meet you here, but I haven't been able to get a hold of him. His phone's been disconnected."

My face fell. "I'm sorry to have to be the one to tell you this, but Frank's dead."

"What?" Wallace asked. "How?"

"Whit." The word came out sharp and hateful.

Wallace shook his head. "That's too bad. Frank was a good man." He looked at Mack and the others. "We should all talk."

After Mack introduced all of us, Wallace introduced his group. There were eight others that I could see, two of them girls. Besides Dante, there was Terrance who looked to be in his early thirties and built like Mack. Vivica, who was Wallace's daughter, looked to be in her early twenties and was absolutely stunning. Tall, slender, with skin darker than her dad's, her black hair had been pulled back in a ponytail. She also looked strong enough to kick the crap out of anyone who got in her way.

Then there was Naomi, who looked to be in her late teens. She was their technical and security pro. She had a very pretty face, but she seemed insecure about herself. Although, she was standing next to Vivica and anyone would be insecure standing next to her.

There was also Archibald, who preferred to go by Archie. He looked to be in his late teens and was very tall and very, very thin.

James looked like he was in his late thirties. He was their scholar and looked the part. His black hair was perfectly styled, he had glasses, and he was very proper.

Charles was in his late twenties. He had a handsome face, was very toned, and apparently had amazing accuracy with his bow and arrow.

Lastly, there was Lou, James' son. He was only fourteen years old and had the cutest smile. He seemed very shy, especially around girls. He kept his hand in his pockets and his eyes on the ground.

Once all the introductions were made, we all sat down. Charles stayed standing near a tree and kept glancing behind him.

Wallace must have noticed Charles. "Charles, I think it's safe to bring her out here." Charles nodded hesitantly and walked into the trees.

He came back a minute later with a young woman in his arms. Marie immediately jumped up and went over to her.

"What's wrong with her?" Marie asked him.

Charles looked at Marie, unsure whether he should talk to her or not.

"Tell her, Charles," Wallace said.

"She tripped a couple of days ago on a rock," Charles said. "She has a huge gash in her leg. It doesn't look good."

"Set her down over here," Marie said, pointing to an open area. She went over to her bag and got her medical kit out. When she got back to the woman, she felt her forehead. "She has a fever. What's her name?"

"Denise," Charles said. "She's my wife."

Marie ripped open Denise's pant leg to reveal the gash. Marie let out a little gasp. "It's badly infected." She pulled out her supplies and cleaned the wound. I couldn't watch what she was doing; my stomach couldn't handle it. Charles looked sick watching it, but he held tightly to Denise's hand and wouldn't leave her side.

"While they work on that, we should talk," Wallace said. "I'd been expecting all of you a few days ago."

"We've had some setbacks," Mack said, shooting a quick look at Alexander.

Eric's dad was doing much better but still hadn't gained back his full strength. I began to wonder if he ever would. Who knows all the things Whit did to him while he was held captive?

"Emmie," Dante said, "have you realized you're the revolutionary for your city?"

I shrugged. "Everyone seems to think so. It's hard to wrap my head around it."

Dante sat next to me. He put his hand on my arm. "You'll get used to it. It took me a while to accept it."

Eric looked at Dante. "Did you have a prophecy, too?"

"Yes, and so did the other two cities out there," Wallace said. He leaned forward and rested his forearms on his knees. When Wallace saw the look on our all faces, he smiled. "I was hoping Frank would be here to help explain it all, but it looks like I'm on my own."

Marie had just finished bandaging up Denise, so Charles brought her over to sit with the rest of us. Once everyone was situated, Wallace continued.

"I'm sure River Springs has its own version of what happened years ago just like our city does. Now I will tell you the full story. Well, at least the full story I know. I'm sure information has been lost or twisted over the years.

"As I'm sure you know, years ago the world became corrupt. The entire world was destroyed except a small region of what was once known as the United States. Four men were trying to figure out how to run things. That many heads working together, as you can imagine, didn't go very well. They ended up deciding that it was in the best interest of those left to divide into separate autonomous cities. Not long after the divide, a person from each city had the same prophecy."

"What else did the prophecy say?" I asked Wallace, scooting closer to Eric. It was freezing. He wrapped his arm around me and pulled me close. Dante raised his eyebrows at us.

"Well," Wallace said, "it said that there would be one from each city that would try to lead others astray. In the end, all four of them would come together to start something bigger. To make a drastic change."

"To start a war," Alexander said quietly.

"Yes." Wallace nodded gravely. "To start a war."

"War?" I shook my head in disbelief. "We're supposed to start a war? There are only twenty of us."

"For now," Wallace said. "We should be joined up by the other cities soon. And we hope to enlist more from each of our cities. It'll be a slow process. I'm not saying that we're going to war tomorrow. But over the next few years, we'll continue to grow, and continue to build. The wheels are already set in motion. We can only pray that we can get situated before any of the presidents find us and attack."

"So, these other cities, are they meeting us here?" Tina asked. She and Dee were huddled together near me and Eric.

"Not yet," Wallace said. "Frank and I arranged for our two cities to rendezvous here and then continue through the mountain."

"Through the mountain?" Derek asked. He had been staring at Naomi the whole time. Either she didn't notice, or she was doing a good job of ignoring him.

Wallace pointed behind him. "Only a few miles from here, we'll come up to the edge of the mountain. There's a canyon that we'll take leading us through it."

"How long will it take to get through?" Dad asked. He had noticed Derek staring at Naomi and rolled his eyes.

"As long as the weather doesn't get too bad, should be a

little over a week," said Wallace. "The other two cities will be coming from the other side. We should still get there first, though. One of the other cities had a … problem arise."

"A problem like ours?" I asked grimly.

"Worse," Wallace said. He shivered, but it wasn't from the cold.

The thought of something worse than what Whit did made me sick. What kind of people were out there in the world? How could a person get filled with so much hate that they could be capable of such horrendous things?

I had a feeling the number of people I'd meet that would be capable of such things was only going to increase as my life went on.

CHAPTER 46

The first few days through the canyon went without much incident. On the fourth day, we were hit by a nasty storm. I'd never been in a blizzard like that. I could barely see what was in front of me. We all held onto the person in front of us with Terrance leading the way. The guy was a natural at directions and navigation.

The storm slowed us down a bit. It was awful, the wind fast and harsh. My skin burned from being so dry. I thought we wouldn't make it, but on the seventh day it eased up.

When we finally made it through the mountain, the canyon we'd been walking through opened, leaving us in a valley. When I looked around, I gasped.

"What is it?" Eric asked.

"This place. I've seen it before in a dream." I looked up at the mountain and saw the area where I had been standing with everyone. It was a little alcove in the mountain. A ladder hung down from it.

In front of me lay a huge field of white snow with the

mountains surrounding the area. The air felt cold, but crisp and clear. Above us, not a cloud was in sight in the light blue sky. That meant there wouldn't be a storm any time soon, which made me happy.

I took a deep breath, inhaling the scent of the pine trees that lined the mountains. At the opening of the canyon were some tall, white towers with huge arms on top. The arms were spinning slowly in a circle.

"I've seen it, too," Dante said, stepping up next to me.

I turned to him. "Were there people in your dream with you?"

"Yes," Dante said, looking up at the alcove. "Most of the people that came with me."

"But not all of them?" I asked, quietly so only he could hear.

He looked at me, his eyebrows raised. "You have some extra people, too?"

I nodded in response.

"We'll have to get together sometime and talk," Dante said. "Without everyone else around."

"I think that's a good idea," I said.

"Over here," Wallace said, walking to a cave in the mountainside. When we went inside, I noticed a door in the back wall. Wallace tried the knob, but it wouldn't open.

Mack walked over to the door and held up a handgun. "Want me to try?"

Wallace shook his head. "There should be …" He looked around the cave, scanning it for something. He went to the wall and ran his hand along it. He finally stopped at a protruding rock and pushed in. The piece of rock moved to the side, revealing a small hollow. Wallace stuck his hand inside. "A key," he said, pulling it out.

Wallace went back to the door and unlocked it. The hinges groaned in resistance as he slowly opened the door. "Naomi, can you hand me a flashlight?"

Naomi riffled through her bag that she carried and pulled one out. "Here."

Wallace took it and flicked it on. "There should be a power switch in here somewhere." He and Naomi went inside, leaving us all in the cave.

"Power?" Derek asked. "How could there be power out here?" Right as he said it, lights turned on inside the room.

Wallace stepped out of the room. "Windmills. There are a bunch of them outside. I wasn't sure if it would start up, but luck is on our side today."

"Windmills?" Dee asked.

"They're those huge white towers out," Archie said. "The wind spins them around, creating electricity."

I looked over at him. I think that was the first time I'd heard him speak since we had met. His voice was surprisingly deep.

"What's in the room?" Steven asked.

"Why don't you all come in and find out?" Wallace said with a smile.

I was surprised when we walked into the room. It turned out to be an entire building, with multiple rooms. It was set up as a headquarters with different areas for electrical equipment, weapons storage, and conference rooms. There was an area in the back for an infirmary. The possibilities with the area were endless.

"Where do we start?" Vivica asked, leaning against a wall.

"From the beginning," Wallace said. "We'll have to set it up piece by piece. I think we should divide all the tasks up and go from there."

"Are you going to be our leader then?" I asked Wallace.

"If that's what everyone wants, I can for now," Wallace said. "We'll put it to a real vote once all the cities get here."

"Well, let's vote for a temporary leader, then," I said. "All in favor of having Wallace Brown be our president for now?"

Everyone raised their hands. I smiled and reached my hand out to Wallace. "Well, it's unanimous. Let me be the first to congratulate you, President Brown."

President Brown took my hand and shook it firmly. "Thank you."

After everyone congratulated him, President Brown gave out assignments to everyone. Once he was done, he had me and Dante follow him outside. We went up the ladder and stood in the alcove, looking over the field.

I stood on the same rock that was in my dream and looked at the field of white below. It was wild to think that one day the area would be filled with buildings and people. I just hoped it would be better than River Springs and that we'd be able to work together in unison.

Dante touched me on the arm and held something out to me. It was a small, blue flower. I took it from him and smiled.

"I heard you both mention something about a dream," President Brown said, looking at us. When we both nodded, he looked out over the valley. "What happened in the dream?"

Dante and I both took turns, telling him about our dreams. They were almost identical, just with different people standing near us. One major difference was that President Brown stood next to Dante just like Vice President Oliver stood next to me, but President Brown didn't fade away like Vice President Oliver did in my dream. It was like his fate was already sealed before he died.

President Brown put his hand on his chin, rubbing his thumb underneath it as he spoke. "I think those dreams confirm the two of you being the chosen revolutionary from your cities."

"Do you think the other two had the same dreams?" I asked. President Brown looked over at me. "The chosen revolutionaries from the remaining two cities?"

"Probably," President Brown said.

Dante shrugged as he put his hands in his pockets. "Guess we'll find out when they get here."

President Brown clasped his hands behind his back, his expression thoughtful. "This is it. A new beginning and a new chapter in our lives. One day, this will be a city, full of people willing and wanting to help and serve. We need to make sure we get people who are reliable, hardworking, and willing to fight."

"What should we call it?" I asked them. "Our new city?"

"Well, this area is to protect the people and make them safe. A haven, so to speak," Dante said.

President Brown laughed. "That's exactly what they wanted in the beginning."

"But they failed. We won't," I said, my voice confident. "This is our new haven."

"Well, then," President Brown said, looking over the valley below. "Welcome to New Haven."

Other Books by Sara Jo Cluff

YA Dystopian:

NEW HAVEN SERIES:
RECRUITS
RECKONING
RISE

YA Contemporary:

Filler Friend

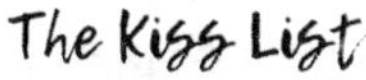

Middle Grade:

THE IMMORTAL LIFE OF COTTON WYLEY

ACKNOWLEDGMENTS

First and foremost, thanks to my husband Chad for encouraging me to write this book. I never would have done it if it weren't for him. He challenged me to write it for NaNoWriMo in 2011, and after some back and forth, I finally agreed. That whole month of November, we'd come home from work and Chad would play Batman: Arkham Asylum on the PS3 and I'd write until well after bedtime. It was a crazy month, but one of the best experiences of my life. It kicked off my writing career. So, thank you Chad! (And Batman for keeping Chad entertained during the month.)

A very special thanks (and lots of love!) to my mama. She's been the biggest fan of this book since the beginning (I'll let you and Chad fight for that spot). I love having you in my corner. You're the best mom and cheerleader an author could ask for!

Dad, thanks for telling everyone everywhere you go that your daughter is an author. I know the ladies at the Del Taco in Saratoga Springs are very proud of me!

Princess Buttercup, I can't go without thanking you. I know it was truly confusing when Mom and Dad came home every night, went into the basement where Dad played video games and Mom wrote on her laptop she wouldn't let you sit on. But we survived! And you've been my writing companion ever since. Though, you still can't sit on my laptop.

Thanks to all my friends and family who read the first

draft of this novel. I'm so sorry you had to read that, but I appreciate all your encouragement along the way! Shauna Porter, Makenzie DesRoches, Debra Wyatt, Pattie Harper, Sherrie Kirkham, Jovan Bonkosky, Kaylyn Cluff, Lindsey Cluff, Ozeanna Hortin, Amanda Craven, Casey Cheney, Jennifer Jones, Erin Young, Jessa Gagnon, Jaclyn Weist, Shannon Speirs, Evelyn Hawley, Michelle Shade, Elizabeth Jameson, Becky Morton, and probably a ton of others I'm forgetting. I mean, it's been eight years since I've written the dang thing. I love you all!!

Dr Pepper, thanks for fueling my writing. I couldn't have done it without you!! I must say, we make a great team. #PepperPack #Ambassador #DrPepperislife

www.ingramcontent.com/pod-product-compliance
Lightning Source LLC
Chambersburg PA
CBHW060552310726
48982CB00008B/1095/J
9781732183247